The Adima Chronicles:
ADIMA RISING

The Adima Chronicles:
ADIMA RISING

Steve Schatz

Absolute Love Publishing

Absolute Love Publishing

The Adima Chronicles: Adima Rising

Published by Absolute Love Publishing
United States of America

This book is a work of fiction. Names, characters, places, and incidents either are the product of the author's imagination or are used fictitiously. Any resemblance to actual persons, living or dead; events; or locales is entirely coincidental.

Cover design by Brandi Lyons

Paperback ISBN: 978-0-9833017-5-2

2nd Printing, 2016

Dedication

To my heart I hold dear … Becky, who loved the story from early on and encouraged me to continue.

And to my beloved … always to my beloved.

Acknowledgements

This has been a long process since nature first whispered in my ear that there was a job to do. Many have helped. Clemente and Delaney Jayne gave useful information and an important perspective early on. Bo, for dependable friendship and counsel for more years that I care to count. Heather was instrumental in opening the doorways to let the messages come through. Erica has provided encouragement and friendship for many years and provided a solid affirmation of the usefulness of the book. Denise Little provided an essential boost at a critical time. Thanks to Cheryl Curtis for friendship, suggestions, and being my black beard even though it required reading an early, rough draft. A special thanks to my publisher at Absolute Love Publishing, Caroline Shearer, and my editor, Sarah Hackley.

Pronunciation Guide

Belecha: Bell – a – **ha** (but with a little snot to the ha, like Bach)

Kiva: **key** – va (rhymes with diva)

Techta: **Tech** (ch sounds like the ck in Back) – ta; means "little toad"

Kroledutz: Crow – la – **Dūtz** (u like goo)

Pelcha: **Pel** – ha (with a ch sound like Bach); means "prairie dogs"

Tinglen: **Ting** – len; Billy's name

Pecheme: Peck – ĕ – **may;** James' name

Heliotom: **He** – Lee – ă – tome; Tima's name

Adima: ă – dim – ă

Radelam: Rad – a – **lam** (like calm or bomb)

Sodrol: So – **drawl** (roll the r a bit)

Mealim: May – a – **lim** (with hints of a double e, like seem)

Oloho: Ŏ – **low** – ho

Arnalea: Ar – na – **lie** - ă

Atomasa: ă – toe – **mă** – sa

Heyatoma: Hey – a – **tome** (like home) – ă

Eliaya: El – ee – **eye** – ya; means "beautiful patterns"

ONE 1

The chill bit through Rory's jacket. At night, the desert air cooled quickly. He scowled and tossed another stone. "This sucks," he sighed.

Tonight was supposed to be special. After a childhood spent moving from one archaeological dig to another, Rory's family had finally settled down in one place. Rory finally had friends, real friends who he wouldn't have to leave before the next year started. Friends who didn't see him as just the short, stocky, weird kid who hated sports and had two dads. Friends who he could finally share his ritual with.

Rory looked around at the empty pit and shook his head. Camping by himself was not what he had in mind for an end-of-the-school-year party.

Sure, they had excuses. People who disappoint you always do. Billy was grounded … again. Tima's mom was freaked about something … again. James bailed as soon as he heard Tima wasn't coming. Nothing new. End of 9th grade and all alone. Just like the end of every other grade. Different place … same story.

Why not bag it and go home? A snack. A real bed. It'd sure be more comfortable. He hesitated. The letter from his mom had come that afternoon.

It'd been nine years since Rory had seen her. Nine years since she'd gotten tired of hopping from dig to dig and country and country, making up stories with Rory while his dad spent the days excavating ruins with grad students. She'd left when he was five.

Months had passed since she had so much as called, and now, all of a sudden, she wanted a son. Rory wasn't buying it, but his dad said she might win in court. He was probably talking to the lawyer now, trying to stay calm, and figure out what to do.

This is better than listening to all that, thought Rory. *Even if I am alone.* He looked down into the pit. *At least the hole isn't too bad. Turned out pretty good, actually. Maybe the best one yet.*

Every year since his mother had left, whenever they got to a new dig, Rory would find the place he felt was right and start a hole. He didn't really know why he was digging, except that everyone else was digging and he wanted something of his own. As he grew, he got better at digging and planning, knowing how to make the right shape and get the sides nice and straight. That's when he developed the ritual.

The first night the hole was deeper than he was tall, he'd build a fire at the bottom and he'd spend the night. He'd watch the stars and the sunrise, and celebrate his accomplishment. The first time he did it, he was only seven. Dad had tried to talk him out of it, but he couldn't. The next morning, Rory had felt spectacular. He'd done it every year since except one – the year of jungle fever - when he and Dad got so sick they couldn't get out of bed for two weeks and couldn't do much for two more weeks after that. That was the year they had met Leon.

Officially the camp cook, Leon had spent a month nursing Rory and his dad back to health. When they went back to the States, to the visiting professor job Dad always took as he wrote up his findings and planned the next expedition, Leon came along, moving not only into the house, but into Dad's room. It had taken Rory a while to get used to the idea of having two dads, but now it was just how things were. The only time Rory regretted living with his dad was at the beginning of the school year. Every year it was a new school, a whole school full of kids he didn't know, and every year he was the new kid trying to make new friends.

It wasn't easy. Until this year. This year, they weren't moving on again. The knowledge that he'd get to stick around for longer than a few months had set Rory's mind at ease, and he'd made friends much more quickly. This year, he still dug his hole, but this time it was in his country and he hadn't dug it alone.

And he wasn't supposed to be celebrating alone either, except they had all canceled.

Rory stared at the cracked screen of his phone. He had figured Billy would be in trouble. Billy was always in trouble, but he didn't think it would stop him. First day of school, when Rory was sitting out under some cottonwoods, cold and hungry, but not wanting to go inside to the cafeteria and deal with all the faces he didn't know, this short blond kid had come over, sat down with a grin, and tossed him half a burrito.

"Hey there," he'd said, his green eyes twinkling. "I figured, before everyone else warns you to stay away from the eeevil Billy Fuller, I'd come over and say hi. Have a burrito. I made it myself, and I'm a pretty good cook." Pausing for a moment, he'd added, "You really got two dads?"

Rory had sighed and looked back at Billy, hoping this wasn't some weird way to start a fight. The kid was smaller than him but wiry. He looked like he'd been in some scrapes, and could hold his own in a fight. Rory was a good fighter because he was strong, and he had a lot of experience winning fights, but he was sick of fighting. Still, he wasn't going to let some smart-mouth kid talk bad about his dad and Leon.

"Yeah," said Rory, staring hard at Billy. "I got two dads. What of it? I'm thinking about getting a hamster, too, but I haven't decided. You got an opinion you want to share?"

Billy grinned. "Huh. Neat. So, do they both try to tell you what to do or can you play 'em against each other? That's what I'd do. The fathers I mean. I'd just ignore anything a hamster tells me to do." Still smiling, he shook his head. "If you listen to hamsters, it's all over for you, man." Then, he gestured with his half of the burrito to Rory's. "Eat. It ain't poison."

Rory shook his head. "Leon and my dad are like a tag team match. Can't play them off each other. No way. Believe me, I've tried. Big mistake." Looking closely at Billy, he added, "Why are you evil?"

Billy shrugged. "I ask too many questions. Plus, my ma is the town drunk … or at least one of 'em. I don't mind saying it, and I don't really mind when others say it, but I also don't mind saying what everyone else is too. Most people don't like that." He took a big bite of his burrito and eyed Rory's. "Look, are you gonna eat that burrito or not? I didn't spit in it. Promise. But if you're too delicate, hand it over. I'll eat it myself."

Rory grinned in spite of himself. He took a bite of the burrito and his eyes started to close. It was one of the best burritos he'd ever tasted and that was saying a lot, since Leon was a master in the kitchen. Rory chewed and swallowed. He opened his eyes and found Billy staring at him with a smile.

"Good. Right?"

Rory nodded. "Most definitely good."

Billy grinned. "The secret is the beans. I make my own beans." He lowered his voice and looked around, like he was divulging a state secret. "That's what gives it the special taste. The way I give the beans that flavor is I pre-fart them. You see, beans always give you the farts, so I figure, you eat some cabbage and chilies while you're cookin' the beans and that gives you the mucho gas. Then, every hour, I lift the lid and let a whole volley of farts loose on the beans. Gives 'em that perfect flavor."

Rory stared at Billy, a mouthful of burrito half eaten in his mouth, not sure whether to spit it out or bust up laughing. Billy finished his half, wiped his fingers on his jeans and lay back, looking at the sky. "I was thinking of selling them at the county fair. Don't know if I should call 'em Billy's Butt Blasted Burritos or Fuller's Fart Fluffed Yummies. What do you think?" He sat up and stared at Rory with a completely serious look on his face, like Rory's answer would change the world.

Rory finished chewing, swallowed, and considered. "What about Burritos Especial? No need to bring your butt into the picture." He grinned. "And if you decided to put a graphic on the side ... somehow, I don't think you'd increase sales by ..."

Billy raised an eyebrow. "You'll never know. Might be the purtiest butt around."

Rory shook his head, laughing. "Don't care. Not the connection you want to make to sell the product."

By that time, lunch was over and Rory had his first friend. Billy spent plenty of time at Rory's house. He wasn't that interested in Javier's archeology, but when Leon was cooking, Billy was there helping. He also helped Rory do and finally understand math. Billy had a way of describing, then making him work the problems, that made it make sense. When Rory went up the hill to dig, Billy would help, constantly asking questions and making suggestions. Billy and Rory ate lunch together most days, usually sitting outside, Billy talking nonstop about other kids or teachers or whatever program he was currently obsessed with and Rory throwing in a quip every now and then. But now he wasn't here.

Rory stood on the lip of the hole and considered. Maybe he should just go back home and try this some other night. Tonight wasn't going to be what he had hoped for. It was going to be just him – like always. First night had always been special. He didn't want to be pissed off. That would ruin it. Then he thought again about what he had left at home. *Nah, this is better than dealing with that*, he thought.

Rory jumped down into the hole and lit the fire. It caught quickly and soon the pinion sap was bubbling, letting loose one of Rory's favorite smells. Inhaling with pleasure, he sat back against the rocky side of the hole and watched the smoke rise up toward the stars. Slowly, he started to relax. So what if no one came. This was good.

Rory looked again at their handiwork. The hole was deep and wide, with good, straight walls. He and his friends had dug and carried and hacked the hard earth for months, and now it was finished. Over seven feet across, nearly six feet deep, with a flat sand floor.

"I'll make a ladder with that lumber in the shed next week," he said. "Then it will be finished."

An owl hooted, scaring dinner out of hiding. Rory laid his head back against the hard packed dirt wall and closed his eyes.

"Arr iiiiieeeeeeee!!! A dark form dropped down from above, a deep growl rising to a scream as it reared up, long arms reaching.

Rory's head jerked forward, then back, and slammed against the wall. "Oww!"

Then he saw his attacker. "Billy! You jerk!" Rory rubbed his head and glared.

Billy snorted. "Mess your pants, Compadre?"

"No, but I got a nice lump, butthead. How'd you get out? I thought you were grounded for life."

"Life wasn't all that long this time. Suzie called an hour ago. She got in trouble up in Denver and Mommy ran right out to save her baby from the evil police." He grinned. "Of course I promised to stay home and think about what I had done."

Rory cocked his head. "What did you do this time?"

Billy grinned. "Can't remember. Oh, wait. There was something about Ms. Horselick and a portrait in my math book."

"You missed one?"

"Front cover. I forgot to take the book jacket off. She did and …"

Rory hooted.

"She's gonna make me buy a new one. $50!"

From above them, a sharp voice barked, "You two wanna keep it down? I thought the plan was to enjoy the quiet of the desert. If I wanted to hear brainless boys babbling, I'd have stayed home and watched the news."

Rory and Billy looked up. Tima stared down at them, hands on her hips, her face holding back a twisted smile.

Tima had plunked herself down at the table next to Rory in history class during his first week at school. A good head taller than Rory, with beautiful, curly, black hair and a self-assured manner, she would have been intimidating were it not for her sparkling smile.

"You moved in down the block from me and my mom," she'd said. "I'm Tima." Then, she stuck out her hand. Rory wasn't used to talking right away and wasn't used to shaking hands with other kids, but Tima had a way of making anything she did seem like it was just the way things were done. So, he shook her hand.

"Tima?" he asked.

She nodded. "Short for Septima. Mom named me after Septima Clark."

Rory tilted his head, questioning.

Tima laughed and waved dismissively. "Look her up. She's the teacher, not me." Then she shot him a fiery look. "I mean it. I'll ask you again. You better have an answer." She smiled a slow grin, but Rory wasn't going to test whether she'd make good on her implied threat. He'd looked up Septima Poinsette Clark when he got home.

A couple of weeks after Rory had started to dig the hole, he looked up from swinging the pick to break up the gravel-studded earth and found Tima sitting on the growing pile of dirt.

"What are you doing, Rory?" she'd asked.

"Digging a hole," he replied, panting, glad to have a break. The pick was heavy, but it was the only thing that busted up the dirt into small enough chunks that he could haul it away.

Tima nodded and cocked her head. "What's a citizenship school?" No explanation, no expression, just the question hanging in the air.

Rory considered Tima, sitting so calmly on the growing pile of dirt and rocks. "What do I get if I know the answer?"

Tima cracked her knuckles. "Better to ask what happens if you don't."

Rory thought some more about whether or not Tima was someone he wanted as a friend, then nodded. "A school in the South that taught people how to read, write, do math and about citizenship. They needed to do that because most Southern states had a literacy requirement to try to keep African Americans from voting. Septima Clark ran the education and teaching program that ran the citizenship schools." He winked, and then returned to slamming the pick into the ground and wrenching up big hunks of rock-studded earth. Tima simply stood up, picked up a shovel, and started shoveling dirt into the wheelbarrow.

They had worked together the rest of the day. From then on, Tima often came up the hill and pitched in. If Billy was there, they'd split up the tasks – Rory with the pick, Billy with the shovel, and Tima hauling dirt. Once the hole got too deep for the wheelbarrow, it went slower. They had to haul the dirt out with the bucket. One day, about a month later, when it was just Rory and Tima, and they were heading down the hill after an afternoon of digging, Tima turned to him.

"Rory?"

"Yeah?"

"Why are you digging a hole?"

Rory shook his head. "I don't know. It's just something I do."

Tima thought about that a moment and nodded her head. "Well, okay then." She kept walking.

"Okay what?" Rory asked.

Tima stopped and looked at him. "If that's good enough for you, it's good enough for me. See you tomorrow, Rory." Then she turned off toward her house.

Rory had stared after her, amazed that someone would help him day after day just because it mattered to him. He'd never had friends like that before.

TWO 2

Tima stood on the lip of the hole, looking back and forth from Billy to Rory. She scanned the desert around the hole, nodded to herself that no one was around and leapt with the poise of an athlete down in front of them. "What happened? I heard someone scream."

Billy nodded. "Yeah, some little girl saw a shadow and wet her pants. She ran home to change."

Tima punched him in the arm. "No girl screams like that. That was a widdle boy if I ever heard one. Seeing as you're here, I understand why. I nearly scream every time I catch your face full-on. You probably popped out and Rory didn't have a chance to look away. Lucky he's not blind."

Billy started to reply, but Tima held up her hand, pulled her phone out, and dialed. She spoke sharply. "James. Get dressed and get up the hill. We're all here. Yes, I know what time it is. It's time for you to get your buns in gear." She put her hand on her hip and tapped her foot against the packed sand while he responded. "James Nomura, you are *not* going back to sleep. If I don't see you walking out your back door before I count to 10, I'm coming to get you. And you know I will." James was still explaining why he couldn't come when Tima hung up and faced the two. "He says he'll be right up."

Rory couldn't help grinning. This was getting better and better. "But I thought you …"

Tima brushed that away. "Mom's already asleep. She gets nervous. Then she gets over it. I left a note. It's all good." Tima's mom was a writer. "She just got trapped in a story. When she gets stuck, she gets depressed, and that makes her more stuck."

Tima didn't talk much about her mom's problems to anyone except James. Rory had asked her about it a couple of times, but Tima didn't want to get into details.

"No worries," she'd said. "It isn't like I'm burying it. I have a therapist I talk to. Mom has a therapist. I talk to James and his mom. I'm handling it. It is what it is."

"Besides," she'd added, wiggling her eyebrows, "Every family has something."

Rory had let it drop. He knew better than just about anyone how tiring it got to explain about families.

Tima and James were a pair – not boyfriend and girlfriend – but where there was one, the other was usually within easy reach. It was a funny match. James, with his glasses, lanky build, and orderly ways, was as quiet as Tima was loud. A third-generation farm boy, James was more comfortable with cows and herbs than people. Tima was an artist, and she painted wild swirls of color and texture on huge canvases, rocks, timbers, and nearly anything else that took her fancy. After the day's chores, Tima would usually go to James' house and they'd do homework together or sit and talk.

Tima had introduced Rory and James, but James hadn't done much digging on the hole. "Sorry, Rory," he'd said, even though Rory had never asked. "I spend all day digging, so coming up here in the afternoon to dig a hole … It just doesn't work for me. If you really like digging, though, feel free to come on down the hill. We're putting in a new field of peppers."

Rory had taken him at his word, and never expected to see him at the hole. One afternoon, though, after they'd started hauling the dirt out with the bucket, Rory had found James busy next to the hole with a tripod, a pulley, some rope, and a post-hole digger. Rory had already learned that James was a wait-and-see guy, so that's what Rory did.

Within the hour, they had a well-designed system for raising dirt by the bucketful and swinging it over to the growing hill of rock and dirt. James had tested it a couple of times, smiled, and nodded to Rory. "See you later. Time to irrigate the corn." Then he'd headed down the hill, waving without turning back around in response to Rory's surprised, "Hey, thanks!"

James had called to cancel a few minutes after Tima had called to say her mother was having one of her moods. Rory had known James would cancel. He was even more certain that even if James was asleep when Tima commanded, he would be heading up the hill toward them in 5 ... 4 ... 3 ... 2 ... 1 ... BANG. They all heard James' back door slam and knew he was trudging up the hill to join them. Rory smiled. From all no-shows to everyone here in a just a few minutes. How great was that? New Mexico was going to turn out all right after all.

Tima looked around and nodded. "Most excellent. Billy, pump up that fire. Look at you. Did you just wear that raggedy hoodie? You know it gets cold at night. Here – I figured as much." She threw a wild-colored, woolen thing at him, and Billy, who would have stepped aside and let the thing fall into the fire had it been anyone else, caught it and pulled it over his head without a single comment about how much it looked like it had been rolled in one of her paintings. With Tima, and only Tima, Billy minded.

Tima looked around. "Okay. Who's got eats?"

Rory pulled out his pack. "Leon cooked a bunch of stuff."

Tima grabbed it and started pulling out goodies. "Look at all this! You and your dad must be scarfin' all the time."

Everyone dug in while the pinion sap in the logs popped and sent showers of sparks up toward the amazing spread of stars. James dropped down from the side, grumpy at first, but cheering up when he saw the spread of munchies.

"You called right after I finally went to bed," he said. "Dad got home late. There was almost a riot at the council meeting."

Billy perked up. "Really? I always thought those meetings were snooze fests. Anyone get punched?"

James shook his head. "Nah, Dad threatened to have the sheriff start giving tickets for disturbing the peace. $50 a pop." James smiled. "Amazing how people shut up when talking costs them something."

Tima nodded. "What caused the fight?"

"Some guy named Cisco bought Rattlesnake Ranch and wants to change the zoning so he can build a kiddie park to lure tourists off the interstate."

"What's Rattlesnake Ranch?" asked Rory.

"It's that boarded up tourist trap on the edge of town," replied Tima. "It closed years ago." Turning to James, she asked, "Why does anyone care? Gets the place cleaned up."

James shrugged. "Outsiders, noise, competition. Plus the guy is an obvious sleaze – small time operator looking for a quick buck. Dad's sure he's up to something, but can't tell what. He's turning the whole thing over for a community vote. Said he wasn't going to have just the council decide."

Billy grinned. "Maybe we should go next meeting. I'd hate to miss a total meltdown."

Tima glared. "Government is not a wrestling match for your entertainment."

"Be more people participating if it was."

They all continued to munch and talk.

This is everything I'd hoped for, Rory thought, looking around at the hole, the fire, and his three friends. A smile started to spread across his face.

Just then, a grinding screech tore from the fire, and a wave of energy as powerful as a bomb slammed all four of the teenagers into the rocky wall. Almost as one, they turned and clawed at the dirt sides of the pit, instincts taking over with a primal desire to get to safety.

Rory turned his head back in horror and saw a thick, black cloud belch out of the fire and congeal like gelatin into the shape of a hideous creature. Ear-splitting shrieks tore from the flames. A heavy, burning stink of plastic, fear, and rot filled the space, making it difficult to breathe. The four desperately fought to find a way up, out, and away.

The smoke around the creature twisted into oily, arm-like clubs that whipped out and slammed them back to the ground. The thing loomed above, a churning tornado of fury, blocking out the stars. Terror and confusion washed over them. Rory felt the creature suck away his strength and his will.

Rory tried to turn his head, to look away from the vile sight, but he couldn't. His muscles wouldn't obey. His head throbbed. The inky, smoking thing wrapped tighter and tighter around his chest, around his throat. He tried to pull at it, but the smoky arms dissolved beneath his fingers, only to squeeze again as soon as his hands were through. He couldn't breathe. His mouth wrenched open to scream, but no sound escaped. Yet all around him the shrieks of the beast deafened him.

This can't be happening, he thought. *Not possible. Home is just down the hill. Dad and Leon will hear the screaming. They'll come running. It can't be. It can't really be ...* Rory couldn't breathe. Blood roared in his ears. *This is it,* he thought. *Death by ... by what?*

He couldn't think any more. His lungs were begging for air. Black spots filled his vision. Beside him, grunts and moans from the others told him they too were getting crushed as the creature pulsed above them, roaring unintelligible threats and curses.

Red-hot pain shot through his chest. Tentacles sunk through his chest, grabbed his heart, and squeezed. Rory curled around the pain, gasping as the pain exploded. *Can't breathe. Pain. Darkness. Fading ...*

A tremendous roar shook the ground. The next instant, a blinding flash of light and a burning wave of heat propelled the creature backward, blasting through it and tearing it apart. A nerve-twisting scream split the air, slammed into Rory, overloaded his brain, and dropped him into sweet, black unconsciousness.

THREE 3

When Rory opened his eyes, everything was quiet. He looked around, listening. Nothing unusual. He felt for a lump on the back of his head, where he had hit the ground. Nothing. Confused, he struggled to his feet and heard sound to his right.

Billy sat up, rubbing his neck. "What was that?"

Tima moaned. "I thought we were toast for sure. That thing wanted to wipe us out."

Everyone stared blankly, stunned for a moment. "Maybe there was some toxic spray on the wood," said James. "I smelled burning plastic. Where'd you get it, Rory?"

Rory glared at him. "You're kidding, right? That wasn't something on the wood. I don't know what it was, but it was alive and it tried to …"

"Couldn't be," said James firmly. "It had to be some weird hallucination from the smoke."

"And we all had the same hallucination?" asked Billy. "What kind of hallucination squeezes the breath out of you? Get real, James. That thing was killing me. I don't know how we're still alive. No way we all just went night-night and had the same big, bad nightmare."

"It wasn't a dream." A voice spoke from the shadows.

They spun toward the sound, bits of sand flurrying at their feet. Billy reached over and grabbed a thick branch and held it out like a club, his wiry arms pulsing with adrenaline. Tima moved into a judo stance, ready, watching, and steady. They stood their ground, prepared to fight or try once more for the wall.

"Calm down," said the voice. "I'm not the beast. I saved you."

An old man with large, dark eyes stepped out of the shadows and stopped in front of the fire, keeping his distance. He wore a loose leather shirt and leggings. His gray hair had hints of black and was pulled into two long braids. His wide mouth, corners turned up slightly, tried to hide a smile. A carved, square stone hung from a cord around his neck. He was the spitting image of Native Americans in school history books.

"Name's Belecha," he said. "Bell like ding dong and aha like a surprise, but put a little snot in it. Sorry about the attack. I didn't think they would sense you so soon. I also figured you'd be safe in your kiva."

All of Rory's attention fixed on the man and his wise, wrinkled face. It was like the rest of the world went out of focus. He couldn't see or even sense the others. Only he and Belecha, with his deep, almost infinite eyes, were there.

Rory shook his head to try to clear it. Didn't work. Instead, the world seemed to spin.

In a gentle, but commanding voice, Belecha said to him, "You better sit down, Techta. You're about to fall and if I try to catch you, you'll get spooked. I let you fall, you'll bang your head. Either way you lose."

Knees losing their strength, Rory slid down until he was sitting on the hard ground. The rocky surface felt safe and secure. Very real, after too much weirdness. He looked up at the man who seemed friendly but carried himself with the confidence of a seasoned warrior.

"What was that thing? Why did it want to kill me? Who are you? What do you want?"

Belecha held up his hands, his long, thin fingers and pale palms standing out in the firelight. "One question at a time and not too much. Looks like you haven't decided whether to pee, puke, or pass out."

Rory took a breath. "Okay. What was that thing?"

"An energy sucker. We call 'em Kroledutz. They feed on the energy of living things and particularly like to munch on people. They usually just take a sip now and then. That way, they can keep feeding on a person for years."

"You call that sipping?" yelled Rory, pushing against the ground to stand.

Belecha made a calming gesture with his hand. "I said usually. You're a special case. You, it wanted to kill."

Rory felt panic rising. "Kill me? Why?"

Belecha shook his head. "Too much to explain now. Important thing is that I got it before it told the others where you are."

"Others!" Rory leapt up and headed for the side of the pit. "There are more? How many? Where do they come from?" He had to get home. Nice, safe, normal home.

Belecha touched his shoulder. "You'll never learn anything if you start shouting every time I tell you something."

Rory jerked away. "What! That ... that ... thing just about ripped my heart out of my chest! And there are more? And you think I should be calm! No way. I've got every reason ..."

Belecha's body burst into a towering, glowing orb. Waves of energy washed over Rory like a blast of sun at mid-day. "HUSH!" The word shook the ground.

Rory hushed.

Belecha continued in a commanding roar. "Pup! You got too much to learn too fast and if you don't learn it and learn it good, you're gonna be toast ... very messy toast. Most likely, you'll be dead meat in one, maybe two days. Maybe, just maybe, if you shut your mouth and open your ears and try to kick start that brain, you'll still be in one piece in a week."

Rory's mouth gaped. Belecha, shrinking toward normal size and shape, reached out with his long fingers and gently closed it.

Belecha nodded. "Better." He gestured toward the fire. "That was just a rover. Mostly Kroledutz hang out in packs – we call 'em nests. Most people on this planet can't see 'em, but they've been here since before humans were fighting over bananas. They've grown strong the last few thousand years, and now they're planning to take over. You and your friends are the last chance to stop them."

Rory protested. "Us? We can't fight something like that. Why don't you all leave us alone? I promise I won't say anything. None of us will. Just leave us alone!"

Belecha shook his head, sadness in his eyes, and placed a hand on Rory's shoulder. "It's up to you and only you. I know you don't believe me, but you chose this path. Now you have to try, because if you do not, it will be over before it begins. The Kroledutz won't rest until they have ripped you apart. They don't care if you fight. They'd be happier if you didn't – easier for them. They only want you dead. After you, they will feast on your friends. Finally, they will finish their destruction of everyone and everything on this planet. Ready for the worst news? You probably can't stop them. You are probably already dead, just waiting to fall. The only chance, and it's a small one, is if all four of you work together, learn very fast, don't die, and we all are very lucky."

Rory suddenly remembered James, Billy, and Tima. He broke his gaze from the old man and looked around. A glowing fog filled the hole. Through it, he could barely see the others frozen in place. Fear rising again, he looked back at Belecha, clenching his fists. "What did you do to them? Let them go!"

"I didn't do anything to them, Techta. You and I have stepped out of your world for this conversation. They are the same. Think of this as being between moments of time."

"That doesn't even make sense. How can you ..."

Belecha shook his head. "I'm not going to explain it now, Techta. It's been a long night for you, so let me stick to the essentials. There's a thing that needs doing, and you and only you can take the first step. Take that step and you might just survive. Might. You decide and the others will come, too. Either way, it's in your hands."

"What do you want me to do?"

"Tell the others. Make the choice. Then, you must *state your intention*. The rest will follow."

Rory looked at this mysterious old man with the impossible story and shook his head. "This is not turning out to be the evening I expected."

A grim smile tugged at Belecha's mouth, reaching the crinkles of his eyes. "Don't you like surprises?"

Rory shot him a look. "How come you know all this?"

Belecha winked. "Well, the first reason is that I am wise beyond my years – and that's saying a lot. The second reason is that I'm a Watcher."

"What's that?"

Belecha rolled his eyes. "Hmm … a Watcher … what would a Watcher do? Let's think."

In an instant, his body disappeared, leaving only his eyes floating before Rory. They grew, turning into huge, glowing orbs. Belecha's voice boomed from the darkness. "I watch, bright boy." The ground shook with his words, and Rory felt dizzy.

"I've been watching and planning for more than 5,000 years, and if you can't activate the Stone by the next full moon, we don't get another chance. Tag – you're it!"

With that, the eyes exploded, sending whizzing, whistling streams of color spinning out in all directions.

Rory stared at the colors shooting by and, for the second time that evening, fainted.

FOUR 4

Rory opened his eyes. Tima was kneeling next to him. Relief filled her face as he shook his head, trying to focus.

Billy was standing with James looking down at him. "You okay?"

"Wha ... What happened?" moaned Rory.

"Dunno, dude," replied Billy. "One minute, some old guy appeared. Next minute, he was gone and you were on the ground."

Rory started to push himself up.

"I don't know if you should move," said James.

"I'm not going to just lay here. What if something else plans on showing up?"

"You have a point," said Tima, raising an eyebrow and looking around while helping him sit up.

Rory realized he was squeezing something so tight in his left hand that it was digging into his palm. He opened his fingers and stared. In the light of the moon, he could see it was the stone that Belecha had been wearing around his neck. There were carvings in each corner and a hole in the middle.

Tima looked at the stone and back at Rory. She reached for the stone. "What's this?" Taking it, she studied it closely on her palm. "Looks old."

"Nailed it, Tima," said Billy, grinning. "Course, most rocks are pretty old."

Tima shot him a dirty look. "The carvings, dummy." She cocked her head, looking at Rory closely. "What happened to you Rory? Something's up."

Rory knew if he told them, there was no turning back. He shook his head. "Probably nothing ... I mean it must have just been a dream ..."

Billy laughed. "Rory, you are the world's worst liar. There's something you aren't saying and we're gonna get it out of you one way or another. Might as well get it over with. Give."

Rory sighed, started slowly, and it all poured out – the Kroledutz, that it was up to them to save the world, every crazy sounding thing – even the parts when Belecha grew huge and the end, when his eyes exploded. When Rory finally stopped to take a breath, he looked around, trying to judge their reactions. James looked, as usual, like he was calculating something in his head. Tima looked curious. Billy was grinning like it was Christmas.

"Someone's yanking your chain, but it's a great yank. Think how much trouble they went to. I've got to see this."

James nodded. "We all saw the guy, then he was gone. If it's a prank, it's a good one."

Rory was stunned. "If! You mean Mr. Scientist doesn't think I'm nuts?"

James smiled and shook his head. "Never make a decision without considering all the possibilities. What do you think, Tima?"

"We need more information," she declared. "If he wanted us dead, he could have let that cloud thing finish us."

Billy nodded. "Totally. We were screwed."

Tima nodded. "But what do we do?" She handed the stone back to Rory. "Did he say what you were supposed to do with it?"

Rory shook his head. "He just said we had to make our choice and state our intention."

"Maybe you should rub it," said Billy. "You know, like Aladdin and the lamp."

"Maybe you should ask your dad," suggested James. "He's an archaeologist. He might know something about the carvings and if they tell you what to do."

"Maybe you should all bark like dogs and roll around in the dust," said a voice from near the fire.

"Can it, Billy," scolded Tima.

"That wasn't me!"

"Look," said James, pointing toward the fire pit. Above the fire, a small ball of smoke shimmered. "Did you use wet wood? The fire shouldn't be smoking that much." Suddenly he looked very worried. "Maybe it's another one of those cloud things."

Tima shook her head. "Nah. That came pouring out, like it couldn't wait to get us. This is just hanging there."

Rory got up and went to the fire pit, waving his hand through the ball of smoke. "It isn't smoke from the wood. Look, it doesn't move."

"Watch where you are putting your hand, youngster." The voice came from the center of the ball, which quickly expanded into the old man they had seen before. Belecha was grinning.

"I wish I had a camera. You little pelchas look like you've seen a ghost."

"Well, isn't that what you are? A ghost or something?" asked Tima.

"It's gotta be some kind of trick." Billy walked around Belecha, looking carefully. "Someone is waiting to make us all do something totally embarrassing, then laugh their butts off."

Belecha sighed. "You always were a difficult one to convince, Tinglen. Even when you were an old man, you wouldn't believe a wolf was a wolf until it chewed your leg off."

"My name is Billy, not whatever you called me, and what do you mean, when I was an old man?"

"Later on that. Let's just say I've known you all for a long time in a lot of places that you don't remember – yet. So I know that right now each one of you is trying really hard to come up with a story that explains why you didn't just see an old man pop out of a ball of smoke. Right?"

Rory was relieved that the others were seeing whatever it was. Billy looked suspicious. Tima seemed content to see how everything played out. James … well, James' mouth was hanging wide open, and his eyes were filled with panic.

Belecha looked at James and spoke soothingly. "Don't you go crazy yet, Pecheme. You start yelling and running around, and you'll never find out what's going on."

It was exactly the right thing to say. James could never stand to leave a puzzle unsolved. He didn't say anything, but stopped looking like he was about to make a run for the hills.

"Listen, hombres," said Belecha. "Here's how it goes. There are a lot of things you need to do and even more that you need to learn. If you get it wrong, the world ends and so do you." He slapped his hands together like he was crushing a mosquito. "That quick."

He held up a hand to stop both Billy and Tima's questions. "I'll explain, but we don't have much time, so first off, you have to believe I'm not blowing smoke." He looked down at his body, which still wasn't completely formed and was glowing faintly in the moonlight, and grinned. "Well, I guess I am blowing smoke, in a way."

"You're blowing something," said Billy.

Belecha gave him a hard look. "You all have to see what the problem is. We're going to take a little trip. You want to back out afterward, you have that option, but first you have to see the what and the why."

"Where are we going?" asked Rory.

"Not far, you might even recognize it."

"Who's driving?" asked Billy. "Can you pull a car out of that fire, too?"

"No driving. We aren't going in body. It's about energy. We'll travel the web."

"Web?" asked Tima.

"You'll see. You won't have to take it on faith for long. This once, do what I say. Will you grant me that?"

They looked at each other, considering.

"Look, I blew away the beastie just a little while ago. Now, I appeared in a ball of smoke. That's got to count for something. Your bodies will never leave this spot. Promise. So what's there to lose?"

Rory nodded. Tima, looking thoughtful, nodded, too. James gritted his teeth. "I'm in."

Billy shrugged. "Sure. Knock yourself out. If this is a trick, it's a good one."

Belecha grinned. "It's a great ride. I promise. Now everyone, sit down around the Stone, each one of you facing a corner, and touch that corner with a finger."

They followed his directions. Belecha faded into a glowing ball and floated above the Stone. "Okay, pay attention, and hold onto the rings."

A roaring sound, as loud as a hurricane, filled the hole.

"What rings?" shouted James.

A shimmering mist filled the air, blocking out the stars.

"You'll see."

The roaring increased, and Rory felt a pull on his hair. The ground began to shake and Belecha began to rise, pulling them up off the ground. As he did, the Stone grew. From each corner a large ring extended.

"Hold on tight!" Belecha shouted. "It's time to go web riding, and I don't have time to find you if you let go."

They held on, rising through the swirling, shimmering mist until, like an airplane breaking through the clouds, they cleared the haze and saw, stretched out in every direction like a fish net made of star fire, pulsing threads of light.

"Welcome to the real world, pelchas," said Belecha. "Let's go for a ride."

FIVE 5

Faster and faster, they rocketed along a strand of light up toward a thick cluster of threads. Looking down, Rory saw a glowing track beneath them, a moving sidewalk of light going at enormous speed.

"What happened to the earth?" James asked, sounded nervous.

"Hold tight to the Stone!" shouted Belecha. "You'll see."

Shimmering clouds billowed all around them. Occasionally, they saw small points of light in the distance. Once or twice, large glowing spheres hovered above them as they whisked by.

"We're going to drop down now!" yelled Belecha. "You'll feel a jerk and then a fast fall. Hold tight! There will be a small bump when we get there."

Rory squeezed the ring. The others did the same.

"Now!" shouted Belecha. A plunge, then a bump, and they were sitting as they had started, around the Stone, now small again on sandy ground. Nearby, the end of a wooden ladder poked up through a rough dome rising three feet off the ground. A few cottonwood trees to the west showed where a river wound through the desert landscape.

"This doesn't look much different than home," said James, scanning the landscape with some relief.

Rory spoke up as he recognized the change. "But it's day. When we left, it was night and the moon was up."

"Gold star, Techta. I figured you'd rather be able to look around, so I aimed for early morning."

Tima looked around, then turned to Belecha. "Okay, that was some ride. Now, why don't you tell us where we are and why?"

Belecha looked down his long nose and nodded approvingly at her. "You have always focused on the issue at hand, Heliotom."

"I've never met you before. You know that."

Belecha smiled. "Let's handle your first question, then. That's the easiest." He glanced at Billy, who was looking around suspiciously. "Tinglen, you aren't as stupid as you look. Where are we?"

Billy glared at him.

"I'll give you a hint. You've been here lots of times, broken a few windows." He waved his hand at the scene. "Ignore the roads and buildings."

"There are no roads or buildings," said James.

"I don't mean imagine here with no roads. Imagine the places that you are used to without all the stuff people have built in the last hundred years or so."

Billy squinted his eyes and looked around. Then, it hit him. "This is where Rattlesnake Ranch is!"

"You mean the place where that guy wants to build the mini mart?" asked Rory.

Billy nodded. "Yup. Great place to mess around. No one minds if you cause a little damage."

Belecha grinned. "Well done, Tinglen. Now-"

"How'd you make everything disappear?" James interrupted, panic sweeping across his face. "I've been here lots of times since I was a kid. The road runs right in front. Where is it? Our farm is just down that arroyo. I should see the windmill in the south field." He pointed to the gully. "I should see it from here," he added, his voice rising. "Why don't I see it?"

Tima put a hand on James' arm, calming him. Her dark eyes grew brighter as she looked around. "Where are the power lines?" she asked, her voice full of wonder. "And listen – no sound from the freeway. You can always hear it in the distance."

"You know where you are," answered Belecha, "now you should be asking when you are. It's before your calendar was invented, but we are about 5,000 years in your past."

Rory was too stunned to speak, but Tima only grew more fascinated. "Okay," she said, looking around again. "That makes sense. But why? Why are we here?"

"To show you, we have to go there." Belecha pointed to the dome.

"You have your show hidden in there?" asked Billy.

Belecha looked at him and smiled. "It isn't a show, at least not the kind you're imagining. No tricks. But, yeah, we need to go in there. You have to be in the kiva to see what I want to show you."

"You used that word before," Rory said. "What's it mean? What's a kiva?"

"What do you think you've been digging all these years, Techta?"

"So it's a big hole," said Billy. "Why the fancy name?"

"A kiva is not just a hole. It's a powerful place. A sacred place."

"How come?" asked Billy. "Seems like a hole to me."

"Focus," answered Belecha. "A kiva focuses energy. Think of it like a lens. If you grind a piece of glass right, it can focus rays of light. If you hold it near something small, that small thing will look big – like a magnifying glass. If you aim it toward something far away, that thing can look close – like a telescope. You with me so far?"

They all nodded.

"Well, a kiva focuses energy, not images. It allows you to see things you couldn't see without it. You can tune your kiva, just like you grind a lens."

"How?" asked Rory.

"If you use it right, it keeps getting better."

James appreciated the value of quality tools. "Are you saying this is a good kiva?" he asked.

Belecha nodded. "The difference between this and the hole you kids dug is the difference between a science kit telescope and something at an observatory. It's the same basic thing, but this one works much better."

"Okay," said Billy. "How do we get in?"

"Just a minute, hot shot. You are about to step into my parlor. Not many people have ever been invited in. So, a few rules. First, I know it's a challenge, but you need to put a cork in your pie hole … all of you. If you have to ask a question or make a comment, think about it. Every single thing you say in the place affects it."

Billy looked thoughtful, and then nodded. "You got it. I'll wait until we're out to tell you what I think."

Belecha rolled his eyes.

Tima poked Billy in the side. "We'll keep quiet."

"Good. Second, don't try to explain what you see. Lots of it won't make sense. Let it be. Analyzing puts a wall between it and you. Don't. Dive in. You got questions, ask later. Got it?"

They looked at each other and nodded.

"Last one. Before we go in, take a few breaths and focus. You need to be in the proper frame of mind. Walking into a kiva with a messy mind is like walking into a clean house with mud on your shoes."

Rory closed his eyes and tried to set aside his questions and worry. After a couple of minutes of deep breathing, he opened his eyes and looked at the others, then at Belecha.

Belecha looked closely at the foursome and nodded. "Good. Not so grubby. I'll go down first and light the fire."

Belecha led them to the ladder and climbed down, his buckskin pants quietly swooshing against the rungs. Soon they saw flames flickering. "Okay," he said. "One at a time. Don't hurry. You are doing more than just climbing into a hole, so pay attention."

They hesitated, not sure who should go first. Finally, Billy stepped forward and started down. Before his head disappeared, he grinned and saluted. Then he was gone. Tima went next, keeping her focus on the sky above her as she climbed down. James hung back, but Rory pushed him toward the ladder. He didn't want James to have second thoughts up here alone. James grimaced, drew in a big breath, and went down. Finally, Rory started down.

As he stepped onto the ladder, Rory felt a vibration coming up through the wood into his hands and feet. The ladder was an old-fashioned thing, with rough branches lashed between two thicker poles. The uprights had been worn smooth, probably from thousands of hands passing over them. In spite of the fire below, it was dark and Rory had to feel his way, reaching down each time with his foot to find the next rung. The vibration made it feel like he was climbing down into an enormous, throbbing engine.

From below, he heard Belecha chanting and beating a small drum. It seemed like Belecha was introducing him to the place. The drumming and chanting buzzed in his ears, mixing with the vibration of the ladder as he reached down with one foot, then the other, again and again. His reaching foot finally felt sand and he stepped off the ladder and faced the others, the flickering light dancing across their somber but dazzled faces.

The kiva was dark and cool, a round, open space about 21 feet across, with a few cubbyholes dug into the walls. The walls were smooth, as if they had been plastered, and in the dim light, Rory could see several large glyphs, including the four symbols from their stone, painted on the walls. The domed roof was about 15 feet high in the center, coming down to about 12 feet along the walls. Belecha sat on a large, flat, rock that rose several inches above the ground, a rough cut wooden drum with a painted hide head laying on the rock in front of him. A rattle covered with patterns of lines and more glyphs lay beside the drum. The fire was behind him, casting shadows that danced on the walls. To Rory, it seemed the shadows were moving with the rhythm of the drum. He noticed the fire was under the opening, so that the smoke rose from it out to the sky. A low wall behind the ladder had several pots and baskets carefully stacked behind it.

Belecha stopped drumming and pointed at a place on the wall in front of him. "Sit," he ordered. The four looked at each other, then followed his order, sitting on the sand floor. Rory stared at Belecha. Gone was the wise-cracking trickster. This was an old Grandfather who held the knowledge of the ages.

"You are more than bones and the skin you see in the mirror. You have each decided to come to this world at this time because at this moment, a very old mistake can be set right. To understand what I am saying, you must see the energy world that supports the world you know. Don't try to make sense. Seeing will be enough for now."

Belecha pulled out a small pouch, reached in, then threw a handful of powder into the fire. A small, glowing ball of smoke formed and slowly rose. Instead of moving up and out of the kiva, the ball moved to the center of the roof, directly above Belecha.

Rory sneaked a glance at the others. Tima was staring at the smoke, her eyes shining and a calm smile on her face. James was looking around the kiva, trying to find the source of the smoke's glow. Billy was staring at Belecha, watching for any tricks. Rory looked at Belecha, who nodded at him and gestured with his chin to the smoke.

"The story is up there. Tinglen will be along soon." He grinned at Billy. "He would never believe it if he didn't watch me until everyone else sees, so we'll open it up and then wait for him."

Rory nodded and looked toward the smoke. Belecha spoke in a deep, vibrating voice. "You see the world of sticks and stones and think that's all. In your heart, you know it's not, but you don't know how to see anything else so you allow yourself to be distracted by your world's noise and excitement and the crowd of voices in your head. Still, the world of energy is here all the time, even when your brain refuses to register it. Now, see what you've been missing."

Belecha clapped his hands two times. The sound filled the kiva and left their ears ringing. He clapped again. On the third clap, the ball of smoke quickly spread across the curved ceiling of the kiva and began to glow more and more brightly. As Rory watched, he realized it wasn't the smoke itself that was glowing, but rather what was inside the smoke. Light threads, like the ones they had seen on their way there, pulsed brightly in the air above them.

The air vibrated with the sound of the claps. Like the glowing lights, the vibrations were growing stronger. Rory felt them in the ground and the wall he was leaning against. As the light threads grew, they began to pulse in time with the sound. They moved across the ceiling, aligning themselves, crisscrossing to form a web. It seemed the web was growing larger and larger, expanding up and out. Rory knew he should be able to see the ceiling in the light the web was giving off, but he could not. The ceiling had vanished into a vast dome of stars and beyond them, glowing spheres, and through it all, spun the web of light.

Rory turned to the others to see if they saw the same thing and gasped. They were wrapped in threads of shimmering light that streamed out from their bodies, then up and around the walls and into the web that floated above. "Can you move?" he asked.

Tima grinned broadly. "Uh huh, but look." She slowly waved her hand in front of her body, moving like she was under water. As if it were water, the air shimmered and moved with her motion. From her arms, threads shot out and up the walls. "Isn't it beautiful? Try it."

Rory moved his arm and was amazed to see the same lights coming from his arm and hand. James, who was slowly waving his hand in front of his face, said, "I can't understand how ..."

"Pecheme!" Belecha cut in. "Let it rest. Think later. Feel now."

Rory glanced at Belecha, and his mouth dropped open. The old man was hardly recognizable as human. He was shimmering points of lights wrapped in glowing threads. Rory looked at Billy, who shrugged. "I never stopped looking. I hardly blinked. He did it in slow motion. I could see it happen, like those time-lapse movies where you see plants grow and flowers open, but I couldn't see how he did it." He turned his head and grinned. "Still, I say go with it."

Rory nodded. Billy was good at seeing through lies, but he also could recognize truth. Rory set his questions aside, reveling in the brilliance of the light.

"This is the world of light, the world of energy, in my time," said Belecha. "It is vibrant and easy to tune into. However, it is not like this in the time when you live. That's the trouble. That is why you are needed."

"What do you mean?" asked Tima. "How can something like this change?"

"The threads you see are the trails of energy that connect certain entities to their source. The entities are called Adima or Light Weavers." Belecha slowly moved his arm through the air. Rory watched as the threads shifted and moved, weaving together in the space overhead.

"I am Adima," Belecha continued. "You are Adima. It is as much a part of you as the color of your hair. Actually more a part of you."

James cut in. "I see threads from your rattle," he blurted, "and your drum and ..."

"I know, Pecheme. I used the word entity, because Light Weavers take many forms. Some are living, some are not. Trees, rocks, and things that have been made, like my rattle, can be Adima. They all create, and when they create, they weave the web of light. You will learn more later. For now, I want to show you what things look like in your time."

Belecha began a slow chant, shaking his rattle at the web. As they watched, the threads moved slowly in the sky, as if waving in a soft breeze. The stars behind the threads, however, moved swiftly, like fast motion movies of the sun rising and setting.

"Time is skipping forward like a rock across a pond. You are seeing hundreds of years pass," explained Belecha.

As they watched, the number of threads began to thin. Where the sky was once glowing with the sparkling waves, now there were only a few strands against the blackness.

"We slow even more now, so you can see what is happening. Choose a thread and watch it closely."

Rory picked a thread to watch. As he did, he saw a black dot appear on it, then several more. As he watched, the thread broke and the end waved randomly. Black dots appeared all over the remaining part of the thread and it soon disappeared.

"I saw one dissolve," said Tima, before Rory could speak.

"It didn't dissolve," said Belecha. "What did you see?"

"Black dots. First one, then more and more. The thread broke and dissolved."

"What you saw was the problem. Those weren't dots. They are other beings. We call them Kroledutz. They are

Energy Suckers. Just as Adima create and spin light and energy, they feed on it."

"That's what attacked us last night?" asked Rory.

"That was a single one. There are now countless numbers of the creatures," replied Belecha.

"Why are there more now than in your time?" asked Tima.

"The Kroledutz helped create a stain on this world long ago. That gave them the power to spread like weeds. The Adima could not stop them then, so most of us left."

"Left?" asked James.

"Yes," answered Belecha. "We can follow the thread back to the Spheres – the source, any time. When you know it's going to be cold and nasty for a while, sometimes the best thing to do is go inside and sit by the fire until spring."

"And you think it's spring now?" asked Tima.

"It's possible. Even if it's not, we have to force the issue. The Kroledutz are closing in for a final takeover of this world. If you four can't fix it quick, it won't matter if four more come later. There won't be a way in." Belecha turned to the four. "You are this world's only hope, and you only have four weeks."

Rory looked at the others. None of them appeared enthusiastic about such a task.

"Before you decide," said Belecha, "you need to see the Kroledutz up close and personal. One more ride, and then I'll take you home."

SIX 6

Belecha pulled the Stone from a hidden pouch and laid it in front of them, giving Rory a piercing glare. "You left this where we landed. Let me make an important point about this Stone – life or death important. When you are traveling, this Stone is your one and only ticket home. Without it, I can't get you back."

"I thought you told us we weren't traveling with our bodies," said Billy.

Belecha picked up a pebble and threw it at Billy so fast he didn't have time to duck. It hit him right between the eyes.

"Ow! That hurt."

"How can it hurt if you don't have a body?"

Billy rubbed his head and glared at Belecha. "I dunno. You're the one with the answers."

"Then pay attention. What travels is the energy of your form. That is the most important part of your body. You just aren't carrying around the bag of meat. That's sitting back in your kiva."

Tima looked thoughtful. "What happens if someone sees us back there?"

"Won't happen. Hiding a place from unaware people is pretty easy and I did it before we left. However, the energy form has limitations. It can't carry something physical from here to your time and place. You need your physical bodies for that, and to defeat the Kroledutz you have to bring something from this kiva back to your time." He raised his chin. "I'm not telling you what it is yet."

"So how do we travel with our bodies?" asked Rory.

"You have to activate the Stone. Once you activate the Stone, it becomes a portal and you can travel to any time, place, or dimension with your physical body. Until then, it keeps your energy form stable, especially when you are traveling, especially now when all this is new to you. That is why you have to pay attention to the Stone. If you lose it before you learn a lot more, you are stuck. You can't get back, even with my help."

"Keep track of the Stone. Very important. Got it," said Rory.

"If this kiva is at Rattlesnake Ranch and what we need is in it, why can't we just dig for it in our time?" asked Billy.

"Think back to the times you've been here before. Did you see the kiva or any sign of it?"

"No. There's only that old building that's falling down. Most of the ground is covered with asphalt – I guess it was the parking lot."

"So, how deep do you think we are now?"

All four looked around at the sand walls, but it was James who spoke up. "Based on the time it took to climb down, I'd say we are 12 to 15 feet down."

"Right," said Belecha. "Add to that the several feet of dirt that has covered it in the past 5,000 years, and you'd have quite a bit of digging to do. Think you can do that in your time without anyone noticing and asking what you are doing?"

"No," said Rory. "And even if we could, it wouldn't help. The moment we uncovered it, we'd lose access to it. There'd be archaeologists all over the site in a flash. We couldn't take anything."

"Exactly. You need to activate the Stone, so it becomes a portal, so you can travel here and bring back the key. That is your task."

"How do we do that?" asked Tima.

"To activate the Stone, you must survive four challenges. I can take you, but I cannot help. You four must get through them on your own or die trying. By facing each challenge, you will learn something you need to activate one of the corners. Four corners, four challenges –– get it?"

"What's in it for us?" asked Billy. "This sounds dangerous. Why should we risk our lives for a bunch of glowing threads?"

"You risk your lives either way," said Belecha. "The Kroledutz are looking for you. Now, one of them has found you. I got that one, but more are coming, and it won't take them long to find you. You four stand out. They're coming for you. If you fail, you die. But, if you do nothing, you also die. They won't leave you alone until they rip you apart. Then, they'll turn to everyone else in your world. Is that a good enough reason?"

"Can't we just refuse to play?" asked James.

"No. You'll find out why on one of the challenges, but the Kroledutz won't ask if you want to fight. They will attack and, if you stand there, that's fine with them. It will make it faster and easier to destroy you."

James' face looked sick as he shot a glance toward Tima.

"Like I said, you need to see what you'll be facing before you make any decisions. One more trip. Then I'll take you home." Belecha stood up with a graceful strength that heightened his powerful image. "Ready?"

Everyone turned to James. He took a deep breath, then nodded. "I'm ready."

"Put your hands on the Stone." ordered Belecha. "Hold on. This will be fast, but we won't land like we did here. I'm not sure what might be there to greet us so we're going to stop at a holding point."

"What's that?" asked Rory.

"Think of it as an observation platform. When we get there, keep your eyes open, and your mouths shut." He looked at Billy. "I mean it. One noise at the wrong time and you may not make it back."

Billy nodded. "Got it."

Again, the roaring filled their ears, the shimmering energy cloud filled the kiva, and Belecha faded into a ball of light. He rose and hovered over the Stone. The four teens looked at each other, and grabbed onto the Stone. Following a thread that glowed more brightly than the others, they were quickly pulled up into the web. Soon, they were flashing along a dazzling ribbon of light.

As they sped through the web, Rory saw the same glowing spheres floating beyond the ribbons that he'd seen before, but this time he also saw the countless threads and ribbons that started at each one. The spheres seemed to be wrapped in them. It was the most beautiful thing he'd ever seen, and the rush of speeding along the ribbons, the buzzing of the energy all around was the most glorious feeling he'd ever had.

"This is awesome!" Rory shouted, mouth stretched wide in a grin. "I was born to ride these ribbons."

"Quiet!" called Belecha. "Remember: no talking." He looked down, checking where they were and nodded. "Okay. Hold on!"

They felt a dropping sensation, then a sudden stop. They were just outside a big shopping center in Albuquerque, but the angle was wrong. They weren't in front of it so much as above it, as though they were observing the center from inside a tall building. Looking below them, though, Rory saw only empty air.

Belecha gestured to the mall. "Look at the people," he whispered. "Look for the threads. Relax your eyes and do not focus on what you expect to see. Allow your mind to see what is there."

Rory looked at the people, but instead of focusing and giving each a label, "she's pretty" or "cool shoes," he tried to open his eyes and shut his mind's mouth. As he did, he began to see a cloud around the group he was looking at. At first, his mind tried to explain, and it went away. He tried again, looking and not explaining.

Slowly the threads began to come into view. They were not the bright threads he had seen coming out of his hands, his friend's bodies, or Belecha. They were dimmer, and dark blobs hovered around many of them. As he watched, the picture came into greater focus. The blobs were creatures! The same as the one that had attacked him in the kiva!

The creatures were sucking on the threads of the people down below or floating around, looking for an open thread to grab. Some people had more than one creature attached to them, clinging to them like enormous black leeches. These people had almost no threads left at all they were so dim. As Rory watched, one went out completely.

They were feeding on them! Sucking out the energy. Killing them! It was horrible.

"Stop them!" Tima whispered. "We have to stop them!"

Belecha made a cutting motion with his hand. "I told you quiet! That's an entire nest. They've already eaten almost all the light available here. We stand out like a sun in a dark room. You want to be lunch, Heliotom?"

A huge dark shape suddenly appeared in front of them, blocking their view. Smells of rotten meat, burning plastic, and sweat filled the air, making Rory dizzy. Fear and sadness washed over him. It was like when the thing attacked them, but worse. Much worse. He opened his mouth to scream, but could only gasp in panic.

A screeching, grinding noise roared into Rory's brain. It was laughing! He forced himself to look, noting the red orbs for eyes, the hooked, cruel beak.

"Ah, Belecha!" the creature rasped. "How good to see you after so long. I see you brought treats."

Belecha stepped in front of Rory and the others, growing larger. As he expanded, he grew brighter and brighter, pulsing with power.

"Radelam!" he boomed, his voice making the air shake. "You foul creature, go! We have no use for you!"

Radelam let loose another hideous laugh. "I'm not leaving yet, Belecha. I haven't had my fill." The creature sniffed the air around the four, drawing attention from below. "Ah!" it roared, as more creatures lined up behind it. "You have brought more than treats! You have brought a Stone! Sodrol! Fool! You seal your fate and theirs as well! This ends now."

The thing hurled itself at them as the masses behind rose to attack as well. Belecha threw his arms wide.

"El atlecha at la echem a sta!" he shouted. A burning, bright light shot from his body and reached up to the sky. He glowed brighter, blazing light and color.

With a scream, the Kroledutz fell back, several burning and bubbling. Belecha turned and wrapped himself around the four.

"Hold tight!" he shouted. With that, they leapt up a glowing ribbon and rocketed along a path into the sky.

Rory looked back, but there was no sign of the mall or any of the creatures.

"We're back," Belecha said. "Get ready." They dropped and landed with a thump, back in the hole. Back in their time.

Stunned, they looked at each other, then at Belecha, who had returned to his usual form.

"What-"

"How-"

"Why-"

They all started to talk at once. Belecha held up his hands for silence. When he spoke, he spoke haltingly.

"Look bambinos, I knew Radelam was in the area, but I didn't know he was so close. I didn't know he had an entire nest. This is worse, much worse, than I thought."

Billy was vibrating with anger. "They were killing those people!"

"Yes," Belecha answered sadly, the wrinkles of his face crinkling deeper. "Now you see what they are and what they do when they feed." He looked at the four. "That is what you are facing. It is horrible, and if you do nothing, you and everyone you know are going to be Kroledutz food within the month."

"What can we do?" Tima asked. "We don't know how to-"

Belecha broke in. "I can't talk any more. I have to get back to my kiva. That little trick back there took more energy than I've had to use in two thousand years. You are safe for now, but remember: You must fight or you die. If you choose to fight, you must complete the four challenges. It's the only way. One challenge a week for four weeks. Tonight is the full Turning Moon. Next full moon is the Whale Moon. It will all be over by then, one way or the other."

"We can't win," protested James. "There's no way. Even if we fight, we can't do anything against something like that."

"It won't be easy," Belecha replied, "but it's possible. I wish you had more time or I could give you more hope, but that's not happening. Why don't you at least give it a shot? Commit to one challenge. You make it through alive and you're on your way. You don't, no more worries. If you don't at least try, though, you're dead anyway."

Billy spoke up, still mad. "I'm in. I don't like anything that thinks I'm a snack. I want to know enough to kick that Radelam's butt."

Tima looked at Billy. "I'm with you. That was the worst thing I've ever felt. If they're coming for us, I'd rather have a shot at doing something about it."

Rory nodded. "Things like that don't just go away." He turned to James. "I know this isn't your kind of thing, but all four of us have to do this together and you are one of the four. We can't do this without you." He looked at Belecha. "That's right, isn't it?"

Belecha nodded. "Four or nothing. Four corners, four challenges. Only you four will work."

Rory looked back at James. "One try? Please? Just the first one. Then, if you want out after that, at any time, none of us will stop you." Rory looked at the others. "Agreed?"

"Agreed," said Tima and Billy.

James was silent and looked again toward Tima, holding her gaze with unspoken words. Finally, he sighed and nodded. "Alright. One shot. Then I stay in or go, but it's my decision. And none of you stops talking to me or anything. Deal?"

They all nodded. Then, they turned to Belecha.

Bent, looking very old and tired, he attempted a grin. "Good. Be back here next Sunday at 11:11 – time of the half moon – and we'll take a trip. For now, I've got some healing to do." He started to transform into the shimmering ball of smoke, then stopped. His face reformed.

"Techta, you got the Stone?"

"You bet!" Rory held it up. "After what we just saw, I'm never letting loose of this. When Radelam opens wide for a bite, I want it right here."

Belecha grinned. "Good for you, and good for him. You'll probably give him the farts." With that, Belecha turned once again into the ball of smoke and was gone.

SEVEN 7

The next morning, Billy headed to Rattlesnake Ranch. Belecha's kiva was deep under the ground there and he wanted to see if he could spot exactly where. He knew it wouldn't be like the other times though. Now that that Cisco guy was there, he'd need an excuse to poke around. Luckily, he'd woken up with a great idea. If he could convince Cisco to hire him, he could earn some money and check out the place as much as he wanted.

When Billy arrived, no one was around. A new construction trailer had been moved in and a bulldozer with backhoe sat on the cracked asphalt beside it. The old chain link fence was still there, but every kid in the area knew how to get through it. Billy walked his bike around the back of the yard to one of the easier ways in, where rain runoff had carved a deep groove in the ground. Stashing his bike out of sight, Billy climbed under the fence and walked into the yard.

The backhoe was parked near where Billy figured the kiva had to be located. Billy walked around it, admiring the machine. His brother was a mechanic in Cortez, a few miles away, and occasionally had worked on dozers like the yellow monster Cisco had. Last summer, he had even let Billy drive one and work the back scoop. He wondered if the key was in it. Maybe he could … but no. If he was taking a spin on the dozer when Cisco drove up, there was no way he was going to get a job.

He looked to the west and thought back to last night. He tried to place himself where they had stood. After a while, he was sure. "This is it," he said to himself. "Right under here is the kiva."

He heard a car coming so he walked out to the middle of the yard. Standing between the gate and the trailer, he folded his arms across his chest, put a bored look on his face, and waited.

As the car screeched to a halt outside the gate, Cisco jumped out. "Hey punk!" he yelled. "Get off my property!" He hurriedly pulled out his key and tried to unlock the gate.

Billy just smiled. "Good morning, Mr. Cisco. My name is Billy Fuller, and I need a job. I've figured out a few ways I might be able to help you." He widened his grin. "One is to show you how I got in. There are a bunch of ways that most folks around here know. So, if you are keeping anything in that trailer you don't want people to see …" He saw Cisco look at the trailer with alarm. *Bingo.*

"Of course, if you don't want to know …" Billy started to turn. "And you don't want to know how to get the poor folks, who are most of the people in the county, to come out and support you when the community votes, then I guess I'll be on my way."

"Hold on, Kid," Cisco called, finally unlocking the gate and pulling it open.

Billy turned back and shook his head. "I'm not just a kid. I'm a bad kid and everyone knows it. I know how to keep vandals out 'cause I'm experienced at vandalizing. Plus I hear you're having some problems getting your project approved at the council. I can help there, too. I can get the poor folks to support you because I am one of them. I know all the rowdies in the county and I know how to reach 'em." He paused. "I'll work hard. I figure I'm worth at least $10 an hour."

Cisco widened his eyes and looked shocked. "Ten bucks an hour? That's way too high."

You'd say the same thing if I had asked for two dollars, thought Billy. Out loud he said, "Yeah, well, I know the people. I can do what others can't. I can go all over the county and talk to the people and get them to the next meeting to root for you."

Cisco kept shaking his head. "Tell you what, Kid. I'll pay you five bucks an hour, cash. Take it or leave it. Plus, you'll be learning all I know about how to make it big. I've spent years working small time deals, but I always kept my eyes open for a big opportunity like this. You watch, and you'll learn how to do it, too. That's worth a lot more than the $5 an hour. In fact, that's a lesson in itself – keep your expenses low, especially before the cash starts to flow. I'll give you that for free."

Billy worked on looking like he was holding back tears. "Only five? I'll have to work for you for weeks to pay off a debt I owe. How about seven?"

"Nope," Cisco said, moving to get into his car. "Five is all I got for you. Either take it or get off my property."

Billy smiled to himself as the car rolled by. *I knew he'd go for it. Guys like this can't help taking candy from a kid.* Billy waited until Cisco got out of the car. Then, remembering to look sad, he nodded. "Okay, you win. But I got to get paid every day."

"No problem." Cisco looked up and thought for a moment. "I guess it's summer and school is out. Let's say from 10 in the morning to two in the afternoon every day. Here, working where I can see you."

Billy pulled a horrified face like he never intended to actually have to work for the money. "But I figured I'd spend the mornings going around the county and talking to people and coming up with a plan to get your proposal ..."

Cisco interrupted. "I ain't paying you to talk or think. I do that just fine. If you come up with a plan while you're pulling nails and cleaning salvage from the old building, we can talk about what it's worth." Cisco grinned, certain he had won. "Take it or leave it, Kid."

Billy sighed deeply. "I'll take it."

"I'm doing you a favor, Kid. I hope you appreciate it."

Billy tried to look grateful. "Oh, I do. Thank you, Mr. Cisco."

"Be back here tomorrow at 10 ready to work. Don't plan on lazing around. I got a big, mean guy named Matt who will be making sure you don't rip me off."

"Yes, sir. Thanks a lot."

"Now get outta here. I've got things to do." He walked away without a backward glance. Billy watched as he climbed the steps to the office door, unlocked it, and stepped inside. A minute later, lights came on and the air conditioner kicked in.

Billy slipped back under the fence, grabbed his bike, and headed home grinning. He had an in. "He's got something in that trailer, and I'm going to figure out how to take a look. I'll just act stupid for a while, and he'll get sloppy. When he gets sloppy, I'll be waiting!"

EIGHT 8

"Mijo!" Leon called, coming through the office door, "It's your dad."

"Thanks," said Rory, turning away from the computer.

Javier was in Florida dealing with the custody suit. While he was gone, Rory was researching the glyph symbols on Belecha's stone. His dad had been able to give him a few pointers on where to start looking before he'd left town, but he hadn't had time to do the research with him.

Leon held out the home phone. Wood chips and sawdust clung to his hairy arms. As Rory took the phone, he noticed a few had found their way into Leon's beard. "Work must be going well," he said.

Leon nodded and smiled, laying one hand on Rory's shoulder. With his strong fingers he gave Rory a quick squeeze. Then, he turned and left. "Hey, Pa," said Rory, turning back to the computer. "How's the gooey South?"

"Not so good." Javier sounded tired and depressed. "It's like the humidity keeps everyone from doing anything too fast, including think. How are you and Leon?"

"Fine. Leon's almost finished with his carving. How bad is it?"

"Kathy says she isn't interested in money."

"Right. She only cares about me."

"Actually, yes, that's what she's saying. That and getting you to Florida is the only way to save your soul."

"What! She actually said that?"

"Yeah. Several times, and she's not budging. She seems to have really found a place for herself down here with this guy and the church he belongs to. She wants you here with her."

"That's nuts! I don't want to live with her." Rory paused. "I mean, one time … maybe …" Shaking his head, he rallied.

"But not now! Not when things are so good and we've finally settled somewhere!"

"I know, Son. I don't want that either, but it isn't looking good. I talked to a lawyer today. She said that under Florida law your mom has a good chance. Most of the judges here like to give mothers custody. And then when the judge considers that you have two fathers ..."

"Won't they listen to me? My voice should count for something."

"The court will listen to you. They want to talk to you, but they want to talk to you here." His dad paused. Rory could tell he wouldn't like whatever was coming. "They want you to come for a month."

"What! No way! I need to ... I'm supposed to meet everyone in the hole on Sunday night. We're supposed to ..."

"I'm telling you what they want. Nothing is decided yet, but I'm pretty sure you are going to have to spend some time here."

"I don't want to go!" Rory yelled. "I won't go! They can't break up our home!"

"Rory, if you get mad and start yelling, your mother will win. The only way the court will listen to you is if you show you're worth listening to. You have to stay calm, be mature. Do you understand?"

"Yes," Rory sighed. "I understand."

"If you can do that, despite what the lawyer says, I think we have a chance, especially if we show that this is an old pattern of hers; your mom falls into a new place, decides she wants you with her, and then a few weeks or months later decides she's done with the place and leaves, all thoughts of you coming to stay vanishing with her." Javier paused. "Besides," he added, "we have you, and I'm very proud of you."

"Thanks, Dad." Rory took a deep breath. "Alright. When is this going to happen, and how short can it be? I won't do a whole month. I can't. I'll run away first."

"I'll talk more with the lawyer tomorrow. We're going to meet with the judge and make a case for a shorter trip. I hope we can convince him to keep it to under a week."

"Yeah, I bet a week with me will be more than she can stand."

"Now Rory, you have to behave."

"I'm not going to set fire to their house or anything, but just because I don't act much like a kid around here doesn't mean I don't know how to. She doesn't know me anymore, and I'm going to do my best to be a sulking, smelly, messy, demanding, noisy teenager. Heck, I might even get to like it so much I'll try it when I get back here."

His dad laughed. "Not a chance. Try that act, and I'll let Leon deal with you."

"Man! Life just isn't fair!"

"I'm crying, Rory. Real tears. Now, let me talk to Leon. It may be another couple of days before we get to see the judge. Then I'll be back."

"Okay, Dad. Thanks for fighting for me. If I had to move away from you …"

Javier broke in, "Rory, you are my son. I love you. Of course I'll fight for you. That's my job. I won't pick up your dirty socks, but this … this is on my chore list and I'm glad to do it. You're worth it."

"Thanks, Dad."

"Now get Leon, and don't mess up my office. I want a full report on everything that's been happening when I get back."

"Sure thing." Rory went to the door and called down to Leon. "Leon! Dad wants to talk with you." He listened until he heard Leon pick up the other phone receiver and say, "Hola, Corazón …" Then he hung up.

Turning back to the computer, Rory thought about Belecha's warning that they only had a month. "I hope we have a whole month, old man. It looks like the poo is going to start flying a lot faster than that."

<u>NINE</u> 9

They met again on Sunday night, nervous but determined. Belecha, in human form with his same leather clothing and long braids, looked at the four teens. "Are you clear on what's going to happen?" he asked. "I don't want Pecheme to go all squirmy when he finds himself in a different place."

James glared at Belecha. He wasn't happy to be here, but he never backed down from a commitment. Tima touched his arm to calm him. She answered Belecha. "We told you we'd do this."

Billy looked at the old man, measuring him. "Once. We agreed to give you one shot."

Belecha grinned. "You still think I'm making this up, don't you?"

Billy shrugged. "We'll see."

Belecha nodded. "When we land, you head straight up the hill toward the fire. You'll meet Mealim there. She's the teacher for this challenge. I'll stay with the Stone and keep the portal open."

"Why aren't you coming?" asked Billy.

"Two reasons. Well, three. First, if I keep the portal open, you'll get back faster – if you live. Second, you have to learn the lessons and go through the challenge on your own. If I'm there, you won't look for your own solutions, you'll look for mine. That won't work."

Rory noticed he wasn't saying any more. "What's the third reason?"

Belecha looked a bit embarrassed. "Well, Mealim and I go back, and she's got a pretty sharp tongue, and she likes to use it on me."

Billy whistled. "The great and powerful warrior is afraid of someone?"

"Just wait 'til you meet her," he deadpanned. "If you want my advice, be polite."

Rory, ready to get things started, clapped his hands together. "Let's do this."

As before, all four of the teens sat around the Stone. Once the energy threads appeared, Belecha reached out grabbed one. With a quick jerk, the group was speeding along a wide ribbon of light through the web. The same rush of freedom filled Rory, and he was disappointed when Belecha called out too soon, "Get ready ... Now!"

They bumped down in a rocky clearing along a rough mountain trail.

Standing, Rory looked around. This felt different than New Mexico. There was more water in the air and less oxygen. He could tell they were in high mountains. Belecha pointed up the trail toward the top.

"That way. I'll wait here."

"I think I see a fire," said Tima.

"Go on," ordered Belecha. "She's expecting you."

Billy flashed him a grin. "Sure you don't wanna come?" Belecha gave him a stern look in return. "No worries. I'll give her a kiss for you."

"Try it, boy," Belecha muttered, mostly to himself. "She'll rip your lips off."

They headed up the steep trail. "Rory," Tima said, looking up at the sky, "do you notice that the stars are different?"

Rory glanced up and then stopped, staring. "That can't be!"

"What?"

"I can see Taurus, and look, there are the seven sisters – the Pleiades. My dad used to point them out all the time because so many ancient people have origin myths about them."

"What's so strange about that?" asked Billy.

"The Pleiades aren't visible in the summer, at least not in New Mexico."

"Really? Where can you see them?" asked Tima.

"In the southern hemisphere. We would see them when we were on digs in Peru. In fact, that's what this feels like, the high mountains of the Andes."

Tima nodded. "I had a feeling we were in a different place."

They continued up the path. The thin air and the steep grade made conversation hard. The path swung around a huge rock wall and began to circle again up into the darkness. At the base of the bare stone wall was a small cave. In front of the mouth of the cave a fire burned. Between the fire and the cave sat a figure. A pot that hung over the fire bubbled and gave off a wonderful smell.

Looking up as they approached, a small, compact woman stood and stirred the pot. The aroma reached out to them. "Who's hungry?" she asked with a welcoming smile.

As one, they stepped forward, any worry and shyness torn away by the sudden growling of their bellies. Soon, they sat in a semi-circle, just inside the cave, busily inhaling bowls of the wonderful stew.

As he ate, Rory studied the cave. It didn't go back far, but its roof was blackened from thousands of fires. The walls had been worn smooth by hands passing over them over the years. There were paintings on the walls that resembled the symbols etched on their Stone. The ground was sand, comfortable to sit on, and, he suspected, not bad to sleep on either. The cave and the fire and the food all gave a feeling of safety, security, home. He felt he had been here before and was glad to come back. The others also seemed to relax.

The woman was old and calm and remained quiet. Her lined face smiled gently as she watched them eat. She seemed glad they were there and happy they were enjoying the food. When Rory's eyes met hers, she smiled extra big.

"So, you're traveling with the old raccoon?" she asked.

"Raccoon?" asked Rory.

She nodded. "Belecha. He's a raccoon if there ever was one. Plenty smart. Plenty mean if necessary. Always getting into things and leaving a mess." She chuckled and looked down toward where they started. "I guess he was too scared to come up with you."

Billy grinned. "He said he would get in the way of our learning."

"Humph. More likely he knew he'd get in the way of my cooking pot when I tossed it at his head. He's a trickster, that one. How'd he get you to come? "

Tima answered. "He told us the Kroledutz would kill us and everyone we know if we didn't learn how to stop them."

"We told him we'd give him one chance to convince us," said Billy. "Is that what you're going to do?"

The old woman's face changed. Rory had seen that look on the face of teachers. It never came before anything pleasant. In an instant, Mealim unbent and expanded, transforming into a huge, horrifying creature, filling the entire opening of the cave. Her eyes burned with flames. Her mouth unhinged and gaped open, revealing what looked like a boiling universe of stars and suns. An earth-shaking roar of rage tore from her mouth.

Now Rory understood why Belecha had stayed behind. They all cowered back, looking for a way to escape. The thing that had been Mealim was blocking the mouth of the cave. There was no back exit. They were trapped.

Rory's mouth went dry and he looked at Billy, thinking he might have some ideas, but Billy shook his head. Rory had an inspiration. He dropped to his knees in front of the thing and bowed deeply.

"I'm ... we're ... we didn't mean to be disrespectful," he stammered. "We just don't know what to believe, and we were hoping you could help us." He bowed again, motioning frantically to the others to do the same. One by one, they caught on and bowed.

Slowly, very slowly, the fiery creature began to fade and fold in on itself. Before their frightened eyes, the thing again became Mealim. It was as if they had all imagined the transformation. As they watched, even the stern look on her face relaxed and before them, bent and smiling, once again was the calm old lady. Now, though, they knew better than to be fooled by appearances.

Mealim spoke as if nothing unusual had just happened. "I am not here to convince you. I am here to offer you pieces of the story, pieces that will help you meet your challenges. Then, it is your responsibility to do what you wish."

She peered closely at each of them. "Sit," she ordered, waving off their bowed poses. "I am going to give you three things, three key things. Each of your challenges will include these same three things. Listen closely. The first is a story."

"Is the story true?" asked Tima.

"There is no true. There is useful or not useful. The second thing I will give you is a piece of the puzzle. The third will be a challenge. You will solve the challenge by using the information in the story and the piece of the puzzle." Looking at the four skeptical teens, she nodded to herself. "Words won't do. I will begin by showing you – showing you who you are."

Mealim closed her eyes and struck the ground with her stick. As the staff struck the ground the first time, she began to grow. Her body stretched taller and thinner.

The staff struck the ground a second time, and her face and arms disappeared. She was transforming into a writhing snake standing on its tail, reaching up to the sky, silhouetted by the fire that was again roaring higher, filling the entrance to the cave. The Mealim serpent stretched taller than the mouth of the cave. The staff fell to the ground, striking the ground a third time.

The air filled with a glowing, sparkling mist. The Mealim snake, writhing in the entrance, transfixed Rory's gaze. Fog, filled with pulsing points of light, billowed in front of his eyes, making it harder and harder to see her. He realized she was fading. He could see the sparkling points in the mist in front of her. Behind her, he could see the fire blazing higher and higher through her undulating body.

"What's happening to me?" James screamed.

Rory tore his eyes away from Mealim. James was fading away, too!

"I can see right through my hand!" yelled James in a panic.

"Dude, calm down," said Billy.

"Ahhh!" screamed James. "You're fading, too."

Rory looked at Billy. Even with the light of the roaring fire, Billy was fading away.

"We are all fading," said Tima. "Look at your hands."

Rory looked down. He could see right through his hands. Then, as he watched, they vanished. They weren't invisible. They had simply dissolved into the mist. The rest of his body was fading, too, but somehow he was still there, just in a different form than any he had ever experienced before.

He tried to take a deep breath, but he couldn't. He didn't have lungs. It was a weird sensation. Not particularly bad; it wasn't like he was dying. He couldn't breathe, but he didn't need to. It came to him. *I'm part of the mist.*

"Can you hear me?" Tima asked.

"Of course," replied Billy.

"Where are you?" yelled James.

Rory realized he could see in all directions, not just one like usual. The entire cave was filled with the glowing mist, and he was everywhere in it.

Tima's voice cut through his thoughts, calm and thoughtful. "Can you see in every direction?"

"Yeah," said Billy, excited. "It's like I have eyes in the back of my head – the sides and top, too."

"But you don't have a head," yelled James. "None of us do! We don't exist."

Mealim's voice cut through his panic. "Of course you exist. If you did not exist, how could you be making such a racket?"

This did not calm James. "You stole my body! Give it back! Give it back!"

"James," reasoned Tima. "Calm down. We are obviously supposed to be learning something here, and you're not helping."

Mealim's voice came from the front of the cave. "Exactly. Now, I will explain."

Three claps rang out, and the four teens, once more in their familiar forms, dropped to the ground. The mist vanished, and Mealim slowly appeared before them. She spoke, her voice like a rush of wind roaring through uncountable years. "I have shown you. You have felt it. You have experienced what you truly are. These bodies are the clothes you wear for an instant of experience. I have not asked you to understand. I have forced you to experience. You now know."

Even as he shook the dirt off of his hands, Rory felt each word vibrate through him. He knew what she said was true.

Mealim picked up her staff again and pointed to the spot in front of her. Shaken, each of them slowly took their places. Mealim drew a large oval in the sand and spoke as she drew. "From the beginning of existence there has been aware energy. This energy has two very basic drives – to share and to experience. In order to share, energy came together, forming Spheres."

"Spheres?" asked Tima. "Not one?"

"Countless Spheres formed," Mealim replied. "At first the energy moved together into one, but as differing interests arose, new Spheres formed." She slowed her words slightly. "Energy seeking certain experiences is drawn to similar energy to form a Sphere. There are as many Spheres as there are interests. It's like in your school, where there are groups interested in sports, in singing, in theater."

Mealim began to draw lines extending out from the egg-shaped oval in the sand. "The second drive is to experience – to learn and create. In order to experience, each Sphere extended energy into worlds, becoming entities."

"You mean that everything we see is an extension from these Spheres?" asked Billy.

"No." answered Mealim, shaking her head. "Everything is not of the Spheres. On this planet, countless objects exist, and only a small number come from a Sphere."

"Are the Adima extensions of the Spheres?" asked Rory.

"Yes. Every Light Weaver is from a Sphere. We are not sure, but we suspect that the Kroledutz are also Sphere extensions. However, no Adima has ever seen a Sphere that would extend such creatures."

"What happens when Adima die?" asked Rory.

"When the energy has experienced what it wishes, it returns to the Sphere. The energy again becomes part of the Sphere and shares the experiences with the whole." She looked at them. "This process continues as it has continued from the beginning of the Spheres until now."

She sat down, her head at their level. "That is the end of the story."

TEN 10

"What do the Spheres have to do with us?" asked James, calmer now that he was back in his familiar body.

Mealim nodded, as if expecting the question. "Most of the time, a Sphere forms a single Adima to have an experience. However, some experiences require a group of entities, each with its own role, but all working together on a specific task. That requires a special kind of Adima and a Stone."

"Like our Stone?" asked Billy.

Mealim nodded. "Yours is one of these Stones." She smoothed out the sand and drew the familiar rounded rectangle. As she drew the glyphs in each corner, she said, "Within each Sphere there exist glowing seeds. Just as a plant starts with a seed and a different seed will create a different plant, sometimes Adima form around one of these light seeds. When an entity has a light seed at its core, the seed affects how that being forms and grows. The seed shapes the being and gives special powers."

"Do you have a seed at your core?" asked Rory.

"I do not. Seed bearers are very rare. We call them Sodrol. They only form when the Sphere has decided that a very specific experience would be useful. Then, from the Sphere, a Stone is created. The Stone attracts the seeds that are needed. Around the seeds, the Sodrol form.

"The Stone represents a specific task. The hole represents the Sphere that decided to initiate the adventure. The carvings on your Stone indicate the types of seeds needed. Each seed will be at the core of a Sodrol, the entity formed with the special powers of that seed."

James opened his mouth, but Mealim explained before he asked.

"If you want to build a table, you need a saw, a measuring tool, a hammer, and nails. A chainsaw won't help. If a Sphere wants a particular experience, it chooses the tools that are best suited.

"This Stone," she continued, "calls to a specific group of Sodrol and can only be used by them."

"So, it's like it's a lock and only the Sodrol have the combination?" asked Rory.

Mealim smiled. "A combination is a good description. To use the Stone, the Sodrol must learn the combination to activate it. However, each Sodrol can only unlock one part of the combination. In order to unlock that part, the Sodrol must become aware of its own true nature – the Seed at its core. Until they all know who they are, they cannot activate the entire Stone and use it."

James looked at her, knowing, but dreading the answer. "Are we the Sodrol for this particular Stone?"

She nodded. "Each one of you has at your core one of the seeds represented by the glyphs on the Stone. You have come from a Sphere to complete this specific task. It was your choice before you began this life. Each of you has a unique role in completing the task."

Tima spoke up. "How do we know who we are – which one is which?"

"Even if we know, what do we do to activate the Stone?" asked Rory.

Mealim smiled. "That is my piece of the puzzle, my second gift to you. I will give you three pieces of information. You may not understand them, but they are all useful. You may only have the information I give you. I will not answer any questions. Do you understand?"

They all nodded.

"Good. Here is the first piece of information. You can only discover your own nature – the seed at your core – during a challenge. During each of the four challenges, you will find yourself in impossible danger. You have only one hope for survival and that is the knowledge held by a particular Sodrol. To save the lives of all, the one Sodrol who holds the key knowledge for that challenge must realize and accept his or her true nature. If that happens, the way to escape the danger will be clear. If not, all will perish and return to the Sphere. Each challenge will require a different Sodrol; the others will not be able to see the solution. As you face the challenges, each of you will be forced to see into yourself and learn your true nature and take action based on that knowledge."

Mealim looked hard at each one in turn. "You can only see and know through action. That is why I forced you to experience your true form and did not try to explain. You cannot learn your seed by analyzing. When your mind tries to explain, it puts a wall between what is and you. You cannot know by thinking. You must experience and act to truly know. That is the purpose of the challenge – to force each one to act and so to know."

"But if we don't figure it out, we die?" asked James.

"You will cease to be outside the Sphere. This experience will end."

James opened his mouth to protest, but she stopped him. "I will not argue or discuss. Time is short now and if you argue, you will not have the information you need to survive." James looked sick, but he kept quiet.

"Second. By surviving the challenge, the particular Sodrol learns who he or she is and also intuitively how to activate the corresponding corner of the Stone."

Panic was growing in Rory's chest. This was not just some field trip! There was a very good chance they were not going to make it home. He looked at the others. Tima was concentrating completely on Mealim's words. James looked like he was about to hurl. Billy looked back at Rory and shrugged. "We'll deal," he whispered.

Mealim was speaking again, pointing to each corner of the Stone. "The third piece of information I will give you is the definition and strength of each of the four glyphs."

She pointed to the crude thunderbird. "This is the bird who draws strength from the air. It brings the tool of perception. Just like the eagle and the hawk, it can see the smallest creature either through pinpoint sight or by observing slight changes in patterns to see through the masks and camouflage others use. The bird can see the truth from great distance and, once it sees, can also see the direction or path the prey takes. The bird dives with deadly accuracy to arrive where the prey will be, not where it is now. The bird sees what is truly there, waits its time, feels and thinks ahead of others, and takes swift action."

She pointed to the crooked line. "This is the snake. It draws its strength from fire and brings the tool of change. Just as fire changes air and wood to flame and ash, the snake molts, leaving behind its old self without regret or fear. The snake knows what is essential and what can be discarded. It grows through change and understands that change also means choosing what is kept and what is cast away, for nothing changes without leaving behind a skin.

"This one is the buffalo." She pointed to the glyph. "It is of the earth, bringing forth patience and nourishment in the long and short rhythm of the seasons. It is attached to the strength of nature across all times and dimensions. It holds the knowledge of the rocks that wear down to sand, melt into magma, erupt into air, and form into rocks again. It has the explosive power of the fire at the earth's core. It can summon the calm of the mountains that measure their lifetime in millions of years."

Finally, she pointed to the glyph of the fish. "This is the whale. The whale brings the tool of crossing boundaries. It is of the water, but it breathes air. It is the largest animal, but lives on tiny plants and creatures. It can travel the depths of the ocean, but must come to the surface. The whale appreciates the essence of each of the other Sodrol and can see through their eyes. It can cross and combine viewpoints to see a new direction and solution in the most impossible times."

Mealim stood and nodded. "This is all I have to teach you. Your challenge is before you. Farewell."

Then she transformed into a ball of light and began to disappear, just like Belecha. The teens sat stunned. As she vanished, the fire exploded upward and out, filling the entrance with roaring flames. The air grew hotter, forcing the friends against the cave's back wall. The fire grew.

Billy looked around. "There's no way out the back. I've been checking since we got here."

"The air isn't going to last!" yelled James above the roar. "We need to get past that fire or put it out."

Rory looked at the raging inferno, thinking over the words they had heard. "This is the challenge. She told us we have a way to overcome the challenge. One of the four glyphs."

"She said we would know which one," Tima added.

"She said one of us would know," James corrected. "She also said it was not about thinking, but about knowing." He seemed to be calmer, now that there was a problem to solve.

The fire reached higher and ever closer. The air was getting hard to breathe, it was so hot. The howling of the flames filled their ears and the smoke burned their eyes.

"Maybe we can put it out somehow," suggested Rory. "There's a lot of sand here. Maybe if we throw it, we can clear enough of a path to get out."

"No way!" shouted Billy. "We don't have time. The air is almost gone."

"I agree!" yelled James. "At this rate, we'll pass out any minute. I already have a monster headache. Lack of oxygen."

"Me too," said Billy. "Head's killing me. 'Course, in about three minutes, it'll be the flames so this is as good as it gets."

Tima punched his shoulder. "Shut up. We have to find an answer. They don't want to kill us. They want us to solve the challenge. What were the four glyphs?"

Rory closed his eyes and pictured Mealim drawing in the sand. "Bird is from the air and brings the power of perception. Snake from fire, brings the power of change. Buffalo is earth, with time and patience. Whale from water and crosses boundaries."

"Remember," said Tima, "we have to decide what glyph applies and who the Sodrol is for that glyph."

James nodded. "I think we can eliminate buffalo and bird. No bird could fly through that fire and patience is not what we need now."

They were all gasping for air, their faces red and gleaming with sweat. Rory looked around, eyes burning with smoke and regret. "Look everyone, I'm really sorry. It was my idea to dig the hole and I got us into this and now-"

James punched him in the arm. "Shut up!" He glared at Rory. "It's not over 'til it's over and there's no use spending our last minutes whining. We each decided. If we get out of this, we'll each decide what to do next. Now shut up, and let's deal with it."

Rory looked at the others. They had the same look on their faces – desperate, but determined. Rory nodded.

"Okay. Thanks."

"So, whale or snake," said Tima.

Billy had a flash of inspiration. "It's snake, of course."

Rory remembered Mealim turning into a snake. "That's right, she showed us."

Billy nodded. "And the snake is fire, and that's our problem."

Rory panted, feeling dizzy from lack of air. "Its power is change and knowing what to leave behind, but what does that mean?"

"Well first, we better be like snakes and get our heads down at ground level," James rasped. "There's not much air left."

They all lay down as the fire battered them with heat.

Gasping, Rory thought back to Mealim's words. "We have to look inside. It's not something we all can figure out. One of us is the Sodrol and knows the answer."

The fire roared. Talking was too much effort. There was not enough air. They fell silent, looking at each other in the burning light as the smoke and sparks filled the air. Rory closed his eyes and tried to go inside, but he couldn't come up with any ideas or answers. *This is it,* he thought.

Rory opened his eyes. Tima was staring at him.

"Our bodies," she rasped. She started to pull herself up, using the wall of the cave, staring at the blazing inferno. "We are going out straight through the fire."

"What?" protested James. "We'll fry."

Tima was certain. "Not if we lose our form and become those clouds of Energy. That is what she was showing us. Belecha told us, too. These bodies are illusions."

Rory straightened too. "Yeah, but how do we turn into the cloud? We only changed when Mealim or Belecha did it to us."

"No," said Tima. "They helped us, but it is what we are. I know. I can feel it." She looked at Rory. "It's me. This is my seed." Her eyes were sparkling. "What we have to do is leave behind our view of our body. All we need to do to walk out of here is to walk out of here. The fire is real, but our bodies don't have to be."

James shook his head. "That's ridiculous. Of course we have bodies. You try to walk through that, and you'll be toast before you get near it."

"We can do this," said Tima. "I'll show you. Everyone, follow me." Closing her eyes, Tima walked, head high, closer and closer to the fire.

"Tima! Stop!" screamed James.

Tima didn't stop. She walked to and then into the fire. As the flames closed around her, her body melted. It didn't burn. It faded into a sphere of glowing mist that Mealim had become. Then she was gone. The three boys looked at each other.

"Do you think ...?" asked Rory.

"She's dead!" croaked James.

"Shut up, James," came Tima's voice from the other side of fire. Her face poked through the flames. "If you guys don't want to end up as bar-b-que, you better get moving because this fire is about to totally blow."

The boys struggled to their feet. James hung back, unable to take the plunge. Rory and Billy looked at each other, grabbed James' hands, and raced toward the fire.

"Noooooooo!" James screamed, holding them back from the flames. The smoke and heat and roar of the fire filled their senses. James' fear was too strong. Even with both of them pulling, he was rooted like a tree. Rory looked at Billy helpless, trying to think of something as the smoke filled his lungs.

Then, through the fire, came a long, thin, glowing form. Like a python, it wrapped around all three. "Come on, you wimps," said Tima fiercely. "I told you what to do and I am not going to have you blow it the first time out."

The Tima snake pulled them toward the flames. James could not stop it. The fire roared closer and closer and then, they were pulled in, flames closing all around.

Rory felt a floating sensation and looked down. They were in the middle of the fire, but he no longer held James' hand because neither he nor James had a hand to hold. He was floating and was as much a part of the fire as the sand beneath the fire and the stars above.

He heard Tima's voice. "Come on, you're almost through. Just follow my voice."

Suddenly, he was out, floating in the clear mountain air, feeling, more than seeing, the stars above, the mountains all around, and the fire, now behind them.

Tima's voice intruded. "Glad you made it. Pretty great, isn't it?"

"This is the most amazing feeling!" James said, awe replacing fear in his voice. "I don't know why I was so scared before."

"We had to give up our attachment to the body," said Tima. "That was the challenge. I got it first, because I'm the snake."

Billy laughed. "If I said that to you, you'd probably punch me. So, do you know what to bring back to make the Stone work for your glyph?"

Tima was silent, thinking. Then, "Of course. Now I see it. It's so obvious. Yes. I know. Let's get back."

Rory was enjoying himself, pointing his thoughts and his 'eyes' in every different direction. "How do we get back into our bodies, if we left them behind?"

Tima slowly faded in on the trail near the fire. "We didn't leave our bodies behind. We left our attachment and our belief in our bodies. We left the idea that our bodies end with our skin, that our body is who we are. Just focus on your body, and it will come together."

Rory tried, but didn't have much luck.

Billy faded in beside Tima. "Try concentrating on your breathing. Feel the breath going in and out. It has to have something to go in and out of, so your body can kind of grow from your lungs out."

Tima grinned. "Your body probably grows from your mouth out."

James faded into sight next to his friends. "That's pretty easy."

Rory still was struggling. Finally, he tried focusing all his attention on his three friends. Instead of seeing in all directions at once, he directed his attention toward them. He looked down and saw his body slowly coming into view. Soon, he was all there. The friends beamed at each other.

James spoke first. "I wonder if they all will be such a snap."

Billy shook his head and snorted. "Yeah, 'cause you were so calm the whole time."

James opened his mouth to protest, but Tima broke in. "Cool it, guys. Let's go home."

Billy grinned. "Sure, snake girl. Hate to think you are boa-ed."

Rory moaned. "Maybe we should leave you here."

"You can't. Remember, we all have to make it through all of the challenges. You leave me here and you'll be toast when you need my expertise -- whatever it is."

"We haven't decided if we are going on any more," said Tima.

They all looked at James. He looked shocked. "Of course we are going on more. Who's going to wimp out? I've got to find out which one I am."

Rory nodded. "I'm in."

Tima and Billy grinned. Then, they all headed back down the trail to where Belecha waited.

"Hey ya!" he shouted when he saw them. "I was about to give up. Thought you guys were toast."

Billy grinned. "Hush up, you old raccoon. Your girlfriend says hi."

Belecha frowned. "Here I was hoping if you lived, you'd be a little less mouthy."

Billy shook his head. "No such luck. Now, get us home before I make a hat out of you."

"Huh. This is getting harder by the minute." Belecha looked at Tima. "You know what to bring back, Heliotom?" Tima nodded. "Good. Then grab hold of the Stone. Let's get you home."

Once more, they sat around the Stone. Tima turned it so the snake faced her. As they all reached out and touched it, the Stone grew and they rose toward the lines of shimmering light, streaking along the web.

Soon, they landed in the hole. Once more, the Stone was small and resting between them.

Belecha spoke. "Now, Heliotom, it's time. Activate the Stone."

Tima nodded. Rubbing her thumb and her forefinger together over the snake glyph, she explained. "The snake sheds its skin, but remains a snake. We learned we can leave our bodies and still have our bodies. So, to activate the snake, use some skin. We constantly shed our skin, but we never notice, because we always are growing new skin. We change completely, but our mind holds us together as an unchanged being."

Belecha nodded. As a few skin cells from Tima's finger dropped onto the Stone, the snake glyph began to glow from within, like a miniature river of fire flowing through the carving. Then it faded, but the corner that held the snake glyph had a shine that none of the others had.

"It is done," said Belecha.

Suddenly very tired, the four looked at each other.

"Let's call it a night," said James. "I'm beat."

They all agreed. Belecha looked at them. "Tell me first: Are you going to try the second challenge?"

Too tired to talk, they nodded.

"I figured you wouldn't be able to turn tail once you got the taste. The real world is better than any half-life fantasy."

Rory grinned, realizing how true this was, even through his weariness.

Belecha clapped his hands together three times, as if calling an end to a ceremony. "Next Sunday. Night of the new moon. Same time. Same place. Be ready." With that, he faded out.

Mumbling their farewells, the four climbed out of the kiva and headed home.

A short time later, Rory slipped into the house. All was quiet. There was a plate of fresh oatmeal-walnut cookies and a note from Leon. "Good adventuring, mijo. See you when you wake up."

Rory smiled, grabbed a handful of cookies and a glass of milk and went upstairs. He looked out the window at the stars for a minute, wondering where he had traveled this evening. Too much to think about, he decided. So, finishing the milk, he pulled off his clothes, fell into bed, and was soon sound asleep.

ELEVEN 11

"Dad!" Rory had been trying to use the star positions they'd seen at the cave to figure out where they might have been during the challenge when Javier came in, weary, but smiling, still holding his suitcase. Rory threw his arms around him. "I'm glad you're back!"

Javier squeezed his son. "That makes two of us." He ruffled Rory's hair. "Any new developments?"

Rory grinned. "A couple. You want to hear about it now, or do we need to talk about Florida first?"

Javier shook his head. "Florida can wait. This is more interesting, but maybe I can shower some of this airport and travel yuck off first. Ten minutes?"

Rory nodded. "Downstairs? I know Leon's been cooking something special, and I'm sure it's better than whatever you've been eating."

"Even what you cook is better than what I've been eating."

Rory poked him in the side. "I'm not a bad cook. At least not as bad as some I've tasted ... Dad."

Javier held up his hands. "Guilty as charged." He turned to go. "See you soon."

Soon, they were gathered around the table. Leon's *sopa seca* had quickly moved from bowls to bellies. Javier pushed back his empty bowl. "Okay, you're up Rory. Let's hear it."

Rory described the journeys with Belecha, first, to his kiva, then to Albuquerque, and finally to the cave and the first challenge, filling in details as Javier or Leon asked. Both of them had enough experience in ancient cultures to question details, but not his sanity.

"So, what do you think?" he asked when he was finished.

Leon spoke first. "Must be hard. Watching, I mean. He must have watched all his friends die. Then, lifetimes of people, without being part of it."

"I never thought about that," said Rory. "He doesn't seem sad."

Leon shook his head. "No, I don't suppose you would see it." He cocked his head and looked at Rory. "I have to wonder why he picked you, mijo."

"He didn't pick me. He said we all decided to come here for this."

"Yes, but he spoke to you first. He said the others would follow if you decided. I have a feeling he has something in mind for you."

"I don't know. It was Tima who got us through the first challenge."

"You said his kiva is at Rattlesnake Ranch, right?" asked Javier, leaning forward.

"Yeah."

"What a find!" Javier's eyes danced, any signs of fatigue suddenly vanished. "If we can excavate it, we could learn a lot about the people of his time. Think of it! Proof of a civilization thousands of years older than any other in North America!"

"No! We can't do that, Dad!" Concern spread across Rory's face. "Belecha said his power comes from the kiva. He doesn't want us to mess with it. Besides, the land belongs to Mr. Cisco. That's where he wants to build that quick market and fun center."

Javier looked alarmed. "He can't do that! It'll destroy the kiva and anything that's inside of it. I'll get an order from the state historical commission to halt it."

Rory grinned. "And what will you tell them? Your 14-year-old son traveled through time, and saw it when it was a kiva?"

"No, you're right." Javier shook his head. "That won't work, but if you can convince Belecha to let us excavate at least a part of it, then we can use what we find to halt Cisco's project. You'll just need to get him to agree. Tell him how careful we are."

"Okay, Dad, I'll ask him, but I really don't think he'll agree."

"Just try. If he says it's okay, I'll figure out a way to get in there and get enough proof of its importance to get the commission to stop work on the site until we investigate further."

"I'll talk with him about it."

"Great. In the meantime, I want to interview you on the details. I want to get as many notes as possible on everything you saw and felt while you were in the kiva. We should start tomorrow. I want to get as much information as I can before …"

Rory looked at him sharply. "Before what?"

Javier sighed. "Before you go to Florida. The lawyer talked to the judge. He insisted that you come and spend time with your mother and be interviewed by both lawyers, plus a psychologist, plus a family services case worker. Like it or not, it's got to happen or we lose before we begin. Be prepared. They are going to ask a lot of personal questions."

"Who are they to ask about us?" Rory asked, growing angry. "Would they ask if you were straight? They're just picking on us because you're gay."

Leon took Rory's hand and looked in his eyes. "Rory. You've got to get that thinking out of your head. They are not picking on you or us. They work with kids because they care about kids. Our family is a new kind of family, and they don't know us. They don't trust new things because they don't want to experiment when kids are involved. So, you have to show them, to teach them."

Rory sighed. "I guess you're right. They don't know us. They haven't been here to see our life. I just hate that I have to defend it. I also hate having to leave right now. There's so much going on."

"We know it will be hard for you," said Leon. "But you are a great kid, and if anyone can show them how well this is working, it's you." He smiled.

"Thanks, Leon," said Rory. "Speaking of showing what we have here, it sure smelled like cake this afternoon."

Leon wiggled his eyebrows, and headed toward the kitchen. "Eeees possible ..." he called.

Rory turned to his dad. "Okay. I'll do it, and I'll be good. When and how long?"

"You leave Monday. You said the second challenge is on Sunday, right?"

Rory nodded.

"Good. Monday I'll drive you to the airport. You can tell me all the details on the way down. If all goes according to plan, you'll be back late Thursday or Friday. That's plenty of time before the third challenge."

"Dad? Is there any chance they'll try to pull a fast one and keep me there?"

Javier looked grim. "I won't say it's impossible, but it's highly unlikely. I won't be there, but you will be in daily contact with Terry, our attorney. She told me that if they pull any tricks like that, we'll go public. She's already talked with the national organizations. You'd be the poster child for gay families ripped apart."

Rory shook his head. "That's not the way I want it."

"Me either. But, Rory?"

"What?"

"You have to know that even when you come back, the judge may rule against us. He may require visitation or decide to give Kathy what she is asking for – complete custody."

"I won't do that."

"It won't be up to you. But, even if the worst happens, we have options. I won't give up."

Rory sighed. "I just wish Kathy would crawl back into her selfish little world and leave us alone."

"Rory, I don't think that's going to happen. She's still your mother, and I think she really wants to prove her worth as a mother to this new man in her life."

"Well, if Belecha is right and we don't pass the challenges and defeat the Kroledutz, it won't matter anyway. I guess that's one good thing about the world ending."

"The world can't end," declared Leon, coming in from the kitchen with a large platter. "At least not until we finish this chocolate-walnut cake."

TWELVE 12

"You want me to say what?" Tima gaped at James and the small computer chip in his hand.

James smiled sheepishly. "It's my little sister's favorite joke. I figured she'd like to have one of her dolls say it. See, I did this one for her teddy bear." He pushed the button on another chip, and Tima heard James, attempting to sound gruff and jolly. "I can BEARLY wait to eat one of your delicious cookies, Lilly."

Tima rolled her eyes. "You're hopeless, James." She pinched his cheek. "But you da cuuutest bearzie wearzie when you do things for your widdle sister."

James brushed away her hand. "It's been rough on Lilly. Dad's really stressed about the business with the council and I've been worried about … well, our stuff. I thought she'd like a talking tea party to play with."

"Okay. I'll do it. What's this chip going into? I should be in character."

James sighed and held out a silly looking, hand-made rag doll with short black hair and a face that had been drawn in. "This one. She calls it Jim Jam."

Tima giggled. "Awwww … he's so cute." She held it up beside his face. "And I do see a certain resemblance."

"Mom made it for her when she was three, and Lilly drew in the face herself."

"Okay, Jim Jam. I think I'm ready. What do I do?"

"I'll push this button and nod … then you say it. Ready?"

Tima nodded. James pushed the button and Tima, talking like a total goon, asked, "Say Lilly, how *does* the water get into the watermelon?" She barely got the last word out before she collapsed back on the bed, holding her side and laughing hysterically.

"Oh, man," Tima said, once she caught her breath. "Thanks. I needed that. Mom's been getting worse, and … well, it's been too long since I laughed like that."

James grew quiet and nodded, then took the chips to his workbench and started to insert them into the dolls.

"Hey James?"

"What?"

"How does the water get in the watermelon?"

James turned and grinned. "You plant it in the spring."

"That's a terrible joke!" Tima laughed, tossing a pillow at him. The pillow bounced off his knees.

"Lilly loves it," he said, clicking the second chip into place. "She'd tell this joke 100 times a day if we let her. The more she tells it, the funnier she thinks it is. The only reason you haven't heard it is that I told her if she asked you, I'd never fix her dolls again." Turning back to Tima, he grew quiet.

"What?" asked Tima. "You've got that look. Just ask."

"I've been wondering. How does it feel? I mean, do you feel …"

"Different? You mean after the challenge?"

"Yeah. I mean now you know. You *know*."

Tima nodded.

"So, how does it feel?" asked James.

"It's different," Tima said, considering, "but it's not. I mean, I've always been this way, but now I know why."

"I don't know, it feels so weird to go back to life as usual after what we went through – whatever that was. Doesn't it feel even weirder to you?"

"I know what you mean, but it's like this: Remember last year, when Mom had her breakdown, and I had to go to a shrink?"

"Yeah."

"For the first few weeks, when we talked she had me tell her about my dreams and we'd talk about what they might mean. She even got me to draw them. That's when I started painting."

"I know."

"Well, one time, we were talking about a dream and suddenly, I started crying – complete meltdown. Then I blurted out that I caused it. I caused Mom's breakdown. It was my fault."

"But, that's not true."

"Of course it's not true; that's not the point! That's what I had been feeling – somewhere deep down. When I got that feeling out and looked at it, I knew that it was wrong. I can't make her sick or make her well. I saw the essential and shed my old guilt like a skin."

"So you were a snake even before you knew it."

"Exactly. And after I shed it, I looked around the office and everything was different – lots better. I felt happy for the first time in a long time."

"I remember that day. You had been so down for so long. Then suddenly, you were back to the old Tima."

"Yup. It was as sudden a shift as during the challenge, but the thing is, even though I had changed in a flash, the world was the same place. When the session was finished, I went down the street and got a burrito. Everything had changed, and nothing had changed. The challenge is like that. Everything is different and nothing is different. I'm still me. I still had to do the dishes last night. And you, you still have to finish your doll operation."

James laughed. "You're right."

"As always."

"I was hoping you'd shed always being right ... or at least stop gloating about it."

"Ain't gonna happen." Tima stood up. "I better go. I need to check on Mom, and I'm starting a new painting. I want to see if knowing changes my style."

James nodded and turned back to his bench. "Okay. See you tomorrow."

"Mom!" called Tima, closing the back door behind her. She listened closely, but got no response. Nodding to herself, Tima tiptoed down the hall and stood outside her mom's office.

Tima didn't want to interrupt her if she was in the middle of getting a thought on paper. The door was closed. Tima stuck her ear up to the door. Nothing. Not even the sound of tapping keys. Tima sighed, knocked, and then stuck her head in the door.

"Mom?"

Grace was sitting at the desk, head in her hands. Her shoulders were shaking. Tima could tell she was crying. This was not good. She had seen this before, when her mother had gotten trapped in depression. Suddenly, anger rose up. She slammed her hand on the desk. Grace jumped and looked up, her face stained with tears.

"Mom!" Tima said, fiercely. "The doctor said you were supposed to get up and go for a walk or something if you couldn't write. You can't just sit here. It just makes you feel worse and worse."

Grace looked hopelessly at Tima. Tears continued to flow down her cheeks. "I'm sorry, Honey."

Tima shook her head. "Don't be sorry. You didn't ask to be sick. That's not your fault, but if I had a cold and went running around in the snow, you'd get mad, too." Tima grabbed her mother's hand and looked in her eyes. "You're sick. We need to call the doctor."

Her mother stared at her. Then, slowly, she nodded.

"Can you make the call?" asked Tima.

"I think so."

"You have to tell him you need to see someone tonight. Even if he's gone home and you have to talk to his service, you have to say you must talk to him right away. Can you do that?"

Again, her mother thought, then nodded.

"Good," Tima said, speaking slowly and calmly. "Now, can you drive to the doctor? If not, I can call James' mom or someone else. It's okay either way. Don't say you can if you can't."

Grace, who had made two decisions already, seemed to be gaining ground. She nodded her head more quickly this time. "I can drive."

"That's good. Now, do you want me to stay with you while you call?"

"No, Honey. I can make the call. I will make the call." Then, as if the minute or so of decisiveness had drained her, she put her head back down on the desk.

"Okay, I'm expecting you to do that right now, Mom. I'll go make you a cup of tea. You tell the doctor's service you must see him or someone else tonight. It's not too late. You tell them that if you can't see them tonight, you'll have to go to the emergency room."

Grace looked up sharply.

Tima nodded. "That's right. You are sick. You know you are. If I were running a high fever, you'd do the same. This won't wait until tomorrow. Understand?"

Grace took a breath. "You're right. I'll make the call now."

Tima turned to go.

"Tima?"

Tima looked back.

"Thank you."

Tima smiled. "It's okay. No fault in being sick. I only get mad when you don't do anything about it."

Tima went out to the kitchen and began to make tea, listening as her mom talked on the phone. Suddenly, she stiffened. A terrible smell filled the air, like rotting meat, burning plastic, and sweat, just like in Albuquerque when Radelam and the Kroledutz gathered to attack.

THIRTEEN 13

"Hey, Kid!" yelled Cisco, from the door of the trailer. "Get your butt in here."

Billy sighed and put down the hammer. Pulling nails in the baking heat inside a falling down building was definitely no fun. "Coming, Boss!" he yelled back.

He stepped carefully across the debris on the floor. Broken glass and boards with nails sticking out littered the floor. Worse, Billy knew, were the snakes that lurked underneath the boards. The shade was a favorite napping place for rattlers. He saw a couple each day.

"Hurry up, Kid! I ain't paying you to sleepwalk," yelled Cisco.

No way I'm getting myself bit for you, thought Billy as he walked carefully through the debris, *no matter how badly I want an excuse to be here.* A moment later, he walked out the doorway, squinting into the sun.

Matt, Cisco's right-hand man, was standing next to the boss. He was bigger than Cisco and just as mean. He'd been using the dozer to fill in the holes Billy pointed out, but he'd made it pretty clear he didn't think Billy should be there. They both glared at Billy as he came out.

"What's up?" asked Billy, walking up to them.

"I finished filling that gap you showed me this morning," said Matt. "Any other ways in?"

Billy thought a minute. "Yeah, there's one more. The fence is loose back over that way." He pointed behind them.

"You gonna show us where, Kid," asked Matt, "or do we guess?"

"Sure, sorry," he said, biting his tongue. "This way."

He led the two men to the place and showed them how he could pull up the fence and slip under.

Matt shook his head. "Not a fill job. Only way to fix that is to wire it back to the post."

"So wire it," said Cisco.

"Got no wire," said Matt.

"Then go to town and get some. I have a list in the trailer of some other stuff we need." Cisco stopped to think. "Stop by the money man's while you're at it," he continued. "Tell him how well the project is going." Cisco glanced at Billy. "Keep the money guys happy and hungry, Kid. Once the money starts coming in, you're golden to them. Let things fall behind or go over budget and watch out. That's why you're here – to keep things moving smoothly. Got it?"

Cisco didn't give Billy a chance to answer. Instead, he turned to Matt and gestured for them all to head toward the trailer. Matt nodded.

Matt nodded whenever Cisco looked at him. He wasn't big on talking. Billy suspected it was too big a challenge for him.

They reached the trailer. Cisco walked inside, calling to Billy over his shoulder. "Get inside, Kid. I want to talk to you, and it's too hot out here to think."

"Sure thing," said Billy, following Matt up the steps.

Cisco picked up a piece of paper off the desk, and handed it to Matt. Matt nodded, then turned and walked out the door. Cisco moved around the desk, and lowered himself into his chair with a grunt.

"So, Kid," he said with a glare. "I've been paying you over a week for just messing around. I gave you this job because you said you had a plan to get my proposal passed. Well, the next council meeting is Saturday, and I still ain't heard no plan. I know you got one so come on. Time to show me what I'm paying you for."

Billy looked at Cisco, pretending to be upset. "It's not like I've been taking a nap!" he protested. "I've shown you how to keep your place safe, and I've salvaged enough materials out of that old building to more than make up for what you've paid me."

Cisco smirked. "That ain't what I'm paying you for and we both know it."

They studied each other.

Billy knew Cisco's type. He was one of those small-time guys who dreamed of making it big, and he figured Rattlesnake Ranch was his ticket to the big leagues. Billy figured he might even be able to do it, if – that is – he didn't get greedy. But, Billy had run into a lot of people like Cisco, and they almost always got greedy. Luckily, though, this was something Billy knew he could use.

"Yeah, I've been planning," said Billy, finally. "I've figured out how you can win at the council meeting."

"Is that right?" Cisco's eyes narrowed.

"Yeah. You just need to get every rowdy and drunk in the county to show up and support you. If you get them there, you'll win, no question. They'll also shout down anyone who talks against you."

"And how do you expect to do that, Kid?"

Billy opened his mouth, and then thought better. "First, what's it worth to you?" he asked.

Cisco glared at him and sat back in his chair. "Right now, nothing. You tell me the plan. Then, maybe, we talk compensation."

Billy didn't think that was fair, but he didn't see any other option if he wanted to keep the job, so he nodded. "Okay, then. Beer Bucks."

"What?"

Billy leaned forward. "Look. The folks I know don't give a cup of warm spit about you, your proposal, or the council. They'll never go to a meeting unless there's something in it for them."

"I don't need a sales pitch, Kid. Get to the point and stop wasting my time."

Billy explained. "You offer to give them a Beer Bucks Club Card for your new store if they come to the meeting and speak for your proposal. The card is good for 10% off all the beer in the Beer Bucks cooler once you open. They also earn Bucks for every six-pack they buy. Once they buy 20, they get a free six-pack."

"That's your great idea? For me to give away my profits? What kind of idiot do you think I am?"

"You aren't giving, you're getting. I know usually you buy beer for $3 and sell it for $6 or more. So, instead of making $3, you make at least $2.40, but you sell twice as much. You only give out about 100 cards so for the price of a few discounted cases of cheap beer, you get your proposal passed and you sell more beer, which will more than make up the difference. You also get a steady income, even when the tourists stop traveling during the winter, 'cause these guys drink all year long."

Billy sat back and watched Cisco calculate the costs and benefits. He waited until Cisco's eyes started shining, counting the money he would make. Then he said, "I figure that idea is worth a few thousand a year to you. I'll give you a break, though. Let's say $100."

Cisco smirked. "We were just talking here, Kid, and I'm already paying you. If this idea works and I see a profit, then maybe I'll think about cutting you in for a bonus. In time. Now, you need to stop gabbing and get back to work. Go wash my car. It's dusty, and I got a date tonight."

"You're not gonna pay me for handing you the way to win?" Billy asked, pretending to look shocked. "That's not very fair."

"Nothing extra. Let that be a lesson, Kid. Free of charge. Never give it away and then ask for money."

Billy shook his head, barely managing to keep himself from smiling. *No surprises there, you crook. I knew you couldn't play fair.*

"Pretty good idea, though, Kid. You might have potential. 'Course, you forgot a few things, 'cause you ain't got my experience." Cisco smirked at Billy. "Pay attention and you might learn something. I got some cards right here. I'll print 'em up today, make 'em look official. Matt and me can hand 'em out over the next few days. But, I ain't just gonna hand 'em out on a promise. People always want to rip you off, so I'll tell 'em they won't be any good unless I sign them, and I won't sign them until I see them at the meeting on Saturday night."

Cisco smiled, settling back in his chair with his fingers laced behind his head and his legs spread wide. He was clearly pleased with himself. Billy tried to look impressed.

"Now, get. Wash the car. Then, you're done for the day."

Billy stood. "Okay, Boss." He headed out the door, thinking: *Just a couple more days. Then, I'll find out what you're hiding.*

FOURTEEN 14

"One night until the challenge, two nights until Florida," Rory muttered to himself. He sighed and tossed a stone into the fire. The moon was coming up and some small creature searching for food rustled the dry brush up near the lip of the kiva. "I wish the world would just go away and leave me alone."

"Careful what you wish for, Techta. You might get it."

Rory threw an annoyed glance toward the fire and Belecha's voice. "You don't always have to sneak up and appear in a puff of smoke, do you? Why don't you just say hello and jump over the side?"

"My the little one is cranky. You got some sand in your drawers?" asked Belecha, appearing beside the fire.

"Life sucks right now. Everyone is having problems, and they all started when you showed up."

"I'm not the cause, Techta. I'm the solution."

Rory tossed another rock. "That's what you say. All I know is everything sucks and is getting worse, and I don't see a way out. The only time anything makes sense is when I'm alone, sitting down here, pretending nothing else is out there."

Belecha nodded. "You're starting to use your kiva to create a sacred space, but you act without knowing why. You come here to get in touch with nature. That's one of the powers of this space."

Rory cocked his head and looked at him. "I come here because it's quiet and no one bothers me … except you."

Belecha grinned. "If that's a hint, give it up. We have things to do tonight."

"But the challenge isn't until tomorrow."

Belecha nodded. "That's right. I'm glad you know your days of the week. Maybe next time I'll quiz you on counting up to 10, but tonight you and I have business. This is for you, not for the others."

"Why me?"

"Well it isn't because of your manners," he said, raising an eyebrow. "You have a special role in this, Techta. The others are part of the team, but you set it all in motion. Just like with your kiva."

"What do you mean?"

"You needed a kiva. You stated you wanted one. The others heard the call and came to help."

"Why do I need a kiva?"

"Remember I told you a kiva focuses energy?"

Rory nodded.

"Well, it also stores energy – kind of like a battery for the energy of the Spheres. It takes a long time and a lot of work to get a kiva right. Only a being that is going to be around for a while needs that kind of tool."

"You think I'm going to live a long time?"

"That depends on what happens in the next couple of weeks, but if you survive, you'll be around a lot longer than a lifetime."

"And that means I need a kiva?"

"A physical entity does not need a kiva. A Watcher needs a kiva. A Watcher needs a place to store the memories and energies of many lifetimes so they can all be brought back to the Sphere when the time comes."

Rory felt a tingle at the back of his neck. "Are you saying I'm a Watcher? I'm not even sure what that means." He quickly held up his hands. "Don't do the eyes and fireworks again."

Belecha grinned. "Good trick, isn't it?"

"Leon thinks watching would be a hard thing, but how hard is it to watch stuff happen?"

Belecha squatted down next to Rory. "It sounds easy, but nothing is harder. A Watcher bears witness – we see the good and the bad. Sometimes, you want to change things so much it hurts, and you usually cannot. Sometimes you can give a push here or there, but you must respect the choices and decisions of the other entities and of the Spheres. They have decided what they want to experience, what they want to learn. We Watchers observe and remember, and we share our observations with the Sphere when we return. We gather the history of existence."

Rory considered his words. "I don't know if I want to do that."

"You can't know. Not yet. There will come a time to choose. At that moment, you will decide." Belecha stood. "Until then, there are a few things you need to learn. Come on."

"Where are we going?"

"To my kiva. In my time. There are things you need to see."

"I can't travel without the others."

"You can't all travel without each other and the Stone. You, alone, I can carry myself. Think of it like a piggyback ride. Now, relax, Techta. Look for the threads and let loose of the body, like you did with Mealim."

Rory took a breath and let it out. He tried to un-focus, like he did in the cave. A familiar pulsing and tingling passed through him. Looking down, he saw his hand was fading. Looking up, he saw threads of energy wrap around Belecha, shooting around and out from the walls.

"Good. You're getting better and faster at this. Let's go."

Belecha faded into a ball of shimmering light and floated toward Rory. Rory felt Belecha all around him. A thread nearby glowed brighter than the others and a part of Belecha reached toward it and then they were rocketing along the ribbons of light. Moments later, they dropped down onto the hard dirt next to Belecha's kiva and slowly came back into form.

Walking to the ladder, Belecha turned to Rory. "Now remember, this is a sacred space. Treat it with the respect it deserves. Think before you talk, and pay attention."

Rory nodded and stood outside looking at the stars and feeling the wind as Belecha climbed down the ladder and lit a torch. "It is ready," called Belecha.

Rory swung onto the ladder, feeling the pulsing vibrations through the wood, and slowly climbed down. Stepping onto the floor, he looked around. The kiva hadn't changed since his last visit, but Rory had. The first challenge had opened his eyes to the energy all around and now he saw how the walls glowed with threads of pulsing light. The rock where Belecha sat glowed with the same lights. Belecha had the drum in front of him and the rattle in his hand. Every time he shook the rattle, ribbons of energy flashed.

Belecha shook the rattle toward Rory and ribbons whipped out and spun around him, then joined the glow in the walls and ceiling of the kiva. Belecha put down the rattle, picked up the drum and began to chant, wordless sounds, twining around the rhythm from the drum. Soon, all the threads in the walls, ceiling, floor, and air were pulsing with the beats of the drum and the rising and falling tones of the chant. Rory felt his being join in. His heart began to beat with the drum, and the threads wrapped around him, pulsing. He felt lifted, buoyed by the energy. He moved toward Belecha, and – as he had the last time he was there – sat before him.

Belecha stopped and put down the drum.

"A kiva is a place of power," he said. "You build it and add to it with creation. Creative action weaves the web. Think of the two words ... creative and action. In a kiva, you act carefully. Any act in a kiva adds to the energy. So, it is important that you treat it with respect. Having a kiva is a gift and a task. You are creating a sacred space."

"You keep saying a sacred space. What is that? Like a church?"

"A building is not sacred because it is a church. It is a church because it is sacred."

"I don't get it."

"Sacredness is active, not passive. What you do in a place makes it sacred, not what you call it. You make a place sacred by only doing special works in that place. You use your intention and your actions. The more you do that, the more it feeds you and you feed it. That is why rituals are good to perform. You do the same thing to set your mind and your energy pulsing in a special way, like I just did when you came in. Sound is a powerful tool. Repetition is a powerful tool. I have done the same thing – the rattle, the chant, the drum – many thousands of times. By doing that, you and I and the kiva focus on what we are doing.

"If you came in here, burping and farting, and ate a burger and drank a soda, you would suck energy from the kiva. That is why it is hard to focus in your world. You try to do everything everywhere. You do not have a place to sit quietly or eat or talk. You do these things wherever you happen to be, so the place cannot help you. A kiva is a special place for creating focus on nature, energy, and creation. It is the place where Adima allow information to grow into knowledge. It is where you are strongest. It is where you go to heal yourself if you are hurt or to learn from the powers of the Spheres and of nature."

Rory looked at Belecha. "How? How do I create focus and learn?"

"You do it by doing it, Techta."

Rory rolled his eyes. "Real helpful."

"Spend time in your kiva and pay attention. If you don't pay attention, even if you are doing something creative, it does no good. On the other hand, if you pay attention and act with intention, you could read a cereal box and you will add energy to the kiva."

"How can I tell if I'm adding to it?"

"You're already doing it. Why were you there tonight?"

Rory's mind flashed on everything that was going on in his life right then, the challenges, his friends' problems, his mother. He felt a cramp deep in his guts and sighed. "It's the only place I can relax and think," he said.

"That's all you have to do, Techta. You go to your kiva, and you focus and relax. That adds energy. The way to improve your effort is to do it with intention. Instead of just jumping in and sitting down, think about what you are doing when you walk up to it. After you climb down, sit and feel the energy, like we did here."

"And that's it? Doing that will help me?"

"No. That is how you prepare. Then, if you want to learn, you must ask. Ask the kiva to teach you. Then, clear your mind and listen."

A picture of his mother beside an ocean filled Rory's mind. "So, I can ask the kiva how to solve my problems or what is going to happen?" he asked hopefully.

"No," Belecha eyed Rory knowingly. "You cannot. It is a teacher. Don't ask for an answer. Ask for a lesson. Then, clear your mind and you will begin to think, then hear, all you need to learn."

"That sounds weird."

"You just faded into a ball of light and are sitting in a hole thousands of years in your past and you have a problem with listening to the teachings of a kiva?"

"Well … I guess not," Rory said, thinking, *At this point, anything's gotta help.*

"Give it a try, Techta. The more you try, the more you will hear. Besides, you are also adding to the power of the kiva. Any creative work you do in the kiva feeds the kiva. Learning is one of the most creative acts you can do."

"I'll try. I will."

"Do that. If, after three weeks, you think you've wasted your time, I'll refund every minute."

"Can you really do that?"

"Maybe, but I bet you won't find out on this one."

Rory nodded.

"Good." Belecha stood and walked to the storage area behind the ladder. "Come over here. I need to show you why we came here tonight."

Rory followed. Behind the short wall were several pots and baskets. Belecha reached back and pulled a small pouch from one of the baskets. He squatted down and pulled several small bracelets made of stone beads and a large necklace from the pouch. The beads of the necklace were carved and painted with glyphs and patterns that reminded Rory of the Stone.

Belecha looked at him. "If everything goes right and you four activate the Stone, you'll come here in your bodies. This necklace is one of the things you must bring back. Also, take any one of the bracelets."

"Why?"

Belecha shook his head. "I'm telling you the what, not the why. The Bird will know the why."

"What?"

Belecha smiled. "Sounds like a comedy routine. This is what. The Bird will know the why."

"I still don't understand."

"You don't need to. For now, just remember to bring back three things. The necklace and the bracelet are one and two. Any bracelet will do, but you can only bring one. Now practice. Stand at the wall, close your eyes, and reach for the pouch. You have to be able to grab it quickly. There may be a lot going on in here."

Belecha put the necklace and bracelets back in the pouch and put the pouch back in a basket against the wall. It took a few tries, but soon Rory was able to quickly grab the pouch.

"Okay, I think I've got it. What's the other thing?"

Belecha walked toward the rock in the center of the kiva. He sat on it and reached down with his right hand and brushed away the dirt near the base of the rock. Rory saw that Belecha had uncovered a small clay brick. Belecha gripped the edges of the brick and pulled it away, revealing a small hole that went under the rock. He reached into this hole and pulled out another rock that fit easily into the palm of his hand. It was shaped like two pyramids stuck together at the base. He held it out toward Rory.

"Look, but don't touch, Techta. You are not ready to touch such a thing."

Rory bent forward to look. The rock glowed like molten lava. Patterns of light moved through it, making it pulse like a living thing. Belecha turned his hand so Rory could see all the sides.

Rory could hardly breathe, it was so amazing. Something deep inside him wanted to touch it, to reach out and feel that glowing object. It was more than he could bear. Sensing this, Belecha closed his hand around the hypnotic stone, placed it back in its hiding place, and replaced the brick. Brushing the dirt back across the surface of the brick, he said, "When you are ready to touch this, you will know."

"What is it?"

"It is called an Oloho - an Energy Keeper. There are only three of these on all levels of existence. It is the most powerful tool the Adima have. Against it, Radelam and the Kroledutz cannot stand."

"How does it work?" asked Rory.

"When the time comes, you will know or you will be told. For now, all you need to know is where it is."

"Understood. I know where it is."

"One more thing."

"What?"

"When you get it … if you get it … don't sit on my rock. I don't want you stinking up my chair."

Rory snorted. "As if. That rock would probably thank me – not having a 5,000-year-old butt perched on it."

"I won't argue that. But I do mean it. It would be a mistake to sit here. Understand?"

Rory nodded. "I promise."

"You and only you must get the Oloho and carry it back. Understand?"

"Got it."

"When you get to your time, give the necklace and the bracelet to the Bird." He held up his hand. "It will make sense at the time. Keep the Oloho yourself. Don't let the others touch it."

"Get the three objects. Give the first two to the Bird. Only I touch the Oloho. Right?"

Belecha nodded and stood up. "That's enough for tonight. Let's get you back."

Belecha leaned forward and tapped him between the eyes and he quickly felt himself fading away. Belecha faded too and wrapped himself around Rory. A ribbon glowed and Belecha reached for it and quickly whisked them back to Rory's kiva. They bumped down and Rory stood, back again in his body.

"Go home, Techta. I'll see you tomorrow night."

Rory turned to go, then stopped. "Belecha?"

"What?"

"My dad wanted to know if he could excavate your kiva – just a part of it. He'd do it carefully and it would help stop-"

"No!" Belecha interrupted with a roar, his eyes flashing fire. "That must not happen! Did you learn nothing tonight? A kiva is a point of power. If you break the form, you destroy it."

Rory tilted his head in confusion. "But your kiva is intact in the far past. It is filled in now and covered with asphalt."

"Time is only a useful tool, Techta. You will learn that. It is a sorting device. Now, let me be very clear." His eyes blazed. "If you breach it here, you breach it there. The kiva connects through time and dimension. The reason I can act in this world at this time is because of the power of my kiva. Without it, I can do little more than watch, and you need more than a set of eyes to get you four through the next few weeks. Filled and covered makes no difference. In fact, it makes it safer, because no one knows it is there. But, if you break the circle, you and your friends are on your own, and you don't want that. The Kroledutz are hunting for you and only my shielding has kept them away."

Rory felt a flash of fear. "I understand," he said. "I'll tell my father 'no.'"

Belecha nodded, relaxing a bit. "Good. Just remember: Keep it simple. He doesn't need to try to find some way around this. Just tell him it is not possible."

Rory nodded. "Okay." Then, he climbed out of the kiva and headed home.

FIFTEEN 15

Leon opened the door, surprise on his face. "Hi, Billy. You're up early."

"Yeah, sorry. I hope I'm not waking you."

Leon smiled. "No worries. I'm up at dawn, but you know Rory is a different story. I don't think he'll be up for at least an hour."

"I know, but I really have to talk to him. It's important."

Leon hesitated and looked over his shoulder. "I don't know."

Billy shook his head. "Look, I wouldn't even try to wake him if it wasn't really important, but it is. Please?"

Leon stepped aside. "If you insist, but I'm saying you threatened me if he gets mad."

Billy grinned at Leon's powerful form. "Deal." He hurried up the stairs and went right into Rory's room and shook him. "Get up!" he yelled. "We have to talk."

Rory slowly cracked open an eye and scowled. "Go away. It's too early."

Billy kept shaking him. "I'm not kidding, dude. You have to wake up. It's an emergency. We've got problems. Cisco is planning something bad … very bad."

Rory rubbed his eyes. "Okay. I'm listening. What's he planning?"

Billy shook his head. "No. We all need to hear this. Call Tima and James."

Rory sighed, and threw back the covers. He knew better than to argue with Billy. "You call 'em. I'll get ready." Then, he headed to the bathroom.

Billy grabbed Rory's cell phone and called Tima.

"Rory?"

"Tima? It's Billy. We need to talk. I'm at Rory's. Can you get over here?"

Tima hesitated. "Not now."

"It's important."

"I can't."

Billy heard the worry in her voice. "What's wrong?"

"It's my mom. She won't get out of bed. It's like it was before. I called her doctor and he sent a nurse over. She's here now."

"Oh. Not good."

Tima sighed. "She'll probably have to go to the hospital again."

"And you're going to Albuquerque with her?"

"No. I'm going to James'. Mom set it up with the Nomuras that I go there if this happens. I just got off the phone with his mom."

"That might actually work. Look, I'm really sorry about your mom, but Cisco's planning something awful, and we need to figure out what to do. I'll call James and see if we can meet over at his house. Can you get there?"

"I guess so. I can't help here, and I think the nurse would be glad for me to get out of the way. I'll meet you there in 20 minutes."

"Good. See you."

Billy called the Nomuras, figuring James would be at the breakfast table. Jocelyn Nomura answered the phone. "Hi, Mrs. Nomura. It's Billy Fuller. May I speak with James?"

"I'm sorry, Billy. James is still out doing chores. Why don't you come over and have breakfast? You can talk to James then."

"That sounds really good, ma'am. But, uh …"

Jocelyn laughed. "But you *all* need to talk, right? Tell Rory he's welcome, too. I imagine Tima's already on her way."

Billy smiled. "Thank you. Thank you very much!" A silver lining appeared for the morning; Mrs. Nomura was one of the best cooks around.

"And, Billy?"

"Yes, Ma'am?"

"Wash your hands before you come," she said with a laugh. "I don't want to see what you've been digging through lately."

A few minutes later, they were all at the Nomura's kitchen table, inhaling the wonderful food. Tima, though, was obviously worried, and Mr. Nomura seemed preoccupied.

"What happened at the meeting last night?" asked Billy.

Franklin Nomura shot him a surprised glance. "I didn't know you were interested in county government, Billy."

"Well, I've been working for Mr. Cisco, so I just wondered."

Franklin slowly nodded. "I'm sure your boss is a happy man this morning. Last night, dozens of people who have never shown any interest in the council meetings showed up to support his proposal. It was quite a zoo. It looks like his proposal will pass next Saturday with no problem."

"Well, I'm glad it will be over soon," said Jocelyn.

"Does that mean he'll start building right away?" Billy asked.

"I'm not sure. The final vote is next Saturday. If nothing changes between now and then, he could start digging as early as next Sunday morning."

Billy nodded and looked uneasy.

After the meal was finished, the four headed up to James' room. Billy turned to Tima.

"How's your mom?"

Tima sighed. "Not sure. I'm supposed to check in with the nurse later to find out if we need to take her to the hospital."

"I hope she's okay," said Rory.

"She's not okay, but I'm worried it's not depression." Tima wrapped her arms around her waist and turned her back on the group. Then, she faced them again. "What if the Kroledutz are doing it?"

James slowly nodded. "Everything is hitting the fan. I've never seen my dad this worried."

Tima's expression changed from worried to determined. "We can ask Belecha if there's anything we can do in addition to the challenges, but we have to stay focused on them. That's what is essential now."

"I agree," said Rory. He turned to Billy. "Okay. Now, what have you found out? It better be completely crucial. I'm up at least two hours before I wanted to be. Tima has her mom to deal with, and James is supposed to be helping his dad. What's the big deal?"

Billy took a breath. "I've been trying to find out what Cisco is hiding in that trailer. He's really careful about locking the door, plus he keeps his important stuff in a locked cabinet."

"So?" asked James.

"Last night, during the meeting, I picked the lock to the trailer. The cabinet would have been harder, but I knew where he kept the key. The meeting started at seven. I was looking at his stuff at 7:05."

"So?" asked Tima.

"So, he's not planning to build a little quickie market and a few rides. He has agreements from three different fast food places and a gas station. It's going to be huge."

"That's not what he proposed," James said. "He can't do that."

"I looked at the proposal. He can. He worded it very carefully. If that proposal passes, he can do almost anything he wants."

Rory was still having trouble waking up. "Well, that's bad news, but it still doesn't explain why you had to talk to us this early."

"I'm not finished. With a place the size he's planning, there's going to be a lot of drainage … dishwashers, sinks … not to mention gas tanks, toilets, and an RV disposal."

Tima nodded. "Sure. If there are a lot of people, they'll make a lot of mess."

"Well, to get rid of all that waste, he's going to have to install a huge septic system."

James agreed. "That's for sure. He'd have to dig a hole …" He started calculating.

Billy broke in. "Right. A hole as big as Belecha's kiva. And that is right where he's planning to put it. Right smack in the middle of the kiva. That's why he has the bulldozer there.

And, I'm guessing that filling that kiva up with sewage would be a really bad thing."

Rory broke in. "I know it is." He nodded his head strongly, growing more alert. "I was in the hole last night and Belecha showed up."

"What happened?" asked Tima.

"He took me to his kiva in his time. He wanted to explain more about what it does. When he took me back, I asked him if Dad could excavate his kiva."

"What did he say?" asked Billy.

He grimaced. "Remember when Mealim got mad?"

James nodded. "That is one thing I'll never forget. I thought we were dead for sure."

Rory nodded. "Well, Belecha can get just as mad. He said if we break it here, we break it there. And if we break it, the kiva loses its power. And if the kiva loses its power, he can't help us and Radelam can do whatever he wants."

Tima shook her head. "That does sound really, really bad."

James agreed. "If that proposal passes, Cisco isn't going to wait. My dad doesn't know why all those folks showed up, but if they vote next week, there's no chance it will lose."

"I know why they all showed up," said Billy.

Tima looked at him. "I thought I smelled a bit of Billy in this. What did you do?"

Billy explained the plan he had laid out for Cisco.

James was mad. "You jerk! We've got to tell my dad and stop this."

Billy shrugged. "We can't. I've been working with this guy. He's crafty and he's mean. If your dad takes him on directly, he'll attack and your dad won't win. Besides, he has something worse planned if he loses."

"What do you mean?" asked Rory.

"In the cabinet was a folder labeled 'Plan B'. It just had a bunch of figures on it, but it added up to a lot of money. I started to look on his computer and I found a folder named Plan B."

"What was in it?" asked Tima.

Billy shook his head. "I don't know. It was password protected. I was trying to figure out the password and got a really bad feeling. I kept seeing things on the edge of my vision and then I smelled that awful stink from Albuquerque. You know? When we saw the ..."

Tima gasped. "The Kroledutz?"

Billy nodded.

Tima looked stunned and for once, her words didn't want to come out.

"What is it, Tima?" asked James, putting his hand on her arm, reassuring her.

"My mom. Two days ago she had an attack, and I made her go to the doctor. Then this morning she was way worse and, both times, I smelled that smell."

SIXTEEN 16

That night, the four worried teens gathered in the hole. Tima's mom was home again, with a new medication and a visiting nurse. Rory had spent most of the day packing and hanging out with Billy, dreading his trip to Florida. James had worked with his dad, not telling him what Billy had found out, but wanting to. Everyone was on edge as they sat in the hole, looking at the sliver of the new moon and waiting for Belecha to show up.

"What happens if Kathy keeps me in Florida?" asked Rory.

Billy shook his head. "I keep telling you. Channel your inner butthead. If you can't make her beg you to leave in four days, give me a call. I have plenty of ideas."

Tima punched Billy's arm. "Being a jerk doesn't come naturally to everyone. Besides, they say you catch more flies with honey than with vinegar."

"Who wants flies? Besides, if you really want some flies, you should use sh–"

Tima broke in. "That's another thing you are an expert at." Turning to Rory, she added, "Give it a chance. It might be okay. Besides, if your mom pulls anything, it will blow her case."

"I think all these problems are caused by Kroledutz," said James. "Dad said he'd never seen people act the way they did last night. It was like everyone wanted to kill each other."

Rory nodded. "That's what I'm thinking. If I get stuck in Florida, I wonder if Belecha can help."

"Yeah, maybe old Belecha can pull our butts out of the fire," came a voice from the edge of the hole. "Maybe he can tell us to duck when we're about to run into a tree, which would be a good thing, because you four sure aren't paying a lot of attention."

They turned. Belecha was shaking his head. "Honestly, you folks are about as aware as a cow pie. In fact, I have personally known cow pies that are more aware than you. It's a good thing Radelam isn't around. You'd be toast before you knew you were on fire."

Billy looked at him. "Well, Mr. Got-the-Answers, what about it? Are the Kroledutz to blame?"

Belecha nodded. "None other. There have been lots of scouts and a few feeders around. When they latch on to someone, that person starts helping spread the darkness. They're hunting for you. I've been throwing as much protection over you as I can."

"What about when I go to Florida?" asked Rory. "Can you help me there?"

"The place doesn't matter. I can do what I do anywhere, but I can only do certain things to help. I can give you some shielding from the Kroledutz. I can point a direction and give you a push if you start to give up, but that's it. Only the physical can act on the physical."

Billy rolled his eyes. "You're like an ugly cheerleader with an attitude."

Belecha grinned. "Hey, Tinglen, you want me to wear pom-poms and a short skirt? I can probably do that, but I promise you won't like the view."

Billy started making puking sounds, but James broke in. "Look. Things are hard at home. I've got to get back soon. Can we do this?"

Belecha nodded. "Sure. Same as last time. I'll get us there, and you go up on your own."

Billy opened his mouth, but Belecha held up his hand for silence. "No, Tinglen, I do not have a problem with who you will meet tonight, but the challenge is for you four, not me. I'll keep the portal open."

"Is every one of these going to be as dangerous as the first one?" Rory asked.

"It's not dangerous if you open up and learn."

James shook his head. "Why does that not make me feel any better?"

Belecha grinned. "Buck up. You made it through one. Techta, you have the Stone?"

Rory pulled it out of his pocket and held it up. "Right here."

"Good. Sit around it. Heliotom, make sure you sit at the snake."

They got into position.

"Let's go," said Belecha, fading into a ball of light and rising above them. Threads begin to emerge from the Stone. One of the threads glowed brighter than the rest, and Belecha reached out and grabbed it. With a jerk, they were pulled up and along the thread, which quickly spread to become a ribbon. They were once again hurtling along the shimmering path.

Soon Belecha called, "Get ready." With a bump, they landed. Belecha, fading in and out, still floated above the Stone. "Up the hill," he said. "He'll meet you. Don't say anything until he starts the conversation."

Heading up the hill, the four looked around. They were near the top of a mountain. There were no trees, but small clumps of wild grass grew on either side of the trail. Many were topped with small, brightly colored flowers.

"Where do you think we are, Rory?" asked Tima.

Rory looked around. "I don't know. This doesn't feel like any place I've been."

Billy stopped, looking at the sky. "You can say that again. Look!"

They had all assumed it was day, since the mountain was well lit. However, as they gazed upward, they saw the sky was lit by a thick lattice of threads and ribbons of energy. When they were traveling, the energy trails were spaced far apart. Here the weaving was so close, the sky seemed to be made up of a blanket woven of light. Extending through the blanket were enormous Spheres that shimmered like they were filled with water in constant motion.

James grinned. "That is, beyond a doubt, the coolest thing I have ever seen."

"Come on," said Rory. "I can't wait to meet who lives here."

They crested the hill. Down the rise, they saw a small village arranged around a central oval. The houses were small, made of mud bricks and logs, so they seemed to be growing from the ground. Above one end of the main oval was a smaller clearing. In the center of the clearing was a circle with a domed covering.

Pointing, Rory said, "I bet that's a kiva." The others nodded, and they walked down the steep, curving trail toward the village.

"It is our kiva," came a voice to their right.

They had come around a bend in the trail. A small spring formed a pool that had been hidden from view. Next to the spring, a rocky outcropping extended into the pool so it was possible to sit on the rock and be nearly at the center of the water. On the rock sat a boy. He had thick straight hair that fell past his shoulders, so black it had hints of purple in the bright light. His skin was a light brown and his cheekbones and almond eyes reminded Rory of descendants of the Mayans he had met in South America. The boy was wearing a skirt-like garment that reached from his waist to almost his knees. On his chest was painted a large oval with lines extending from it. Around his shoulders was a thin shawl with more lines and patterns of ovals. On his head, he wore a headband, from which extended three feathers. He smiled at them, not moving from his place on the rock. "My name is Arnalea. Today is my return day."

Rory introduced everyone and asked, "What's a return day?"

Arnalea nodded, as if Rory had asked the correct question. "It is the day I understand my purpose for this life, why I chose to come to this place at this time. It is the day I decide if I wish to remain or if I would prefer to return right away."

"How can you learn the purpose for your life in one day?" asked Billy. "And how can you know which day? Lots of people never know why they're here. No one ever knows when they're a kid."

"Almost no one," corrected James.

Billy rolled his eyes. "Excuse me, farmer boy. I forgot. Your dad's a farmer, like his dad, like his dad, and you will be a farmer, too. Did I get the song right? Let's just say that no normal person knows when they are a kid." Turning to Arnalea, he asked, "How can you know until you look back on your life?"

"You are mistaken, Tinglen, although you are also correct."

"How can he be both?" Tima asked.

Arnalea smiled. "He is correct that in your world many people never know their purpose. He is mistaken that this is your world."

"Not our world?" James asked.

Arnalea shook his head and gestured at the land around them. "No. In this world, we are born aware. We are aware that we are of a Sphere and have decided to come here for a purpose. At some point in our life, each one of us knows that our return day is approaching. We begin to gather the ceremonial items." He indicated his clothing and headdress. "We create our songs and we talk to the Singer."

"Singer?" asked Rory.

Arnalea continued as if Rory had not spoken. "One day, we wake up and know that this is the day. We have learned the drawings we need to use during our sleep. The One comes to this pool and bathes, puts on the items, and paints the symbols. This I have done."

The four looked at the intricate designs Arnalea had painted on his chest and legs and arms. His unmoving calm extended in waves to them.

"Then what?" asked Rory.

"I have a final task in this world before my return. That is to talk with you. After my task, I shall go to the kiva, where the Singer waits. Together we shall take the path to the cliff."

"What cliff?" asked Billy.

Arnalea stood. "Come, I will show you."

SEVENTEEN 17

Arnalea led the way down to the village. It seemed to be deserted. "They are all in the kiva," he explained. They skirted the kiva and followed a steep path that hugged the side of the mountain. To their left was the stone face, to their right, a sheer wall dropped down to the floor of a valley far, far below.

Tima, usually calm, kept peering over the edge, then squeezing closer to the mountain. "I don't really like heights," she said, "and this path is awfully narrow. This is really high."

Arnalea spoke without slowing. "If you climbed, it would take two full days to reach the floor of the valley and the banks of the river at the base of this cliff. Of course, if you fell, the trip would not take so long."

Billy laughed. "But I don't think you'd enjoy it as much. If you fall, remember to bend your knees before you hit."

"Shut up. You aren't helping." Tima looked sick.

"Actually, you would fall into the river," said Arnalea. "It is wide and deep. At one time it carved out the entire valley floor from this cliff to the mountains beyond."

Tima clenched her teeth. "Oh, joy."

James gave her a soft touch on the back. "I'll grab you if you start to slip."

Tima looked over her shoulder and gave him a quick smile, then returned her focus to the path.

"Careful here," called Arnalea. They had come to a rock column that jutted out. The path was little more than toeholds. He flattened his face to the stone, reaching for handholds to steady himself as he inched around the column and disappeared.

The four looked at each other, not wanting to follow. Finally, Rory shrugged, "Here goes nothing." He imitated Arnalea's movements and quickly made it around the column. Just after the column, a broad shelf opened up. He saw a spring and pool, surrounded by lush green moss and bursts of color from flowering grasses. A short path led up to a slightly higher shelf. At the end of the path was a large, flat stone that jutted out over the edge of the cliff. Over everything hung a deep calm.

Rory felt all his muscles relaxing, as if he had slipped into a tub of warm water. He took a deep breath and sighed. "It's beautiful," he whispered. This did not seem like the kind of place you should talk loud. Arnalea, sitting beside the pool, nodded.

"Rory!" called Tima from the other side of the column. "Are you okay?"

"It's great. Just a few steps around the column. I'm right here. Come next and James can steady you."

"Oh, all right." Tima was not happy about this, but she knew she had to try. Taking a deep breath, she pictured her mother. The vision steadied her. Soon she, then James, and finally Billy were around the column and looking at the magnificent, hidden sanctuary.

"This is a sacred place," said Arnalea. "We come here on our return day. Only the Singer comes more often than that. You are the first ones who have ever come here when it was not their return day. It is an honor and a measure of the importance of your task."

"What do you do here?" asked Tima.

"Mealim told you of the Spheres. She explained that Adima have come from a Sphere into form."

"And we have a light seed at our core," said Tima.

Arnalea nodded. "You four are Sodrol, formed around a seed, but not all Adima are Sodrol. However, all Adima come from a Sphere and after their experience in form, they return."

He waved his arm around the hidden spot, with its clear pool and moss-covered banks. "On the return day, the One and the Singer come to this place. The One bathes in this pool. Then, they both walk up there." He pointed with his chin toward the path leading to the rock. "The Singer sits on the rock. The One goes just beyond to a spot even you may not see until it is your time and stands on the very edge of the cliff. Then, a special thread comes down and the One rides it back to their Sphere. That is the return. At the Sphere, the One dissolves again into the Sphere, becoming part of the energy. They again know and share everything the Sphere has experienced from its beginning."

"So, you die?" asked Tima.

"No. The trip along the thread is for energy only. The form remains on the cliff. That physical existence keeps the entity from completely rejoining the Sphere. However, they share enough to know why they, as elements of the Sphere, chose to come here. They know their purpose."

"Then what?" asked Billy.

"It depends. Often, the purpose is to build a stronger bond between this world and the Sphere. Living an aware life and accomplishing the return is the purpose. Sometimes, there are more lessons the entity and the Sphere wish to experience, so the One will continue. During the return, the One knows. They know if their lesson in this adventure is complete or if there is more to do. When they have returned once, they can go back to the Sphere from any location."

"How do they get back if they aren't finished?" asked Rory.

"During the return, the Singer sits on the rock and sings. He will sing of this world, of the One and their experiences, and of the Sphere. He continues to sing throughout the return. The one uses the Singer's voice as a beacon and again joins with this body. If there is more to learn, the One fully inhabits the body again and, with the Singer, returns to the village."

"What if you know this life and the return was your purpose?" asked Billy.

Arnalea smiled gently. "Then the One only briefly revisits the body and thanks the Singer."

"And then?" asked James.

"The entity follows the thread back to the Sphere. The body, like a cast off piece of clothing, goes away. I have never seen it. In some cases, I believe it vanishes, crumbling into the sand of this earth. Other times, it falls from the cliff to the river below. The body is of this world and its parts continue their journey in another form."

"You die," said Tima.

Arnalea shook his head. "No, we cannot die. We may leave this adventure, but nothing more. When you leave a room and go into another, have you died?"

"Of course not," said James.

"It is no more than that," replied Arnalea.

"But ..." began James.

Arnalea held up his hand. "I do not have long. It is nearly time for me to meet the Singer and when the call comes, I must leave. So, let me complete my task. I must tell you a story, give you another piece to your puzzle, and leave you to your challenge."

Rory nodded. "We need all the information we can get, if this is anything like last time."

Arnalea smiled. "Each one is different. There is no reason to repeat and for you, time is limited."

"For us?" asked Billy.

"Time is the same for everyone," said James.

Arnalea shook his head. "Not for us. We have only two times – before our return and after our return. However, that is part of the puzzle. First, the story."

Arnalea gestured all around. "This place was once a part of your world. Our people were aware of the energy of the Spheres, as they are now. Rumors spread about powerful beings living in the mountains. We were not and are not powerful. We are aware – no more and no less. However, those who were not aware, believed we possessed riches and powers. It does not matter that they were wrong, it is what they believed. For some, it became an obsession to capture our power."

"How did you protect yourself?" asked Rory.

"We did not. What can be taken from ones who have nothing material? What can be threatened against those who know they are eternal? If one had come back from their return with the purpose to defend, we would have, but that did not happen. The Spheres had no interest in protecting us in these forms, and nature's balance was not served by such action."

"Nature's balance?" asked Tima.

"That is for another challenge, Heliotom."

Tima opened her mouth to speak, but Rory put a hand on her arm to stop her. He knew she didn't like leaving a question, but this was not the time for questions. Tima understood and grew silent.

Arnalea continued. "However, this lack of action allowed a mistake to enter the world that has stained it until now."

"This world or our world?" asked Billy.

Arnalea nodded. "Correct question, Tinglen. Your world bears the stain."

"What happened?" asked Rory.

"I will show you." Arnalea reached out his hand. "Touch my hand and loosen your focus on your form."

They followed his instructions. Rory felt a pulsing warmth travel up his arm. He opened his eyes. They were looking down at the pool from far above, like the observation point in Albuquerque, when they had first seen the Kroledutz. He was high enough to see the village and the path leading up to the pool. On a ledge below them, hidden behind a rock so he could see the pool but not be seen, was a man. Rory could see a dark form wrapped around him. In horror, he realized that it was Radelam.

"Radelam!" hissed Tima. "We've got to get out of here."

Arnalea spoke. "We are in no danger. This is a viewing of an event from your world's past, when the Adima, the Weavers of Light, were in full bloom in your world and the Kroledutz had to hide in the corners. That man you see developed a particularly strong hunger for power and Radelam attached to his energy. Instead of eating, he fed him – both energy and ideas. Soon, the man was a leader among his people, but he wanted more."

"What is he doing here?" asked Billy.

"He is here to steal our power."

"You said you had no power to steal," objected James.

"He doesn't know that and wouldn't believe it if we told him."

As they watched the scene below, a chanting rose from the kiva in the village. From the opening, a small girl climbed out, followed by an old man. They stood near the kiva as more and more people climbed out, then bowed and headed up the path. At the pool below them, the girl bathed, then followed the man up the path. An outcropping blocked their view of the girl, but they saw the man sit on the rock, pick up a drum, and begin to chant and beat a slow rhythm.

Tima pointed as a wide, bright ribbon reached down from the sky toward the point where they knew the girl was standing. Almost immediately, a ball of light shot up along the ribbon and was gone. The man continued chanting.

"Was that …?" asked Rory.

"Watch!" urged Arnalea.

After a short time, the ribbon glowed brightly and the ball of light descended. A moment later, it again shot up along the ribbon. This time, the ribbon flew with the ball of light. The chanting stopped. The man stood slowly and looked out across the valley. Then he turned and looked directly at them.

"Belecha!" said Rory.

While much younger, there was no question it was their guide. And although Arnalea had said they were not really there, Rory knew that Belecha could see them.

Arnalea said, "Yes. The Singer that day was the old raccoon. That is why he took the task of waiting until the stain could be cleansed."

"I still don't see a problem," said James. "What stain?"

Arnalea pointed to the hidden man. "Watch."

As Belecha turned and walked back down the path toward the village, the man leapt up, trembling with excitement. Belecha came into the clearing around the kiva. The people still stood there and when they saw he was alone, they raised their voices in happy chants and cheers.

"They see that she returned to the Sphere," explained Arnalea. "This is cause for celebration of a life well and fully experienced."

The hidden man, with Radelam wrapped around him, whispering in his ear, quickly and carefully slipped away.

"Touch my hand again," said Arnalea. "We will see the message that this man, aided by the Kroledutz, took from what he saw."

They again reached out and when Rory opened his eyes, he saw before them a wide, dusty plaza. At one end, a stone pyramid rose to the sky. A mass of people gathered near the base of the pyramid. The man who had spied on the return stepped out of the crowd, dressed as a priest, in ceremonial finery, an enormous headdress and clothes ornamented with gold, shining in the sun. He motioned to his assistants, who dragged forth a young girl bound hand and foot with cords decorated with silver and gold. She was crying and calling out for help, but no one stepped forward to help her.

The man solemnly began to climb the pyramid. His assistants dragged and carried the crying girl a few steps behind him. When they reached the top of the pyramid, he turned and called out to the crowd below in a powerful voice. The assistants picked up the girl and lay her on a stone slab. She frantically screamed to the crowd, but still no one helped. The crowd began to chant with the priest.

Beside him, Rory felt Tima stiffen. "We've got to stop them. They're going to …"

"We can do nothing," replied Arnalea. "We are not here. This is history."

Below them, the priest raised a gleaming dagger over the girl's writhing body. The chanting rose in religious ecstasy. Rory turned his head, unable to watch, but the terrified screams from the girl, suddenly cut off, while the chanting continued, made it clear what had happened.

Tima sobbed.

"Touch my hand," said Arnalea softly. "Let us return."

Back once more beside the calm pool, Tima turned with rage to Arnalea. "Why did you show us that? Why did they do it?"

Arnalea looked at them with deep sadness. "That is the stain on your world. Can you see the cause?"

"He got it wrong," said Billy. "The guy who was hiding here saw the girl return to the Sphere. He thought Belecha was a priest and sacrificed her. That's it, right?"

Arnalea nodded. "With the help of Radelam, he misunderstood and drew a dreadful conclusion. The truth is that the return is directed by the One who returns. The Singer is there only as servant. The observer thought the Singer was in control, had chosen the girl, and was acting to please the gods. The great mistake was that he believed he was seeing ..."

"Sacrifice," said Tima. "Sacred sacrifice to please a god."

"Yes. He thought our power came from sacred sacrifice. His mistake created the stain – a blood red stain. And that mistaken understanding could not have been more wrong. We have no priests who speak for the sacred. We are each the guardian and creator of the sacred. It is our most personal responsibility. We must do it for ourselves and cannot do it for another.

"You witnessed the day the stain entered the world. The day when a person declared it was his choice who lived and who died, instead of it being the choice of each entity. On that day, one person declared he could decide another person's purpose, and people started to believe a priest should take over the duty of creating the sacred. They gave the priest the power to decide who died and when. Sacred sacrifice is the ultimate wrong for many reasons. It steals the entity's true purpose. It gives the power of the sacred to another. It allows a person to claim to know the will of energy for all."

Gesturing toward the world this place was no longer connected to, Arnalea continued. "The horror spread quickly because many who took part believed they were acting properly to please a god. However, this added to the wrong. The ones who took the life did not take responsibility for their act, saying it was the will of God. Giving up responsibility and destroying the purpose of another worked together to drive the stain's dark destruction throughout the world, tearing at the fabric of the web of light. With frightening speed, the pendulum of nature tipped and swiftly swung back toward the time of the Kroledutz. Everywhere,

Radelam and others came forth to feast on the remnants of energy and light and to spread their darkness."

"Couldn't you do anything?" asked Tima.

"You should have fought them!" said Billy angrily.

Arnalea shook his head. "Fighting is rarely our purpose. Besides, fighting and killing to stop fighting and killing does nothing but strengthen the Kroledutz."

"So what could you do?" asked James.

"Leave," replied Arnalea. "All the entities from Spheres had to choose to leave or stay. Most left. Some used leaving to explore a new experience -- there are many experiences of death of the form that one wishes to experience."

"But if the Adima left," Rory asked, "what is this place?"

"The cliff serves an essential function for all. It had to continue, no matter what happened in your world. So, we brought it here. The cliff exists outside your world. There is no direction here - no north, south, east, or west. There is only here. That is how it will remain until the stain can be cleaned from your world."

"How do we clean the stain?" asked Tima.

Arnalea shook his head, smiling. "That is not for this challenge. That is the end of my story, and my time grows short. I must give to you a piece of the puzzle. My piece is to explain how you travel the web."

EIGHTEEN 18

"Belecha takes us," said James, "using the Stone."

Arnalea nodded. "The Stone helps. It is essential for travel with your physical bodies until your challenges are complete. However, it is possible to travel without the old Singer or the Stone."

"Really?" said Billy, a crafty gleam in his eye. "I can think of several ways that could be useful."

"I am not letting you use this for one of your schemes," said Tima, tilting her head at him.

Arnalea smiled. "Time grows short. Pay attention." He drew a square on the ground. "The key to travel in any world is the number of that world. Your world is ruled by four: four directions, four essential elements. That is why your Stone has four sides and there are four of you. Four provides a stable base, which is essential to keep you from each flying off in a different direction. You can have more, but not less. To travel, you need one more point." He held his finger at a point above the square he had drawn. "Add one, and what do you get?"

"A pyramid," answered Billy.

Arnalea nodded. "Correct. Four sides come together to one pointer. You provide the base. Belecha is your pointer. Add one to the number of a world, and you know how many you need to travel. Subtract one from the number of your world, you know the types of travel available." Noting the puzzled looks on their faces, he realized they didn't understand and explained. "For example, your world is a four. Add one, and you get five. You need five to travel. Four to provide a stable base and one to point. Understand?"

They nodded.

"Good. Subtract one, you get three. That tells you the kinds of travel open to you in that world. You can travel in space – any direction – that's one. You can travel in time -- past and future. That's two. Get it?"

"Wait," said James. "What's the third?"

Arnalea smiled. "The third is to return home. You must always be able to come back."

"You keep saying that our world is a four. Aren't all worlds fours?" asked James.

"No. This world is ruled by three."

"How can you tell?" asked Rory.

"How can you tell that a rock is hard? It is something you know when you see it and touch it. When you are aware, you will know the number of a world when you arrive, as certainly as you knew where the sky was in this world, even though it did not look like the sky in yours."

Rory shrugged. "I'll take your word for it."

Arnalea drew a triangle on the ground. "To travel here, we need three at the base, then to add one as a pointer. In this world, we can travel in two directions, not three."

Rory looked confused. "If one direction is coming back, what is the one direction you can travel?"

Arnalea said softly, "We travel to the Spheres. Any other movement is unimportant." He grinned. "Or at least toward the Spheres. We *do* have fun riding the ribbons, even before our return day."

"What happens if we try to travel without a pointer?" Billy asked. "Not plan a direction. Just see where we go. It would be great."

Arnalea shook his head. "Without a pointer, you have a base only. You would be like a chip of wood on a raging river. The web is pure energy. It would drive you from one ribbon to another and you would quickly lose sight of your world. You would wash back and forth forever. The four of you would remain locked together, as you are stable in your connection, but you would never arrive or return."

"Bad idea," said James.

Tima nodded. "Agreed!"

Arnalea stood. "Let's ride the ribbons. I want to show you this world from above."

"How do we do it without the Stone?" asked Rory.

"The Stone helps focus intention, but you can travel without it. Stand facing each other. Intertwine your fingers with the person on the left and right of you. That will form a tight bond. You are sharing your energy to form a single square base." They followed his directions.

"Okay," said Tima. "We're ready. Now what?"

"Since I know this place, I'll be pointer, okay?"

James shrugged. "Sure. None of us know how to be pointer."

Arnalea laughed. "That's not hard. All you do is aim your intention toward where you want to go and look for the path."

"That makes no sense to me, but it doesn't matter," said James. "You're driving."

"Let's go," urged Rory. "I want to see these ribbons up close. I've never seen so many."

Arnalea nodded. "Without the Stone, you have to loosen your focus on your forms."

"Like we did in the cave with Mealim," said Tima.

It took a few tries, but soon they faded into sparkling balls like in the cave.

"Ready?" asked Arnalea.

Rory looked toward his voice. Arnalea had become a glowing, pulsing sphere with a huge number of threads shooting out. He rose above them.

"We have to work together," said Arnalea. "Travel requires intention. You point your thoughts toward a direction and reach out from your core."

"You mean focus on a direction?" asked Tima.

"No ... intention," said Arnalea. "You cannot focus. That brings in desire, which brings in the body. You *intend* to go in a direction, but sometimes, your purpose or the needs of nature are greater. You reach out with intention and follow. Sometimes, it takes you in a different direction than you had planned, but it is always the right way. Watch me, and follow the pull."

Arnalea began to rise, grabbing a thread that reached into the web of the sky. Rory felt a pull and allowed himself to follow. He saw the others, still linked, also rise. Soon, they were among the thick blanket of glowing threads. An over-brimming feeling of happiness filled him.

"This rocks!" he yelled.

"Totally!" agreed Billy.

"It's because we are in direct contact with the web up here. It is pure energy of the Spheres. Look down."

The landscape below had changed. Instead of a cliff, valley, the village, and the pool, there were glowing fires of different colors and intensities.

"Wow!" gasped Tima.

"That's the way our world really is," said Arnalea. "See the kiva?"

"Which one is it?" asked Rory.

"The really bright spot with all the thick ribbons rising."

They looked and saw a brilliant spot that pulsed with light. It looked like a constant explosion of ribbons reaching out.

"The entire village is there preparing for my return. The kiva is always the brightest point, because it is where we do our most sacred work. It is particularly bright now because everyone is there."

"What's that?" asked Rory, noticing a pyramid of searing, bright light a short distance from the kiva.

"Belecha keeping your portal open. See how the light is different than the lights of this world? That is because the Stone is for your world."

"Amazing!" said James.

"Now for some real fun," called Arnalea. They had risen far above the village and all around them, over them, and under them were threads and ribbons reaching in every direction. The ribbons hummed and seemed to be streaking by at enormous speeds. Rory thought of fiber optic cables, where there was always light, but within each cable, pictures, sounds, entire lives hurtled by. "You have to experience thread jumping!"

"What's that?" asked Billy, always up for a new adventure.

"Instead of following a thread based on your intentions, we swing, then let go, and grab whichever thread we can."

Billy was excited. "That's what I was talking about when I said we should travel without a pointer."

"But isn't that dangerous? What if we don't grab one?" asked James.

"Then we spin out of control in the darkness of the universe for all eternity," laughed Arnalea. "So, it's a good idea to make sure you grab one. Come on. A little danger is fun."

"That doesn't sound like fun," said James.

"I'm in," said Billy.

"How do we get back?" asked James.

"Oh, that's easy," said Arnalea. "I know the patterns and colors of the threads from the village. Everything has a unique color. Look for a thread from the village and follow it back."

"Cool," said Rory. "I'm in. How do we grab a thread if it comes near?"

"Reach out with your intention. Imagine that you are joining with the flow of that thread. I know it sounds hard, but it's like everything connected to creation. You have to do it to get it."

"I'm willing to try," said Tima. "How do we start?"

"Also easy," said Arnalea. "I just let go." And he did.

Immediately, they began to plummet down. As Rory looked down, he saw that far below, there were less and less threads and more and more blackness. He felt a rising panic. This might have been a very bad idea. If no one could grab a thread in time …

Suddenly, he felt a strong jerk upward.

"Weee Ho!" screamed Billy. "I got one!"

They were once more whizzing along a thread, this time in a completely different direction. The feeling was fantastic. Billy called out, "I'm going to let go now. Rory, try to grab one."

Rory wasn't sure, but before he could protest, Billy let go and they began to drop again. Rory desperately tried to grab a thread, but none seemed to be responding.

"Got it!" shouted Tima as they again jerked and began to climb. "You have to forget about trying. I kind of looked away from the one I wanted to grab and thought, 'Well, maybe ...' and then I felt it and latched hold."

Arnalea called from above, "Look down again."

They did. The bright energy of the village was nowhere to be seen. Instead, they were tearing along through a multicolored eternity of glowing spheres, ribbons of light and color and threads waving in unfelt winds.

"Now let go, and don't try to grab anything," said Arnalea.

"Okay," said Tima and let go.

Rory supposed they were falling and falling quickly. However, they were so small and everything around was so impossibly big, it felt like they were slowly floating. The sheer number of glowing objects was almost too much to take in.

"We are deep inside creation," said Arnalea quietly. "This is the home of the Spheres. From here we all come. To here we return."

Awed, they were silent.

Suddenly, Arnalea spoke. "It is my time. I am called to my return. Farewell."

"Wait!" yelled James. "You can't leave us here. We don't know where we are. We don't know how to get ..."

But Arnalea was not there, and they were falling. The number of threads around them was quickly thinning, and the blackness loomed ever larger.

NINETEEN 19

"Arnalea!" yelled James. "You can't just ..."

"Quiet, James," said Tima. "He can. He did."

"This must be the challenge," said Rory.

"We're dead!" cried James. "The threads are getting further apart. We're going to fall forever!"

"Well, at least we don't have to worry about hitting anything," said Billy.

"Great," replied James. "We just keep falling through nothing until we die of old age. Much better."

Tima tried to calm James. Using the soft, soothing voice she often used with her mother, she said, "They don't want us to fail. If this is like the last time, we have all the information we need. We'll be fine."

"That's right," agreed Rory.

"Doesn't matter," said James, "We don't know where we are. Only Arnalea knew the way back."

"I think the first thing we should do is try to grab a thread," suggested Tima, still speaking in a deliberately calm voice. "Once we are moving in some direction, we can figure out where to go."

"Good plan," said Billy.

"Everyone, try to reach for a thread," called Tima, dropping the soft tone for a commanding one. "I think they respond to an individual. When I got one, I felt it glow and knew that was the one for me."

They all fell silent, trying to grab a thread. Rory tried to put the fall out of his mind. He imagined taking his desire to grab a thread and wrapping it in a blanket to set it aside. He started to think about tying a cord around the bundle, when he realized the cord he was imagining was beginning to glow and pulse like one of the threads. Remembering what

Arnalea had said, he concentrated on reaching from his center out toward the cord. With a jerk, he felt himself being pulled along its path. He looked at the others, glowing with pleasure.

"I got one."

"Duh," said Billy. "I kinda guessed that, since we're not plunging into darkness anymore."

"Good job, Rory," said Tima. "Better James?"

"Yeah," replied James. "I guess. But we still don't know how to get back."

"Well, the real question is, who is the Sodrol? What glyph represents the seed we need?" asked Tima. "Remember, the reason for the challenge is to make the Sodrol know the seed and act."

"I figure it's Rory. He's the one who caught the thread," said James.

"I don't think so," replied Rory. "I grabbed it, but I didn't have any big revelation. Maybe it will help to figure out which glyph it is. That would help us decide who the Sodrol is. We know it's not the snake, that's Tima. That leaves bison, bird, or whale."

"It shouldn't be bison," said Tima.

"Agreed," said James. "Bison is earth and permanence. This place may be permanent, but it sure isn't earth."

"Definitely," said Billy. "That leaves whale and bird. Whale is crossing boundaries and bird is air and perception. Both could help us."

"We better figure this out soon," said Tima. "We aren't falling, but we are going fast and there's a good chance we are going away from the Stone and our way home."

"There's a bigger problem," said Rory. "Arnalea was the pointer. Even if we figure out what direction to go, we can't head that way. We are the base, but without a pointer, we ride the threads forever. It's not falling, but it's not much better."

"Maybe one of us can be a pointer," suggested James.

"No," said Tima. "We have to stay linked. Otherwise we aren't stable and will fly off in every direction. We need five to travel."

They considered the situation. The amazing web of lights pulsing with energy and the glowing Spheres did not seem as wonderful, faced with the prospect of watching them go by for the rest of time. Rory tried to feel a solution, but nothing came, as they flew further and further into the vast space with no hope of ever returning home.

Suddenly, Billy shouted. "I've got it! It's the bird, and I'm it! I know what we need to do."

"What?" asked Tima.

"I'll be the pointer! Unlink. I need to get into position above us."

"You can't!" yelled James. "If we aren't linked, we don't have a solid base."

"No," insisted Billy. "Arnalea told us what we need to know. We aren't in our world. We're in his world and his world is a three. Remember?"

"That's right!" said Rory.

"So, if you three are the base, I can be the pointer."

"But how can you find the way?" asked Tima.

"He told us that, too. Each place and thing has a special look. Remember, he made sure we saw the color of Belecha and the portal."

"It was a clear, bright, white light," said Rory. "It looked totally different."

"You're right," said James. "But I don't see any threads that look like that."

"Let me get into pointer position. I'll spot one."

It was surprisingly easy to shift positions. Soon Billy was above, and the three were linked below.

"Do you see anything that looks right?" asked James.

Billy scanned the vast web of threads, feeling with all his senses. He saw a movement, a pulsation that, once he caught a glimpse of it, was clearly the same as the threads that had come from the portal. It was dancing and jumping far in the distance, moving away from them quickly.

"I see it!"

"Where?" called Tima.

"Trust me. It's far away and it's getting further. I'm going to have to swing on a whole chain of different threads to get to it. Follow my orders. I don't have time to explain."

Rory looked at the others and decided. "It's your show, Billy. Tell us what to do."

Billy looked for a path. The thread was quickly disappearing. He had to get closer. He saw a thread that seemed to be heading toward the portal thread. If he could catch it …

"Now! Push toward me," he called, and leapt. If he missed this one, they were going to fall a long way.

They all pushed, and just as they flashed by the thread, Billy reached out and grabbed it. They were whipped forward – and it was the right direction! They were heading toward the thread from the portal, but it was still a long way off.

"Great! Now, stay with me. It's going to take a lot of fast jumps if we want to get there."

"Don't worry," said James. "We made the decision. You're the one. Don't waste your time explaining. Watch, decide, and order. We'll do what you say."

So Billy watched the threads, keeping sight of the dancing light that was the path back to the portal. They were still far away, but they were getting closer. He scanned for threads pointing in the right direction. He screamed for the others to leap at the exact time necessary to be where a thread would be when they got there. As he was leaping, he was looking in all directions for the next jump, always mindful of the quarry –– the thread with the color of the portal.

Time did not exist here, so there was no way to know how long they leapt and grabbed, rode and leapt again. The threads got more numerous, which lessened the worry of falling but made tracking the portal thread more challenging. Finally, it pulsed far beneath them, but close enough to grab with one large jump and plunge. If they could swing and fall, he would have it.

"This is it." he called. "Don't freak. It's going to be a long drop and a sudden snap when I grab it."

"We're all good," said Tima. "Ready when you are."

"Wait for it … wait for it …" called Billy. "Swing. Swing hard. We really need some momentum. Now!"

He let go and in a perfect arc, they swung out and down, plunging past a whirlwind of threads.

"How can you see it through all of these?" called Rory.

"Hush, Rory," said Tima.

Billy saw the thread they needed and reached out. It seemed to dance away at the last moment, like it was playing with him, but he adjusted and suddenly they were sliding along the thread. "Got it!"

"You da man!" shouted Rory.

"How do we know we're going in the right direction?" asked James.

"Intention. Think about Belecha and the portal. It will take us. Energy attracts energy."

So they all thought about the Stone and Belecha and the place where they had landed. They hurtled along the thread and soon they saw more threads of the same color and feel.

"You did it!" shouted Tima.

Very quickly, they saw they were over the pyramid of light.

"I'm letting go," called Billy. "I don't know how to land, so it may be bumpy."

"No worries," said James. "I'm ready to be home."

Billy let go and they dropped down in front of Belecha. They stood up, back in form again, and gathered around the old man, who was grinning at them.

"So, Tinglen," he said to Billy. "I guess you aren't so dumb. I always figured you for a birdbrain."

Billy grinned back. "Rather be a bird than an old raccoon any day."

The others gathered around him. "That was great, Billy," said Rory. "I was afraid it was me, and I had no idea."

"Yeah. Good job," said James.

Tima nodded. "Maybe we can take some trips now that you know how to point."

Belecha shook his head. "Sorry about that. Once we get back, you'll need all four to be a base, so you're stuck with me. Besides, I'm a better driver."

"I don't know, old man," said Billy. "Haven't you heard about the dangers of senior drivers? You might lose your faculties and get into an accident. Besides, you probably run the threads with your blinker on."

Rory grinned. "And you never took us swinging. That was great!"

Belecha pulled a face. "Hmmph. You want to take some wild rides? I got tricks you never thought of. I'll show you senior driver."

Tima turned to Billy. "So, you feel it? You know?"

Billy nodded. "Yeah. It's like in math, when I see an answer. I may not be able to explain it to the teacher in a way they want, but I know it's right. I could see the right thread. It stood out from the background, so it was impossible to miss. I knew where it was going to be when we got there." He cocked his head, thinking. "Weird. It felt like I'd done it before, but not as me. I mean it was still me, but I was in other bodies and other lives."

Tima nodded. "Yup. That's the feeling. Like a puzzle piece that you've been turning around and around and suddenly you see how it fits and you push it into place. So, do you know how to activate the bird on the Stone?"

"Sure. Let's get back. It will only take a minute." He turned to Belecha. "You ready to take us?"

"I've been ready for thousands of years. It's you four who have been delaying things."

Rory grinned. "We were just waiting for your smell to die down a little. It's taken this long to be able to get near you."

James held up his hands. "Come on, guys. I'm tired, and I still have things to handle at home. Let's get back."

"Agreed," said Tima. "I want to make sure Mom is okay."

The four sat around the Stone. Tima sat at the snake. Billy sat at the bird. Rory and James looked at each other, shrugged, and sat at the other corners. Belecha took his position above the Stone. "Hang on," he called. They rose quickly and were on their way.

A short while later, Belecha called out. "Here we are. Home again, home again." They bumped down in the kiva. The moon had been a mere sliver when they started. Now, a blanket of clouds filled the sky, blotting out the stars and the little light the moon had provided. It was inky dark. They could barely see each other as patches of deeper darkness.

They turned to Billy, knowing there was one more piece to the evening's challenge. He held out his hand to Rory.

"Give me the Stone," he said.

Rory reached out for Billy's hand. He grabbed it, to make sure he put the Stone in Billy's palm. If it fell, they would never find it in this darkness.

Billy grinned. "Watch this." He took the Stone and threw it high in the air directly overhead.

"Billy!" gasped Tima. They were sure the Stone was gone.

But Billy could now see through the darkness. He watched the Stone as it twirled up and started back down. As the Stone fell past his face, he gave a short, sharp blast of air that rose up from his belly, then caught it in his outstretched hand. He showed the Stone to the others.

As they watched, the bird glyph glowed for a moment, then faded to darkness.

"Wind," explained Billy. "Bird is of the air and the air in my belly was from the challenge. A quick blast and *poof*."

Belecha nodded. "You got it, Tinglen. You never come through when I want you to, but you always come through when you have to. Course, you do tend to be a bit of a show-off."

Billy grinned. "We birds have to show off our plumage and strut."

Rory spoke. "That's great, but now I've got to get home. The plane leaves early."

Tima grabbed his arm. "Be strong, friend. It'll work out."

"I hope so. If I'm not back by the end of the week, send a rescue party."

"We will if we need to, Rory," said James. "You aren't alone."

"That's right," agreed Billy. "And be as awful as you can. Remember everything I taught you, grasshopper."

"If I'm even a bit as bad as you, the entire state will throw me out."

Billy grinned. "That's the goal."

Rory laughed, and the teens started to climb out of the kiva. First James. Then Tima. Then Billy. Just as Rory turned to go, Belecha spoke.

"Just a minute, Techta," he said. "Take this." He handed a small stone to Rory. Rory wanted to look closely at it, but it was too dark. Running his fingers along it he recognized it as a pyramid, roughly cut, with glyphs on each side.

"Other places may have a lot more Kroledutz and you won't have your kiva to run to," said Belecha. "This may help."

"What's it do?" asked Rory.

Belecha smiled. "Makes you smell bad to them. Might as well use your inherent gifts to your advantage. On the energy plane, you will smell like spoiled milk. If they get a whiff of you, they'll have to be plenty hungry to take a taste."

Rory shook his head. "Thanks. I think." He put it in his pocket, then turned to the wall of the kiva, and started to climb out.

Belecha began to fade. When he neared the top, Rory turned and looked down. "Hey, Belecha," he called. "Why do you call me Techta?"

"It's what we called the little toads that would come out after the rain," Belecha said. "They croaked as loud as buffalo, and if you stepped on 'em, the stink would make you barf. Somehow, it seems to fit."

Rory shook his head, and pulled himself over the lip of the hole. "And that's who's watching out for me. Great." He headed home.

TWENTY 20

"What are you talking about, Namuka?" screamed Cisco into the phone. "What kinda crap is this? What do you mean it has come to your attention? Where'd you hear it?"

James' dad had pulled the phone away from his ear when Cisco started shouting. He looked at James' worried face across the kitchen table and smiled reassuringly. Then, taking a deep breath, he put the phone back to his ear. "That's Nomura," he said calmly.

"What?" screamed Cisco.

"My name," replied Franklin, speaking with no trace of the irritation Cisco wanted to cause, "is Nomura, not Namuka. And I specifically did not say who told me because it is an unfounded rumor. I am, instead, going to the source. My question was, 'are you planning to build more than the single store that you outlined at the meeting?' Would you like to answer that question?"

"Who's been talking? What have they been saying? Are you spying? That's illegal!"

"Mr. Cisco, no one has accused you of anything. I have heard an unsubstantiated rumor, and I wanted to squash it before it spread. Now, your response is not exactly what I was hoping to hear. It certainly makes me think there may be something to these rumors."

"Oh, no, you don't. I didn't say anything about any plans. If you want to twist my words …"

Franklin continued to speak calmly, while looking at James. "I am not twisting your words, Mr. Cisco. I am giving you the opportunity to refute the rumors, an opportunity you are squandering. I contacted you immediately. I have not spread the rumor. I have gone to the source to seek clarification, which you have not provided. You have yelled.

Now, one more time, I'm asking you, are you planning to build more than a single business on the Rattlesnake Ranch site?"

"I don't have to tell you nothing, and I ain't going to say any more without a lawyer. Now, you listen to me. You slow this operation down, and I'm ruined and I'm not going to let that happen. I'm going to find out who's messing with me and make them pay, and if you had anything to do with it …"

"It seems this conversation is not accomplishing anything, Mr. Cisco."

"I am a businessman. I'm trying to bring some money into this town's economy. I've taken a big risk and I'm not going to lose. I don't care how dirty it gets. I'm going to win. I've got to win. If that proposal doesn't pass, you'll be sorry. I'll do something else with that land that no one will like. Then, I'll sue this county and you personally."

"You won't win, Mr. Cisco."

"Wanna bet? I got good lawyers and they only get paid when they win and they always get paid. So watch yourself." With that, Cisco hung up.

Franklin set down the phone and took a breath. James looked unhappy. "I'm sorry, Dad. I'm sorry about what Billy did. I'm sorry I told you." He put his head in his hands. "I'm sorry."

"Stop it, James. No apologies. You did right. I'd rather have bad news than surprises. You know that."

"But his plan."

"It's okay if the proposal passes. That's democracy. Even if those people usually don't come out to vote, they have the right. What I don't like is Mr. Cisco not telling the whole truth about his plans, so people don't know what they are voting on."

"And you can't tell anyone or he'll sue you."

"No," said Franklin sharply. "I won't tell, but not because of his threats. It is important to speak the truth, even if the result may be unpleasant. If I start to worry about the result or the possible result, I will never take action."

"Then why won't you tell people about it?"

"Because I do not know it is true. Billy saw something, but he may be wrong. Mr. Cisco did not confirm anything, except that he is an unpleasant man. Now, I do not like him, but that doesn't really matter. I am the chair of the council, and I must behave according to principles, not my personal likes and dislikes."

"So, if all those people come and vote for it, you can't do anything?"

Franklin smiled and shook his head. "I didn't say that. There are a lot of agencies in state and county government that may want to take a closer look at this proposal. Even if we pass the plan, all kinds of roadblocks may pop up. Usually, when the people have expressed support of an idea, I help ease the way through all the red tape. However, I don't have to."

"What about his threat to sue you?"

"Comes with the territory. I get threatened a couple of times a year. He's more unpleasant than most, but no one has ever acted on it. I doubt he will either." Franklin slapped his hands on the table. "Now. Break is over. Let's go out and finish that field. This afternoon, I'll start asking around to see if I can get any more information."

James stood, and they headed out. At the door, his dad turned and put his hand on his son's shoulder, squeezing. "You did right, James. It's good that Billy got that information, but let me take it from here. Mr. Cisco does not care who he hurts and is not someone to be taken lightly."

Then he turned. James, following his dad into the bright sunlight, did not see the look of worry that crossed Franklin's face.

TWENTY-ONE 21

"Tima, can you talk?"

"Rory!" Tima yelled excitedly into the phone. "Are you okay? How awful is it?"

"It's weird, Tima. Really weird. How's your mom?"

"Better. A couple of days asleep, and now she's back to writing."

"That's good." Rory's voice was hushed.

"Why are you talking so quietly?"

"Kathy is always checking up on me. It's like she expects me to run away."

"Are you gonna?"

"Nah. There's no place to go. It's total suburbia here. Every street looks like every other. In fact, even the houses look alike. I'd probably get lost."

"Real middle class plastic?"

"You have no idea. And the people are just as plastic as the houses, and the pastor came by. Oh man is he creepy. His eyes are always measuring you, like he's thinking about how much he could get for you if he sold you."

"Yuck."

Rory sighed, worry entering his voice. "Yeah, but that's not the real problem."

"What's wrong?" Tima asked. "Do you think you're going to have to stay?"

"It isn't that." Rory lowered his voice. "I keep seeing Kroledutz," he whispered.

Tima stiffened. "Floating around, looking for food?"

"No. Worse than that – feeding. They're on almost everyone here."

"What about your …"

"Totally. One's wrapped around Kathy. There's another on her boyfriend, Bill. Same with the three kids. The pastor was almost completely surrounded by this really thick one – nearly as big as Radelam. That's why she did this, I'm sure. She'd never have cooked up this scheme on her own."

Tima shuddered. "How can you stand it?"

"I can't look at anyone. They think I'm being weird and withdrawn, but I'm scared to get near them. It's like they're covered with leeches."

"Gross! You have the rock Belecha gave you, right?"

"Always in my hand. I even sleep with it. I'm scared. It's not like looking at them from a distance. I could reach out and touch one."

"But they haven't tried to go for you?"

"No. It's like they don't see me, but still I'm always on edge. Today I went to see the social worker and she had me go to talk to this shrink. I kept getting glimpses of dark forms. I was trying to be calm, but they noticed it. The shrink asked me why I was so uncomfortable."

"What did you say?"

"I said I was worried I would be taken from the only home I've ever known and my friends."

"Did she believe you?"

"I think so. At least there's one benefit to all this."

"What's that?"

"I'm not mad at Kathy anymore. I mean, how can I feel anything bad about someone who's being eaten alive by one of those things? I think if I ran away, she'd run away with me. I can see it in her eyes. She's trapped and wants out."

"I'm scared for you. If everyone there is controlled by Kroledutz …"

"Yeah. I just want to get out of here and go home."

"Is it almost done?"

"Dunno. They keep marching me to meet more people: lawyers, social workers, shrinks …"

"Fun."

"Not! And when we're at the house, it's like being with a bunch of robots. All cheerful. No talking about anything that matters."

"Awwww, you miss us."

"Got that right. I bet they were boring before the Kroledutz started eating them, but now … If I have to stay, I'm going to eat my hand, just for some excitement."

"Start with your left," suggested Tima. "You need your right to pick your nose."

"Promise." Rory smiled. "You know, I'm actually feeling a bit better. Thanks, Tima."

"That's what I'm here for. I'll send you a bill."

Rory laughed. "Alright. Well, I better go before they come looking for me. Tell the others I wish they were here."

"I bet you'd rather be here than have us there."

"Amen."

"Stay safe. Keep that rock close to you."

"Will do."

Tima ended the call and stared at her purple, flowered phone case, wishing she could send some protection of her own to Rory. She shook her head and turned to the painting she had been working on.

Suddenly, she stiffened. Smoke! She smelled smoke.

"Mom?" she called. There was no answer. Grace was down in her office. She had told Tima she wanted to work on her latest book. Tima realized it had been a while since she had checked on her. She hurried down to her mother's office door. The smell of smoke was much stronger there, mixed with the unmistakable stink of the Kroledutz!

Tima banged on the door, but there was no answer. She threw the door open.

Grace was on the floor, surrounded by stacks and stacks of paper. Her current manuscript and several other manuscripts were scattered across the floor. Several pages were burning. Her hair was wild – tangled and matted. Tears and snot were running down her face. She held a lighter in her hand. Loud, gasping sobs poured from her gaping mouth as she rocked and moaned, then lit the pile beside her.

Tima was frozen for a moment. Then she snapped into action. She ran to the fireplace and grabbed the fire extinguisher. Aiming it at the burning piles, she squeezed the handle. Instantly, everything in the room was covered in white powder.

As the cloud settled a bit, Tima dropped the extinguisher and stepped to her mother. She grabbed the lighter from her hand and threw it away. Then she grabbed Grace's hands.

"Mom." Tima screamed. "Mom!"

Grace looked up at her. "I can't ..." she moaned. "I can't ..."

"Mom!" said Tima, quieter, in a commanding voice. "It is time for you to get up. Stand up. Can you stand up?"

Grace just shook her head and rocked, moaning. Tima let go of her hands and reached for the phone on the desk. She picked it up and dialed 9-1-1.

"Hello," she said. "I need an ambulance. My mother has suffered a nervous breakdown."

She gave the details, feeling detached, as if she was watching someone else make the call. Tima looked around. The room was a wreck, with books and papers thrown everywhere. The fire was out, but all around, Tima felt the dark forms and smelled the stench of rotting meat, burning plastic, and sweat.

TWENTY-TWO 22

Finally! thought Billy, seeing Cisco's car as he pedaled through the gate at Rattlesnake Ranch. Billy had been coming by for two days, hoping the turnout at the council meeting would encourage Cisco to give him a bonus, but the place had been empty and the gates locked.

As Billy rode up, the trailer door banged open. Cisco stepped out while Matt glared from behind him. Both men looked meaner than usual.

"Get in here, you little punk!" yelled Cisco.

Billy shrugged, went into the trailer and sat down. Matt stood behind him, looming like an executioner. Billy willed himself to be calm. He looked at Cisco.

"Where have you been?" he asked. "Celebrating because my plan worked so well?"

"I got a call from Nomura!" yelled Cisco. "Someone's been sticking their nose where it shouldn't be, and I figure the nosiest little punk around is you."

Billy decided the best course of action was to act dumb and deny everything, particularly with Matt towering over him. The game had changed. Now it wasn't about getting a bonus, it was about getting out of the trailer without a beating. "I have no idea what you're talking about, Boss. I came by to see what you wanted to pay me for getting all those people out to support you. Now you're making stuff up to weasel out of it."

Cisco slammed his fist down on the desk. "Shut up! I just spent two days begging some very mean guys to give me an extension on the money they fronted. It'll cost me plenty – in pride and in profits once I get running. Now, I have to win that vote and to do that, I need to know what some little rat has been saying. You've been spying and telling tales. Now you're going to tell me everything."

Billy shook his head. "I deliver and this is what I get? I'm outta here." He made a show of starting to stand. Matt grabbed his arms from behind and pushed him back down in the chair.

Cisco gave him a nasty smile. "You'll leave when I'm ready for you to leave, and when you do, you'll have a few reminders of why it's a bad idea to mess with me." He looked at his enforcer. "Matt, I think this punk needs persuading."

Matt shifted and raised his fist to slam it down on Billy's head. That was what Billy had been waiting for. As Matt lifted his hand, Billy quickly slammed his head backwards, catching Matt full in the crotch. Matt immediately doubled over in pain. Billy continued his motion, swiveling around, up, and out of the chair.

As Matt's head dropped, Billy clasped his hands tightly together and with all his strength, drove them up into Matt's face. Matt fell backward and Billy continued moving – out the door, onto his bike, and through the gate before Cisco could waddle out from behind the desk. He dropped down into an arroyo, knowing that neither man could trail him through the brush on foot. The car was useless off the road. He was safe, as long as he moved fast.

Cisco screamed after him. "You little turd! If I ever see you again, I'll beat your face in. Then Matt will rip you apart."

Billy smiled as he pedaled. "Well, I guess I'm fired," he said to himself. "That's okay. I got what I needed out of those jerks."

Billy considered his next step. He decided it was time to talk with Franklin Nomura and set his backup plan in motion. He headed toward the farm. When he got there, James and his dad were busy planting chili seedlings.

"Hey, James. Hi, Mr. Nomura," called Billy.

James looked up, then glanced at his dad, obviously worried. It was plain to Billy that James had told Franklin everything. With someone he respected, like James' dad, Billy knew that honesty with no delays, excuses, or embellishments, was essential.

"Mr. Nomura, may I talk with you?"

Franklin studied the boy and nodded. "Yes, Billy. I think that might be a good idea." Turning to James, he said, "Can you carry on, Son? I think Billy and I should talk inside."

James didn't like being left out. He thought about protesting, but a glance at his father told him that this was not the time. He nodded and returned to carefully planting the seedlings.

Franklin set down his trowel and stood up. "This way," he said, heading toward the house. Billy followed. They didn't speak until they were inside, sitting at the kitchen table.

"Alright, Billy. What do you have to say?"

Billy got right to the point. "James told you about Mr. Cisco's plans, right?"

Franklin nodded. "I also know that you got the information illegally so I can't do anything with it."

Billy nodded. "Yeah, I was afraid of that." He sat silently for a minute. "You know how I got all those people to the meeting, too, right?"

Franklin nodded again. "That might not have been illegal, Billy, and it was certainly effective, but it was unethical, and I worry that you may not have considered the results of your actions."

Billy sighed. "I know. I didn't realize what he was planning until later. It seemed like the right move at the time."

"It isn't a game, Billy," said Franklin. "You're obviously very good at motivating people, but that's a power and you should only use power for good. The consequences of what you did will affect this area for years to come. I want people to voice their opinions, but they should do it because they've thought about the issues at hand, not because they want free beer."

"You're right."

"You are young, yet it looks like you have made a big impact. That's impressive, but the trouble is, I don't think it's going to be a good impact, and I don't see that there is anything to do about it."

Billy smiled. "Actually, that's why I'm here. There is something we can do."

"What do you mean?"

"Well, in chess, you can't just think about attack. You'll never win that way. You have to think about defense and plan several moves ahead. You have to consider what your opponent will do."

Franklin looked at Billy. "Again, this is real life, not a game, Billy. Still, I see your point. However, you may have underestimated your opponent, just as you underestimated the consequences of your actions."

Billy's grin spread. "Maybe, but I never trusted Mr. Cisco, so when I came up with the plan, I also came up with a backdoor dump."

"Backdoor dump?"

Billy nodded. "A way to kill it, in case I had to."

A hint of a smile flickered across Franklin's face. "I see. And you came here today to tell me about this backdoor dump?"

"Yeah. You see, I based the plan on the type of people I know from hanging around my mom. They're not interested in much, but I also based my plan on Mr. Cisco. He didn't trust me. Dishonest people always figure everyone else is as crooked as they are. I knew he would want to test my plan before the vote. That's why he made everyone come to the last meeting."

"When there wasn't a vote."

"Right. He figured if he got them to one, they'd come to the next, because if the proposal didn't pass, they wouldn't be getting the benefit." Billy's grin widened. "But, he doesn't know these people. Keeping their interest is not so easy. Last meeting they got a cheap beer card and got to create a scene. Now it's out of their heads. The backdoor dump is to put something else into their heads."

Billy realized then that he had been thinking like the bird even before the challenge. All along, he had watched the prey, knowing how it would line up when he got to this point. He'd known, all along, what to do.

"What do you have in mind?"

"Offer them another way to get drunk. I figure if you called the owners of all the bars in the county and told them that Cisco was planning a much bigger operation with cheaper beer, that would get their attention."

"It would."

"Then, if you suggested Saturday would be a great day for a promotion to celebrate the Fourth of July a little early …"

Franklin smiled and nodded. "That group would go to the bars, instead of to the meeting. I believe that would work." He gave Billy a light slap on his back, and his eyes twinkled. "You are a very clever young man. You must be careful how you use your talents."

"I understand that now, Mr. Nomura. Thank you."

"You're welcome." Franklin slapped his own thighs and began to stand. "Now, I have to get back to that field. James is probably wondering what horrors have been happening in here."

"Yeah, he worries a lot."

They both walked to the door.

"Yes," said Franklin, "and he is not the only one. I also am worried about you. Mr. Cisco is a powerful man, and powerful men can be ruthless. You are clever, but you are also young. You have not seen all that men are capable of."

"He's mean, I agree, but I'm watching out for him."

"I don't suppose you would be willing to stay here for a few days, just so we can make sure you are okay?" Franklin eyed him seriously.

"Thanks, but no. I'll be careful."

Franklin sighed and again placed a hand on his back. "I hope you will be, Billy. And please, let me take it from here. I have found that bullies prefer to pick on smaller and younger targets." He smiled. "And I suggest you stay away from Rattlesnake Ranch."

Riding home, Billy felt great about how everything was turning out. Mr. Nomura had made him feel like it might all be okay after all. *I just wish I could see the look on Cisco's face when no one turns up to vote for his proposal,* he thought as he turned onto the road to his trailer.

Looking ahead, his smile vanished. His mom's car was parked across the front yard and the door to the trailer was open. It was the way she parked when she was too drunk to bother with the driveway, but still awake enough to be mean. Georgette must have arrived that morning, drinking all the way, and now there was going to be a fight. If he was lucky, she'd be passed out. If he was unlucky, she'd be screaming and swinging. He shook his head, angry and disgusted. "I better get my money, and get out of here."

Music blared from the stereo as he stepped inside. The place was trashed. Suitcases, boxes, bottles, and garbage were spread everywhere. It looked like three weeks of party, even though it had been clean when he left this morning. His mom wasn't in sight. Maybe luck was with him, and she was asleep. He started toward his room.

"Billy! Is that you, you little puke?" Georgette staggered out of her room. "Where the hell have you been?"

Billy didn't answer. *If I can just grab my money and get out of here ...* he thought. Georgette grabbed him and spun him around.

"Don't you ignore me!" She pulled back her hand to deliver a slap, but he saw it coming and ducked. Her momentum swung her around, and Georgette fell, giving Billy enough time to dart into his room. He aimed for his dresser where he hid his cash. Just inside the door, he stopped.

His room was in worse shape than the living room. All his stuff had been dumped out on the floor. He saw the drawer where he kept his money, empty, sitting on top of a pile. Looking at his bed, he saw an open suitcase and his wayward sister Suzie's stuff spread everywhere. He rubbed his eyes, hoping the picture would go away, but it didn't.

As he stood there, he sensed, rather than heard, a sound at his back and felt something heavy and thick crash into his head. *Probably the phone book,* he thought, as he fell to the floor.

He shook his head, groggy from the blow, and heard Georgette above him, screaming. "Never home! Holding out on us! Keeping money!" He felt a kick, and then another. "Well, that's it! Suzie's come home, and you can go find someone else to sponge off of! You're out!"

Georgette's kicks were wild and she kept staggering, so they weren't doing much damage. For a second, Billy thought he could make a move, get up, and get out of there. Then, he saw Suzie's feet. A boot aimed right for his forehead. He tried to move out of the way, but still caught a good piece of it. As darkness closed in, he thought, *Suzie always was good in a fight.*

TWENTY-THREE 23

"Dad!" cried Rory. "They're never going to let me out of here!"

"Rory, calm down. What do you mean?" Javier gripped the phone and closed his eyes, focusing his attention on Rory's words.

"I saw the judge today."

"Rory, take a breath," ordered Javier. "Stop a minute and take a deep breath. I mean it. Now."

Javier heard Rory suck in a big lungful of air.

"That's good. Now let it out, slowly. I'm here for you. We can talk all night if we need to. I can fly out there. We'll get through this. Now, take another breath."

Rory did so, and then let it out. "Okay. I feel a little better, but it sucks here."

"I know, Son. You're doing a really hard thing. Now, tell me what happened with the judge."

"He was awful. He tried to seem nice, but his eyes were always judging me. He kept asking all of these questions …"

"We knew that was going to happen. Did you stay calm?"

Rory sighed. "It was hard, but yeah, I didn't raise my voice. I kept saying the same thing in different ways – that you and Leon were there for me and cared for me and that Kathy never was, but it was like he thought if he kept asking I'd give up and say something else!"

"I'm so sorry you have to go through this Rory, but it's almost over."

"That's the worst thing; I'm not sure it is! He said he wants me to come back tomorrow. Tomorrow! I want to go home tomorrow, Dad. I want to have time before the challenge. I'm afraid he or Kathy is going to keep me here until the ruling, and I'll miss the challenge, and I'll be stuck here with these weirdos who just walk around looking stupid and, and …" Rory's voice grew higher and louder with each statement, until finally he choked on the last word.

"Rory, stop. Please. You're starting to lose it, and that isn't going to help anyone. I know it's hard, but you have to listen to me." He paused. "Are you listening?"

Rory took another deep breath. Finally, he spoke. "Yeah." His voice, though it wavered, was back to normal. "I'm listening."

"Good. It is not necessarily a bad thing that the judge asked you to come back. That means he is really thinking about this. Remember, standard procedure is usually to give custody to the mother. He is considering doing something different."

"I didn't think of it that way."

"I know. Also, I have been talking to Terry, our lawyer, every day, and she says it is going as good as or better than she had hoped. So, really, it's going well. I promise. Besides, it's already Thursday. You'll be home by Sunday afternoon. That's plenty of time to rest before the challenge."

"Why can't I come back on Saturday?"

"I think you should stay until Sunday. Use Saturday to spend some quality time with your mother. Educate her a bit about our life and what you want to do. Remember: For the first time in years, she *is* trying to show she cares. If you get through to her, she might drop the suit. Then, all this goes away."

"Okay, Dad, but I wouldn't bet on that happening. There's more going on here than that."

Javier sat up straighter. "Like what?"

"Nothing I can get in to now, unfortunately. They're always sniffing around the door when I'm on my phone, trying to figure out what I'm saying. So, we'll have to talk about it when I get home." Rory sighed. "On Sunday, I guess."

"But you're safe?" Javier asked, concern filling his voice.

"As safe as I'll be on Sunday," Rory answered. "Don't worry, Dad. You're right. It'll be okay."

"You're doing great, Rory. I'm proud of you. Call when you need to, and keep up the good work. I'll see you Sunday at the airport."

"I'll be the one with the huge grin. 'Night, Dad."

"'Night, Rory," Javier hung up the phone. He sat for a minute, gathering his thoughts, then dialed the number of their lawyer. As the phone began to ring in Florida, he heard the doorbell buzz, and Leon go to answer it.

"Hello, Terry Belauto here."

"Hi Terry, it's Javier Hurtado. I just talked to Rory and ..."

A shout from the front door stopped him. "Madre de Dios!" Leon yelled. "Javier, get down here now!"

"I'm sorry, Terry. I have to call you back." Javier hung up, and rushed down to the front door, wondering what else could have happened.

At the bottom of the staircase, swaying back and forth, his face swollen and covered in blood, was Billy. Leon had his arms wrapped around him, holding him up.

"Billy!" said Javier. "What happened?"

Billy mumbled a reply, but the effort of getting to the house had taken all his energy. Javier knelt down, lifting Billy's eyelids, checking for a concussion. He could see Leon quickly locating the sources of blood, checking to see if this was a hospital, doctor, or bandage emergency. With many years of experience on remote digs, both Javier and Leon were good at this. Leon looked at Javier after a couple of minutes.

"Banged up pretty good. Head wound. No breaks that I see. Concussion?"

Javier shook his head. "I don't think so." He held Billy's face and looked into his eyes, talking loud and clear, to get through. "Billy! Can you tell me what happened? I think you are okay, but we'll get you to a doctor to be sure."

Billy's eyes opened and he shook his head. "No doctor. It was Mom. Mom and Suzie. They took my money and then ..."

"Shhh," said Leon. "You need a doctor, mijo. I'm worried about these cuts on your head."

Billy struggled to stand on his own, pushing Leon's hands away, shaking his head to clear it. "No. No doctor. Take me to a doctor and they call either Mom or the cops. Either way ..." He looked up at Javier through an eye swelling shut. "Can I stay here? Please. Just for a couple of days?"

"I don't know, Billy. You look like ..."

Billy struggled for a grin. "I look like hell. I know. But I've taken a beating before. It looks bad, but I can tell that nothing's broken. I just need a place to stay. Please?"

Javier looked at Leon, who shrugged. "We could check him more carefully. He's probably right. If we keep an eye on him, he should be okay."

Looking back at Billy, Javier decided. "Leon, why don't you help our guest upstairs? He can stay in Rory's room."

Billy nodded his thanks, then felt himself fall back into the pain of his injuries. Leon scooped him up in his strong arms and carried him upstairs.

TWENTY-FOUR 24

"Dad!" Rory ran through the final security point and into Javier's arms. "I didn't think I'd ever make it back!"

Javier gave him a strong squeeze. "I missed you, Son."

Rory nestled into the hug. "I don't know what I'm going to do if Kathy gets custody, Dad. That place really …"

Javier held up his hand. "I know … it sucks. Now that you're back, it's time you put that particular word aside. I don't want people saying I allow you to swear."

"Ha. Everyone there thinks you're teaching me to swear, instead of the other way around."

"You know the power of words. There are almost always better words to use that really mean what you want to say. Besides, if you get into the habit, one will slip out when you don't want it to. I hope you kept it clean when you talked to the judge."

Rory put his hand on his heart. "I was as pure and innocent as a baby lamb."

Javier's head fell back in mock laughter. "Good thing they don't know you like I do!"

"Yeah," said Billy, with a wry smile. "Everyone here knows you're a baaaad boy."

Rory hadn't noticed Billy, standing a little distance away. His eyes widened as he took in Billy's bruises. "Dude, what happened to you? You look like you bounced down a mountain on your face."

"Mom came home and decided to prove how much she cared. I thought I'd come along to the airport, since …" he hesitated.

Javier broke in. "Billy is staying with us for a while." He looked at Billy. "Actually, for as long as he wants."

Rory grinned. "Cool. Now if anything goes wrong, I know who I can blame."

Billy shook his head. "Try it, and you'll wake up one morning with your head shaved."

"You'd do that, wouldn't you?"

Billy nodded. "Never threaten something unless you're willing to follow through."

"Come on you two," said Javier. "Let's get your bags, Rory. Leon is circling with the car."

A few minutes later, they were all in the car, heading home. Rory turned to Billy. "Are you okay? I mean, other than being uglier than usual, is anything broken?"

Billy shook his head. "No. My ribs hurt and my face hurts, but-"

"It's killing me," said Rory, grinning and throwing his right hand across his heart with dramatic flair.

Billy punched him in the arm. "Anyway, I'll survive, but I'm pissed off. Mom took my money, and they jumped me. I didn't even hear them sneak up, and I'm supposed to be the bird with amazing perceptions. Didn't work that way."

"It's hard to expect it when it's your own family. Can you handle the challenge tonight?"

"Totally. No way I'd miss it. Way things are going, we have to do this."

"What do you mean?"

"Well, last night at the council meeting, Cisco's plan lost." Billy grinned. "I wish I coulda seen his face."

"How did that happen?"

"A little bird suggested it would be a good idea to have a bunch of beer promotions at all the local bars to celebrate the Fourth. Mr. Nomura agreed, and made a few phone calls. Funny thing. None of Cisco's supporters showed up."

Rory grinned. "I'm guessing you don't have a job anymore."

"Nah, but I'd lost it already anyway."

"Well, I guess that takes care of Cisco."

"I don't think so. He stormed out, shouting he was going to get back at everyone in the county." Billy shook his head. "I don't trust him. He's got something planned."

Javier spoke from the front seat. "I've been talking to a friend at the state historical preservation commission. I know Belecha doesn't want us to mess with that kiva, but if Mr. Cisco tries anything, all I have to do is make a call and we can start the process to get it declared a potential historical site. However, we'll have to dig to prove it."

Rory nodded. "I know he doesn't want that, but it's good to have as a backup, even if it isn't much of one."

"Mr. Nomura is worried, too," Billy added. Cisco threatened to mess with him if it didn't pass. James says his dad is spending a lot of time staring out the window, but won't talk about it."

"What's up with Tima?"

Billy shook his head.

"What's wrong?"

"Her mom had another breakdown. She tried to torch everything she was writing. She's in the hospital. They say she's going to be coming home on Tuesday, but Tima is pretty messed up about it."

"I'll call her when I get home," said Rory, his forehead furrowed in concern. "Do you think she'll come tonight?"

Billy nodded. "She said she had to." He lowered his voice. "There's something else."

"What?"

"Kroledutz. They've been showing up a lot. We all can see them now. They have definitely found the town."

"But not us?"

"Not yet."

"Well that's good, but it won't be long, I'm sure. They were all over Florida, too. It was so gross. If I didn't have my rock from Belecha, I'd have been a goner."

Javier caught Rory's eye in the mirror.

"Yeah." Rory nodded to the unspoken question. "That was the 'other thing' I mentioned. They were all over everyone there. Kathy, her boyfriend, the kids. Especially that mean pastor. He was wrapped almost entirely by one of the biggest ones I've seen."

Before Javier could reply, they pulled up in front of the house. Rory jumped out of the car, and rushed inside.

Opening the front door, he was swept up with the scents of home. His mouth watered at the aroma of Leon's *arroz con pollo*. It was great to be back.

"Smells like someone's been cooking me something special," he said.

"You deserve it, mijo," said Leon, coming in from the car and giving him a quick hug. "You've been through a lot. Now, get your stuff up to your room and clean up. We eat in 20 minutes."

TWENTY-FIVE 25

Everyone was worn down and on edge that evening. When Belecha appeared, he looked more haggard and bent over than they'd seen him. He looked around, then sniffed the air. "Let's go. I don't want to call attention to what we're doing. The Kroledutz are all around."

"Fine with me," said Rory. "Let's get this done so I can sleep for a couple of years."

"Tell me about it," said Tima.

"We don't have time for whining! Things are happening faster than I planned. We need to get out of here, and you four need to be quiet."

His words snapped the teens from worrying about their lives to the task at hand. They all nodded and gathered around the Stone.

"Put this world out of your mind. You'll need all your attention to get through the next challenge."

Rory took a deep breath and followed Belecha's command. Soon, the group was flying along a ribbon of energy. They dropped down on hard-packed dirt with nothing around but tall grasses. It was night.

Belecha pointed. "Walk that direction. You'll see a fire."

Silently, they headed off. The bowl of black sky stretched impossibly far and deep above them, stars so thick they looked like clouds. The half-moon provided enough light to walk. They felt, but could not see, the land reaching flat mile after mile in every direction. No hill, no tree broke the landscape. The tall grasses that covered the place caught the wind, filling their ears with the hum of stalk against stalk.

Ahead, a dip in the flat earth, clear of grass, sheltered a fire. They headed toward it, not speaking. The immensity of the empty land made them reluctant to break the quiet.

Coming near, they saw a figure, softly chanting to a steady drum beat, beside the fire. As they came into the circle of light near the fire, the figure stood. He was old, his face wrinkled and hardened like an apple left for days in the sun. His long, white hair flowed around his face and past his shoulders. His simple leather shirt and leather pants were loose and worn.

"Sit," he ordered, pointing to a place near the fire. "You may call me Atomasa. I am the Watcher here."

Rory stiffened. Belecha had said he was a Watcher. Belecha had said Rory would also be a Watcher, if he chose to be.

"What do you mean a 'Watcher'?" asked James.

"A Watcher allows the experiences of a place to touch him. Many lives, many events, many existences travel through a place. A Watcher rejoices in each one and listens to its song."

"Song?" asked Tima.

Atomasa nodded. "Every entity has a song, which it sings through its entire existence. It is the pulsation of its experience."

"In Belecha's kiva, the ribbons vibrated together when he chanted and drummed," said Rory.

Atomasa nodded. "He was singing the song of his kiva. By doing that, he became part of the kiva. That is the power of the song. When you sing the song of another being, you become part of that other being for a time. It is very important that you understand this. Look, I will show you."

Atomasa picked up his drum. He began to chant, his voice rising and falling, and then began to spin a rhythm within the chant with the drum. Breathy noises mixed with the drumbeats, whirring on, sinking and rising.

Listening, Rory began to notice the sound of the wind as it chased through the grasses all around them. The sound of the wind mixed with Atomasa's song and the sound of the drum, growing stronger as his voice grew, lessening as his voice quieted. The rustle of the grasses swirled around him, growing louder and clearer, until Rory could hear individual stalks rubbing against each other.

As he lost himself in the sound, he realized he could feel the grass stalks rubbing against him. He felt he was walking through them, bending with the wind, bowing before it, pulsing with the currents of the wind through the grass. Then, he became one of the stalks of grass. He looked around and saw other stalks of tall grass: his family. He felt his roots reaching into the dry earth and then the cool damp earth deep at the very tips. He saw the moon reflecting on the bodies of his fellow stalks. He twisted to catch the wind, to bend and release. It was like a wonderful dance.

Suddenly, he was sitting again in front of the fire, the feelings and sounds gone. Atomasa was grinning at him. Rory looked around, shocked to have a body and hands and be sitting on the dirt. He looked at the others and saw from their stunned expressions that they had also become grass and then been brought back.

"That was the song of the grass," said Atomasa.

"How did you do that?" gasped Tima.

Atomasa smiled. "Intention. You focus your attention and intention upon knowing and celebrating the entity. Then, you begin to make sounds and listen. Let your intention carry you. Sometimes there will be words or sounds that resemble words. Other times there will just be sounds. Do not think -- feel."

James protested. "That's hard for me. I've trained myself to think things through."

Atomasa shook his head. "Not so, Pecheme. You often rely on the song, but you do not acknowledge it." Seeing James shake his head, Atomasa smiled and asked, "How much water do you put on your fields? Do you use a chart to decide?"

"No. I know what the field needs. It depends on how hot it's been and how the plants are doing - lots of things."

"So you have learned to feel the need of the field. You are, without realizing it, singing the song of the field and of the plants. If you think about it, you will see that you sing the song of many things around you."

James sat quietly, thinking. Finally, he looked up at Atomasa. "I understand you now. I guess that's how we

make most of the important decisions around the farm."
Pausing he added, "But it's nothing like what you just did."

"When you sing another's song with intention and
awareness, you can completely become that entity for a time
and share its experience." He looked around at the four,
sitting before him. They understood.

"Good," he said. "Now, I have a story to tell you. Are you
ready to listen carefully? I do not tell my stories often."

The four looked at each other, then nodded.

"You know of the Spheres. They created themselves from
the matter of the universe. They were and are driven by two
desires: to experience and to share."

"Yeah, Mealim told us about that," said Billy.

"Good, now you have been reminded." Atomasa paused,
making sure the four were still listening closely. Then he
continued. "The desire to experience is the desire to create.
Experience is action is creation, if you are aware."

"What if they are not aware?" asked Rory. "A lot of the
people I saw in Florida were doing things, but it didn't seem
like they were creating."

"When you are aware, every action is creation. When you
are not, nothing is."

"What makes someone aware?" asked Tima.

"Attention and intention. You have probably spoken
without thinking before."

"Sure," said James.

"That's usually when I get in trouble," added Rory.

Atomasa nodded. "That is because you spoke without
paying attention and, often, without considering your
intentions – why you spoke at all."

"So intention is paying attention to the results?" asked
Billy.

Atomasa shook his head. "Not results. Results are in the
future. Intention is of the moment. It is acting with
awareness."

"But is watching action?" asked Rory. "When I watch TV,
I'm not doing anything."

"You see an important difference. It depends on your
intention. A Watcher watches with the intention of knowing,

honoring, and sharing the action. A passive watcher lets experience flow past, and neither watcher nor actor gains."

"That makes sense."

"This world offers a rich opportunity for action and creation. We call this world nature."

"But nature is trees and mountains and rivers – not the entire planet," said James.

"Nature is more than your view. You are not only your arm or your foot. You are the energy of the Sphere that created your form with the intention of an experience. In the same way, nature is the entity that created itself with the intention of this place."

"So nature is everything on the planet?" Tima asked.

Atomasa nodded. "Nature is streams and trees, cities and roads, people and rocks. It is all these things and more. And its life is long."

"They say we're killing it," said James.

Atomasa shook his head again. "Once more, you are seeing only parts of nature. Nature has a long existence. Its primary purpose is to keep a balance, like a person on a wire high above the ground who is constantly catching new objects, yet not falling."

He looked around, listening to the wind, then said, "When you hear talk of the planet dying, you hear a limited perception. The true statement is that nature may not support your type of being and keep its balance. Faced with that situation, nature will simply drop the thing making it teeter. That is not the end of nature, although it may be the end of humans."

Atomasa gestured at the unseen land all around. "In this place, at this time, buffalo are so numerous that a herd can take several days to pass one place – thousands upon thousands of individuals in one mass. The indentation where we sit is a wallow, where countless buffalo have rolled, rubbing a great dip in the ground over time. There are so many, it is inconceivable that their herd will ever fade away, but in time, another herd will come – humans. Nature will not be able to keep its balance with two such vast herds on the planet at the same time, so one will be dropped. The time of the buffalo will be over. They will all but disappear, but nature will retain its balance."

"The buffalo will think it's the end of the world," said Rory.

"Yes," agreed Atomasa. "But it is not. It is the end of their time. The important lesson for you four is the length of your view."

"What do you mean?" asked James.

Atomasa looked at him. "Who are you?" he asked.

"I'm James."

"That is a very short view. In this existence only, you are James. However, I have Watched your energy in dozens of lifetimes. I have seen parts of the energy that is now in you in thousands of lives. Just as nature will not end when it drops humans to keep its balance, you do not end when you drop James and return to the Sphere. You have been. You will be."

"So what?" said Billy, growing impatient. "This is interesting, but what difference does it make?"

Rory looked at Billy. "Be quiet," he whispered. "We haven't seen him mad, and I don't want to risk it."

Atomasa smiled. "The bird is always on the hunt for prey. What does not serve that end is of no interest. Your question makes sense for your perception."

Billy smirked at Rory. "See. I know what I'm doing."

Atomasa nodded. "However, you must be careful, little bird. Perception can be a tool or a cage. You have been caged by the limitations of your time. If you expand your perception, you have access to many lives and much information."

"How?" asked James.

"Through aware action."

James looked confused.

"Each time you travel the ribbons, your perception is expanded. You have been seeing more, even in your own time, since you began to travel, have you not?"

Rory nodded. "I've been seeing the threads and ribbons. I'm also seeing Kroledutz."

"Me too," said Tima.

"That is because your perception has enlarged. Experience in other times expands perception. Expanding your perception opens you to use all the experiences from all your existences. You will know your other lives, so you will not have to learn lessons again." He looked at Billy. "In this adventure, you do not have the luxury of time. That is why it is important."

Billy nodded. "Last challenge, I got the feeling I had been a bird in other lives."

Tima nodded. "I've been seeing how I pick the essential and use fire to burn away the unnecessary since the first challenge."

Atomasa nodded. "You will continue to see more if you pay attention." He looked around at the grasses bending in the wind. "That is my story. Now, I will tell you a piece of your puzzle, and you will be ready for your challenge."

TWENTY-SIX 26

Atomasa drew a square in the dirt. "You know how you use the Stone to travel?"

"Yeah," said Billy. "Four points for our world and three kinds of travel – time, direction, and return."

"And we need five to travel," added James. "The four corners for the base and a pointer. We're the four, and Belecha is the fifth. That makes the pyramid."

Atomasa nodded. "That is correct, but not complete. To be able to defeat the Kroledutz, you must be able to activate the double pyramid. That allows you to access the powers of the other times and dimensions."

"Other dimensions?" asked Rory.

Atomasa nodded. "Nature has many levels. There are worlds that exist outside of the planet you know. You have seen several already."

"The cave," Tima said, nodding. "And Arnalea's world."

"Yes," said Atomasa, "And here. There are many such places. You will need their assistance when you face the Kroledutz. There is not enough power in your time and dimension to turn back thousands of years and fix the ancient mistake. You are only four and are only just becoming aware. I am sure you have wondered how you can stand against even a single nest of Kroledutz. Radelam leads only one of many upon many nests that are massing about your kiva. They know you are weak."

James spoke up. "I've always thought it was hopeless."

"Belecha told us we have to activate the Stone," said Tima.

"I'm hoping that makes a difference, but I don't see how it will help," added Rory.

Atomasa nodded. "Activating the Stone is important, but using the double pyramid is essential. That will open the portal to all times and dimensions, which can channel near limitless power. This knowledge has been in your world since ancient times."

"What do you mean?" asked Rory.

"Think of the pyramids you have seen, firmly rooted in the earth, yet reaching to the sky. Those of your time view them as tombs, pointing direction for those who have left the world. They only see half the structure."

"You mean they go down as far as they go up?" asked James.

"No, they don't." said Rory. "My dad and I have been to pyramids in South America. They don't go down."

Atomasa smiled. "They do not go down in the physical world. However …"

Tima broke in. "On the energy level, they reach down to another point, beneath the point in the air?"

Atomasa nodded. "That is their secret message."

Rory had a sudden inspiration. The Oloho was a double pyramid! He opened his mouth to tell the others of the rock that Belecha had shown him in his kiva, but Atomasa looked directly at him and held up a hand, stopping the words. Rory remembered Belecha had told him not to let the others touch the rock. Maybe he wasn't supposed to talk about it either.

As if he could read Rory's thoughts, Atomasa nodded, then continued. "In order to travel to other dimensions, you must have one more point. A sixth point provides an anchor in your dimension, so you may open the paths to those dimensions and return."

"Wait a minute," said Tima. "We've done that, though, traveled to the other dimensions, and we never had six. It was just us and Belecha."

"Well thought, Heliotom. Have you noticed that Belecha seems very tired and leaves quickly after each challenge?"

They thought about it.

"He has been looking older," said James, "which is funny to say, seeing as he's … well, I don't really know what he is, but he talks like he's been around forever."

"He has been both your pointer and your anchor. That old one has been saving his strength for thousands of years, but it is costing him dearly. He has been using all the power he has. The challenges have been spread out to give him time to gather his power again. That is why you have been able to travel within the dimensions."

"Can we help him?" asked Tima.

Atomasa shook his head. "No. The anchor must be either one from another dimension or a Watcher. It cannot be done by you or anyone you know."

"What happens when we fight the Kroledutz?" asked James. "You said we need to open the portal to other dimensions."

"Belecha will do that," said Rory.

"No," said Atomasa. "It is difficult enough to provide an anchor for travel. It is beyond his power to be both pointer and anchor for the double pyramid during the battle."

"Sounds like we're screwed," said Billy.

"You will understand at the proper time." He looked at Rory, warning him not to say more. "When you are ready, you will be given a second Stone for that purpose. For now, you need only know that powers from other dimensions will help you. Be aware. If you are drowning, look for something that is floating. Then grab it. Do not study it. Do not think about it. Grab it."

Atomasa stood. "I have given you all you need. The dawn is breaking." He motioned toward the sky.

They looked up and saw that the sky had faded from black to the light gray of pre-dawn. In the direction he had pointed, the first fingers of the sun were reaching up to color the sky.

Atomasa picked up his drum and bowed to the dawn. He began to beat a rhythm on his drum. Turning, he headed away from the four, beginning a peaceful chant, singing to the new day. As they watched, he disappeared in the tall grass, although they could still hear his song and the beating of the drum. Soon, the chanting faded.

"Funny," said Billy. "I can't hear him singing any more, but the drum is getting louder."

"Yeah," said Tima. "And where's the challenge? In both of the other ones, the challenge was right there."

They stood up, climbed to the edge of the wallow, and looked around. Suddenly James shouted, fear cutting through his voice. "Buffalo! Herd of buffalo!"

Without missing a beat, Billy replied, "Heard of buffalo? Of course I've heard of buffalo. Have you heard of bananas?" He grinned at James.

"No, idiot!" James yelled, pointing toward the rising sun. "Look!"

Turning, they squinted into the bright light.

"It looks like the horizon is moving," said Rory.

"Looks hazy," said Billy. "Is that fog or smoke?"

"Can't be fog," said Tima. "It's too dry. It might be smoke, but we've already done fire."

"Buffalo!" yelled James again. "It's a stampede! Remember when we are."

"When?" asked Rory. Then it hit him. Atomasa had said that they were in the time when buffalo herds covered the plains. Looking at the horizon, he realized why James was scared. The moving horizon was a wall of buffalo. The drumming they thought they had heard was the sound of the buffalo running. The haze was dust rising from what looked like more than a million hoofs churning the earth. As far as he could see, the huge forms barreled toward them. It was like a range of mountains, except it was moving – fast. And it was heading straight at them.

"There's no path to get out of their way!" yelled Billy.

"Too many," agreed Tima. "But we can't stay here! Those things can weigh a ton. They'll plow us down and grind us into the earth."

"I guess we found the challenge," said Rory.

"Duh!" shouted Billy. "Maybe you're the bird, not me. You have such keen perception." He paused, looking ahead again. "What are we going to do?"

Tima gave Billy a stern look. "It would help if we stopped yelling at each other."

Billy nodded. "You're right. Sorry." He calmed himself and looked at the others. "Alright, what do we know about buffalo and stampedes?"

They turned to James. His dad had cows.

James shook his head. "I've dealt with 10 or 12 cows at a time. For them, you yell or make a noise and they run the other way. This many ... I don't know. We can't make a noise louder than them. Listen to that bellowing."

"It sounds like lions roaring," said Rory.

The wall of buffalo was closer now and closing the distance fast. The teens could feel the ground vibrating from the pounding of their powerful hooves. Yet even as the stampede got closer, Rory could see the horizon still pulsed with more buffalo. As far as he could see, the world was filled with countless, unstoppable, towering trains of destruction, charging toward them. His mind would not think. He was overwhelmed with the sight.

Tima laid her hand on his arm. "Rory. Look at me. You have to calm down." Rory barely heard her. He couldn't tear his eyes away from the roaring wall of pounding death. His terror kept rising. The sounds of the hammering hooves filled his ears. The dust began to choke him. And still they came, more and more of them.

"The challenge is not about thinking a way out," said Billy. "Remember, the purpose is to force the Sodrol to realize the seed at his core. When I knew it was me, I knew what to do." He looked at Rory and James. They both stood frozen, staring with horror at the looming death. "Obviously, the seed here is the buffalo. One of you is the Sodrol."

No one spoke.

Tima cast a glance at James and Rory. They were both still rooted in place, staring at the stampede. The lead buffalo were close now. They could see the matted hair and heaving nostrils, hear the snorts and bellows, feel the ground throbbing with their beating hooves. "Come on, you guys," she said. "One of you is the buffalo – of the earth. One of you knows. Figure out which one and let's get to work."

Neither James nor Rory moved.

"Okay, then," said Tima. Letting out a sigh of exasperation, she quickly walked in front of them, balled up her fist, and punched Rory in the chest. Then she turned to James and punched him too. The guys jumped, finally breaking their gaze from the oncoming beasts, and looked at Tima.

"Pay attention!" she screamed. "Which one of you is it? One of you is the buffalo and knows what to do. I am *not* going to die here! So, stop freaking out and focus on your core."

Rory took a breath, thick with dust, and tried to block out the mountain of towering buffalo. He looked inside, seeking knowledge, an answer, but found … nothing. Just as he was about to give up, he heard James shout over the roar.

"The earth. Of course! We need to sing its song. It's me! I'm the Sodrol."

James dropped to his knees, spreading his hands on the ground before him. Then he began to beat on the earth like a drum. He looked up at the others. "Don't just stand there," he commanded. "They are pounding a rhythm. They are all celebrating the song of the earth. You can hear it, too. Now get down here, listen and feel, and drum."

They quickly dropped to their knees, facing the rushing beasts. Rory placed his hands on the ground. He could clearly feel a rhythm beneath the pounding of the hooves. He began to beat on the earth, in time with the rhythm he felt. As he did, the beat grew stronger. It danced in and out of the sound of the stampede.

Beside him, Rory heard James begin a breathy, sing-song chant. Beating on the ground, Rory heard how the chant rose and fell with the beat. He began to sing, too. As he did, he heard the snorts and bellows of the beasts separate into parts of the song. He beat upon the earth and sang. Together, the teens' wordless chants joined to the rhythms pounded out by the countless beasts, creating a unified sound, a symphony of celebration of the earth.

As the song rose and fell, Rory realized that he was no longer on the earth, but was of the earth. He felt the rocks deep within and the grasses feeding on water and life. He felt the warmth from the sun beating down. He felt the wind blowing across his body and the massage of the powerful herds that danced their throbbing dance across him.

It was the best feeling he had ever experienced, more wonderful even than traveling the ribbons. He felt the songs of all the beings across his life – across endless time and place. The feeling was enormous. Enormous in richness and variety and joy. *I could do this forever!* he thought.

"Rory." He heard his name from far away. "Rory, you need to come back." It was James. James was tugging his arm. Arm. He had an arm. He was not the earth.

"Rory!" Again, James' voice. Rory opened his eyes. He was lying on the ground. The others were crouched around him.

Billy held out his hand. "Time to go, dude. Places to be. People to see."

Rory, still not quite back, reached out for Billy's hand. Billy and James pulled him up.

"What happened?" asked Rory.

"They're gone," said Tima. "James knew. Once we were part of the earth, they passed over us."

James nodded. "You didn't want to come back. I understand. Great feeling, isn't it?"

Rory nodded in agreement. "Amazing." He looked at James. "Thanks."

James smiled. "Any time."

"Do you know what you need to activate the Stone?" Tima asked.

"Sure," replied James. "Just some dirt. The earth is the earth. It doesn't matter when or where. I'll add a bit from the kiva when we get back."

"Good." Tima looked around. "It's so peaceful here. I wish we could stay."

Billy shook his head. "Not our place or time, Tima. We have work to do."

"I know. I wasn't suggesting we stay, but it's a nice break from … back there."

Rory stood and stretched, then rubbed his chest. "Why does my chest hurt?"

Billy laughed. "You got beat up by Tima. Don't you remember?"

Tima punched Billy in the arm. "I did not beat him up. I just needed to get their attention. You, on the other hand …"

Billy held up his hands in surrender. "Not me. I'm already bruised."

"Hurry up and heal. I can wait."

James seemed calmer than Rory had ever seen him. "Let's get back," he said, smiling. "I want to see what's different now that I know who I am."

"I'll tell you what you are …" said Billy.

James just shook his head and smiled. "You're going to have to get a new act. Can't get under my skin anymore."

"*Humph*. Well, it was a fun ride."

Smiling, they headed back toward Belecha. He still had not taken form.

"We hear you've been doing double duty and it's wearing you down, old man," said Billy. "You want me to drive?"

"I'll never be that tired, Tinglen."

Billy shook his head and looked at the others. "Stubborn, ain't he?"

"Hush, Tinglen. I am in no mood for your games. Now, does the buffalo know how to activate the Stone?"

James nodded.

"Then let's get back. You four pelchas wear me out."

Soon they were back. They had left a clear, early morning on the plains, but at home the moon was still high in the sky.

"I've got to get back to my kiva, so listen up, all of you. You must pay attention at all times. The Kroledutz are all around now, and they would love to take a bite before the last challenge. The closer you get, the more dangerous it is, and the more likely they will sniff you out. So don't look for them anymore. Try not to attract attention."

They nodded their agreement, but said nothing. They were all tired, too tired to do anything but go home.

"Last challenge is the night of the full moon," reminded Belecha. "Be here and be ready."

They nodded again and moved to climb the ladder.

Once he was alone, Belecha sent out light to the kiva, feeding power to the place, adding chants of protection. He was tired and weary, but he was worried, too. It had been so long since the stain had marred the world. This was the last chance. The four were learning so much so quickly, but there was so much further to go, and more Kroledutz in their way every moment. Would they even get a chance to face the Kroledutz as aware beings? One misstep and they would be swatted down like bugs.

Belecha looked at the sky and the stars, comparing the ribbons of the thin web of light he saw to the thick and rich tapestry of his time. Eventually, he sighed. "I have done all that I can."

TWENTY-SEVEN 27

"Where's my son? You got him, don't you?" The short lady with bleached blonde hair poked Javier in the chest. "Let me see him."

Javier began to close the door in her face, but with surprising strength, she pushed back and bullied her way inside. A short, sequined tube top exposed a roll of pasty, white flab around her waist. She waved a finger at him, peering around with angry, bloodshot eyes.

"Oh no, you don't!" she screeched. "You got my boy in here, and I ain't leaving without him."

Javier crossed his arms and stared at her. "Lady, I don't even know who you are. Get out of my house right now, or I'm calling the police."

She put her hands on her hips and made a chilling sound. "You got some court case going on right now, don't cha?"

Javier's eyes widened, as she continued. "I might tell them officers something you won't like. You go get my son. Now!"

Realization dawned. Javier looked at her again, disgust filling his eyes. "You're Georgette Fuller, Billy's mom. You beat that child! You wretched, evil woman. Get out of my house!"

Georgette sneered. "I'll leave, okay, but not before we got an understanding. I gotta leave town. Got me a new man up in Denver, and I'm either takin' that boy with me, or you're gonna make it worth my while to leave him here."

"Lady, that poor boy is recovering from the horrible beating you and your daughter gave him. I'm not letting you go near him."

"Fine. I don't care. He's always been a pain. Just give me some money for expenses, and I'll be on my way."

Javier wanted to laugh, but he found nothing about the woman in front of him amusing. "You're kidding, right? I'm not paying you to leave. What I'm going to do is call the sheriff if you don't get out of our house right now." He headed toward the phone.

"Better not. The way I figure it, you should be happy to pay my way. How do you think it'll look to those Florida judges if I say you're the one who beat my boy? I'm sure he's got some nasty bruises by now. Maybe he did something to piss you off. Stole something maybe. I don't know, and I don't care, but you better believe I'll do it. I'm sick of this no-horse town."

Javier stopped and turned to glare at the woman. She smiled. "I thought that would get your attention. So, here's what's going to happen. You got 'til Saturday morning. I want $10,000. If you don't have it, I'm going to the sheriff, and I'm gonna scream my head off. Don't think I won't." With that, Georgette turned and left, slamming the door behind her.

Javier watched her go in silence.

"I'm sorry, Dr. Hurtado," came a sad, quiet voice from the stairs. Javier glanced up and saw Billy standing there, looking sick and embarrassed. "I didn't think she'd actually come after you."

"Listen to me, Billy. It's not your fault. You don't control her."

"What are you going to do? You've helped me, and now she's going to mess up the court case. That means both you and Rory get screwed."

"I don't know what I'm going to do, but I know two things. The first is, you are always welcome to stay here. We like having you around. She can yell all she wants, but the truth will win out in the end."

"What's the second thing?"

"You aren't going anywhere, ever again, with that creature. No one needs to put up with that kind of hate."

"You know you can't pay her, though, right? If you do, she'll be on you every time she needs money and that's almost always."

"I know, Son. I'm going to call my lawyer. Don't worry. He's as good as the lady in Florida, and he knows custody law like I know archeology. Like it or not, you're stuck with us ... as long as you don't mind having two fathers around."

Billy smiled at him. "I have no problem with that." He smirked. "Now, that new brother of mine ..."

"Ha! You'll have to work that out with Rory," said Javier as he headed toward his office. He turned back, serious. "Don't worry, though. We'll figure this out."

"Okay," said Billy and watched him go. Then, he went to the room he was sharing with Rory, grabbed the few things he had and put them in his backpack. Rory was out, probably at the kiva, so he left a note. "Rory. My mom's messing with your dad. Best for me to disappear for a while. See you Sunday night for the challenge."

Then, he quietly went out, grabbed his bike, and pedaled off.

TWENTY-EIGHT 28

"James! Teddy's broken." James looked up from the chili plant he was staking, and squinted through the bright sun at Lilly. She held out her bear and squeezed it. "See? Nothing happens."

James took the bear and poked at the plump belly. "Here's the problem. The chip got turned around. I think someone must have been messing with it. I wonder who?"

"I was trying to make him ask for more vegetables," replied Lilly. "Teddy's got to be more health concus."

"You mean health conscious?"

Lilly nodded. "But now he won't talk to me, and I'm in the middle of a party. Fix him ... please?" Lilly smiled that special smile that always worked on James.

"I'm sorry, Punkin Butter. I'm helping Dad now. I'll fix Teddy tonight."

Lilly knew how to get her way. She turned to her father, who was watching his children with an amused smile on his face. "Daddy. Please, oh please, oh pretty, pretty please! Tell James he has to fix it now? Please?"

Franklin laughed. "How can I say no to such politeness? Will it take long, James?"

James shook his head. "Less than ten minutes."

"Then, go on. Bring me back some water, okay?"

"Sure, Dad."

James took Lilly's hand, and they walked inside. A few minutes later, with Teddy repaired, James headed back. At the door, his mother called to him. "James!" He turned. Jocelyn went to the table and picked up a letter. "This came for your father, registered mail. It may be important. Would you bring it out to him?"

James took it. "Sure thing, Mom."

He headed out to the field, handing his father a cup of water and the letter. Then, he returned to staking up plants. It was hot work, but the chilies were growing well. Finishing one, he pulled the weeds around the next before starting to stake it up.

"I wish the chilies grew as good as the weeds," he said.

His father didn't reply. James looked up. Franklin was standing very still, looking out at the farm, the open letter dangling at his side.

James stood and went over to his dad. "What is it? What's wrong?"

Franklin turned weary eyes toward his son. "It's Cisco. He knew it would be impossible to sue me for being head of the county council, so he came up with another way. He bought that strip of land beside us."

"Why? Nothing grows there but tumbleweeds. It's got no water. What can he do with it?"

"He can claim that his land extends into half our property."

"That's crazy. That's most of the fields and half the barn. That land has been ours for …"

"Over a hundred years," finished his father. "But it was never surveyed. It didn't matter. But, he's not doing it to get the land. He doesn't expect to win."

"Then why?"

"He knows we'll have to pay for a survey and a lawyer, neither of which we can afford. All he has to do is stretch it out for a couple of years, and we'll be broke. He might be able to do it in less."

"He can't do that. This is our land."

Franklin sighed. "Yes, it is, but that man knows how to use the law to his advantage, and he has the money to get his way." He shook his head, looking down at the ground, and sighed. "I think I need another cup of water. I'll go have a talk with your mother. Would you finish weeding this row?"

James looked helpless. "Can't I …" he started. Then, he stopped. He didn't know what he could do.

Franklin shook his head. "Let me talk to your mother. We'll call Norm Fairchild. He knows property law pretty well. We need more information. Right now, what has to happen is for these chilies to grow, and they won't have a chance if they have to fight for their life against the weeds. The weeds will win."

James nodded. "Okay, Dad."

Franklin Nomura nodded his thanks and slowly walked back to the house, looking down at the ground he and his father and his grandfather had turned from rocky dirt to farmland.

TWENTY-NINE 29

"Rory, we got trouble."

"Billy!" Rory shouted into his phone. "Where are you? It's been two days, and we're freaked. Dad wanted to call the cops. Your mom can't ..."

"Rory," Billy broke in. "I'm fine. No sweat. I've lived here most of my life. I know plenty of places to stay." Billy hesitated. "I went by Cisco's."

"Why would you do that? He wants to kill you."

"I didn't walk right up, dude. He never saw me. I've been worried about that Plan B I saw on the computer, so I thought ..."

"You didn't break into his trailer again, did you?"

"I thought about it, but I didn't have to. Cisco and Matt were there with some other guys. Matt was on the dozer and Cisco was arguing with the guys. That's the problem."

"What's the problem?"

"They were arguing about how much Cisco would charge and how much he could take."

"Charge for what?"

"Cisco plans on turning Rattlesnake Ranch into a dump. Those guys he was talking to own franchises along the highway. Cisco's gonna take all their garbage. He's also going ahead with a bigger septic system. The slime ball is going to pump out all their systems and guess where he's gonna put the stuff?"

Rory felt a sinking in his stomach. "The kiva?"

"The kiva," confirmed Billy. "He's going to have Matt dig a hole bigger than the kiva. I saw the markers. Then he's going to fill it with crap and sludge from all the fast food places for 50 miles along the highway. He was bragging it would be the biggest pit of shit in the state."

"Ewww."

"You got that right. He's got to be stopped. Maybe that guy your dad talked to from the state historical commission ..."

"But Belecha said we couldn't dig up the kiva."

"It's getting dug up anyway. The only question is if it's gonna be filled with archaeologists or sewage."

Rory sighed. "I guess you're right. I'll talk to my dad. When are you coming back? We're planning a massive dinner for my birthday on Saturday. Leon's going all out."

"Sorry, dude. Can't make it, but happy birthday. I'll see you Sunday." Billy hung up, and the sadness seeped back into his expression. He would do anything to protect Rory and his dads, even if that meant staying away from them.

A couple of hours later, Javier pulled up to the gate at Rattlesnake Ranch. The gate was locked. Inside, Matt was busy on the dozer, clearing cracked asphalt from the area over the kiva. Javier blew his horn. The door to the office trailer banged open and Cisco came out. He walked to the gate, but made no move to open it.

"What do you want?" Cisco demanded.

"I'm Javier Hurtado. I'm an archaeologist at the University."

"Whoopee for you. Why should I care?"

"I see you're digging."

"Wow! You really are smart. Did you learn that in school?"

Javier tried to control his temper. "Look, Mr. Cisco. I have reason to believe there is a very important archaeological site where you are digging. It may significantly add to our knowledge of ancient cultures."

"So what? You still haven't told me why I should care. I have every cent I could scrape together tied up in this project. This place is my future, and that's way more important to me than someone else's past." He touched his hat. "But, you do make me wonder where you got your information. This is private land. Have you been trespassing?"

Javier glared at Cisco. "I have not been trespassing. You should care because you might be destroying the most important find of our lifetime."

"And that is worth exactly how much to me?"

"There might be some money for use of your land and your inconvenience, but that's not the point. There is a larger picture here."

"Look, Hurtado," sneered Cisco. "The larger picture is that this little hick county already cost me a bundle of time and money. I'm fighting for my life here, and you all messed with me. The people who put up the money don't care about excuses or finds or any of that. They care about money and their percent. I got no choice. That vote left me with no options." He gestured toward Matt and the dozer. "I'm putting in the largest septic system in the state, and there's nothing you can do to stop me." He turned away.

"You can't do that! I can get the state historical commission to put a hold on this project."

Cisco's head turned back with a nasty smile. "Try it, bucko. Think I didn't do my research before I started? By the time you get through the red tape, I'll have the whole place dug up. I know you can't do anything without proof, and you got no proof, do you?"

"Well, I …"

"Well, you nothing. Now, get back in your car and go read about As-Of-Right zoning. I bet you learned to read in that fancy school of yours. It says I can do whatever I want, unless you have something more than rumors from some wackos."

With that, Cisco walked back to the trailer, went in, and slammed the door.

THIRTY 30

"Mom!" Tima ran to her mother and hugged her close. She felt the strength from her own body pouring into Grace's frail form. "I'm glad you're home."

"Thank you, Honey. I'm glad, too."

Tima stepped back and looked at her mother. She didn't look good. Her face was slack and had a gray tinge. Her dark eyes were dull. Her movements were slow, her feet dragging a bit as she walked into the living room and looked around like she wasn't sure where to sit or what to do.

Jocelyn Nomura, understanding this was not easy for either mother or daughter, took Grace by the arm. "Come on, dear," she said. "Let's get you up to bed. You need a nap."

Grace nodded and passively allowed Jocelyn to lead her back toward her room.

Jocelyn turned to Tima. "Why don't you fix us some soup and sandwiches while I get her settled? We can have a little lunch before Grace takes a nap."

Tima nodded and busied herself in the kitchen. Soon, holding a tray full of food in her hands, she pushed open her mother's door. Jocelyn was gathering her things. "I have a meeting with our attorney, so I'd better go. If either of you need anything, give me a call." She bent over and gave Grace a quick hug. As Tima set down the tray, Jocelyn squeezed her shoulder. "She'll be fine. It's just a little hard coming home, but she wanted to be here."

Tima nodded. "Thank you," she said, a small tear falling down her cheek.

Jocelyn gave her a hug. "We're here any time you need us. You know that?"

Tima nodded again, and Mrs. Nomura left the room. Tima picked up her mother's plate and took it to her, sitting beside the bed. "Here, Mom. There's soup, too."

"Thank you, Honey." Tears began to roll down Grace's cheeks. "I'm so sorry."

"Mom, it's okay. We'll be okay."

"I don't know. I don't know if I can, Tima. Everything has gone so wrong. If you weren't here, I think I would have …"

Tima cut her off. "Mom, stop it! Stop apologizing. Stop trying to judge if this is good or bad. It is what it is. We'll get through it – together."

Grace looked at Tima with wide eyes. "How can you say this isn't bad?"

Tima shrugged. "It's … new. It may not be what either of us planned, but we're both learning things about each other and ourselves, right?"

Grace nodded.

"Then how can it be all bad? Different, sure … but it just is."

Grace thought about that as she took a bite of her sandwich. "Maybe. I've been feeling so guilty about making you go through …"

Tima shook her head. "No scars on me from it, Mom." She grinned. "Of course, I figure I have a free pass next time my room is a mess."

Grace smiled, a bit of the sparkle edging into her eyes. Then, they clouded again. "Honey, while I was in the hospital, I made a decision."

Tima tensed. Making decisions during a breakdown was a bad idea. "What?"

"We can't live here anymore. We need to be around family."

Tima felt like something reached into her chest and squeezed her heart. "What do you mean? I love it here. You love it here."

"I can't trust myself, Honey. I can't be sure I won't … won't …"

"Crack up again?" asked Tima, getting mad. "So what? Do you think you won't crack if you're somewhere else?"

Her mother shook her head, begging with her eyes for Tima to understand. "No. I can face it if I," she hesitated, "crack up, but I can't worry about you if I do. I can't take care of you, and it's unfair to ask you to take care of me."

Tima started to speak, but Grace cut her off. "Let me finish. This is very hard. I don't know when or even if I'm going to get better and I can't stand the thought of you here, isolated, if I lose it. I want us to be near family."

"But the Nomuras ... They're almost family."

Grace shook her head again. "Jocelyn is very kind, but they have their own troubles. Besides, here, we are far away from the kind of help I may need. If I have to be in the hospital for a long time, I don't want to be so far from you. I don't want you to be alone. We need to be near family. I've already called my sister in Cleveland. She knows of an apartment in the same complex ..."

"An apartment? You swore you'd never live in an apartment again. Besides, you have told me lots of times how much you hated living in Cleveland."

Grace tried to sound hopeful. "It will be fine. It's what we need to do. I'm going to contact a real estate agent once I feel a little better. I'm sorry, but it's what I have to do ... and soon. I want to go before the end of the month."

Tima was stunned. "But I can't ..."

"You can. We have to. It's not forever, but for now ..." Grace sighed, looking suddenly as if all of the life had drained out of her.

Tima tried to think of a way to stop this, but Grace was fading, her eyes closing. Tima realized that her mother was holding herself together by sheer force of will and that to argue with her now would be useless and cruel. Tima closed her mouth and nodded.

"Let me think about it, Mom, and we can talk later. Now, you need to rest."

She took the plate from Grace and kissed her on the forehead. Grace's eyes were already closed. She mumbled, half asleep already, "Thank you, Honey. I'm sorry, but it really is the only way."

Tima took the tray to the kitchen, blinking back tears, trying to think of a way out. She knew this was the work of the Kroledutz. She tried to think how her snake seed could help, but came up empty. It was clear that leaving New Mexico was not casting aside a useless skin, but losing something essential. She had to make her mother see that. Tima picked up the phone. She couldn't talk to James about this yet; it would hurt too much. So she called Rory.

"Rory … My mom says we're moving to Cleveland … and I … can you come over?"

Rory sounded bad, hardly able to talk. Being close to tears herself, she could hear the tears in his voice, too. "I can't come now. The lawyer just called. We lost." He choked on the words. "Kathy got almost full custody. I have to move to Florida."

"No! When?"

"Monday. I have to be there Monday night, or they can put out an arrest warrant for my dad. Saturday's my birthday. Sunday's the challenge. Then, I go." He paused. "Happy birthday to me."

"What can I …" started Tima, her caretaking instincts kicking in, despite her own problems.

Rory stopped her. "Look Tima, I have to go. I'll try to call you later."

THIRTY-ONE 31

The moon lit up the yard. The dozer, like a mechanical beast from another world, squatted on top of Belecha's kiva. Billy had been watching Rattlesnake Ranch since late Thursday, leaving only briefly to get food and water. He needed to get inside the fence, but someone, either Cisco or Matt, was always there, even through the night, making regular rounds. During the days, Matt worked on clearing away the asphalt from over the kiva. Today, he'd finished. It was late afternoon by then, but he had immediately started to dig, pulling deep scoops of dirt out with the backhoe.

Billy could only watch in frustrated anger as the dozer tore into the earth. Finally, Matt had turned off the machine and gone into the trailer. Billy hoped Cisco and Matt would decide to go into town for supplies and a good time, like they usually did on Saturday nights. He decided to risk a quick food run just before the sun went down. When he came back, less than an hour later, the yard was empty. The gate was locked, Cisco's car was gone, and the trailer was dark. Billy looked for any sign of the men, but they were both gone. By midnight, he was sure they weren't coming back.

He crept down, taking his time, watching and listening. Still nothing. Going around to the back of the yard, he found the opening he hadn't shown Cisco or Matt, in case he needed an easy way in. A pile of rocks near the fence made it look solid, but he knew better. Working quickly, he soon had pulled enough away that he could wriggle under the fence.

Once in, Billy looked around again, listening. No sound disturbed the still, New Mexico night. He headed toward the big dozer, and looked down. The hole didn't look too deep, but he couldn't tell if Matt had gotten down to the kiva or not. He knew if the walls were breached, Belecha's power was toast and so were they. Billy focused on the old man, trying to will him to appear, but nothing happened ... he'd get no help from Belecha tonight.

Pulling a large crescent wrench from his back pocket, Billy climbed up to the engine housing, searching for the lines he needed. One of the good things about having a mechanic for a big brother was that Billy knew his way around an engine. He could loosen the fittings deep inside so the fluids would run out without a pool showing on the ground. The next time the vehicle started up, the engine would fry. It wouldn't stop Cisco, but it would buy them some time.

The job was tricky. He twisted into the engine housing to get at the right nuts and worked quickly. Loosening first one, then the next, Billy had only one more to unscrew and it would be done.

"It's stuck," he muttered, trying to get leverage in the tight space. "Come on ... come on ..."

Just then, the lights in the yard flashed on.

"Get him!" yelled Cisco. "Grab that little punk!"

Billy felt Matt's giant hand wrap around his neck, lifting him up and out of the dozer.

"I owe you for the head butt," Matt growled. Holding Billy, he punched him solidly three times hard and fast in the side of the head.

Some bird, thought Billy, as he began to fade. *Twice in one week.* Then he fell into blackness.

Billy woke up with the hot desert sun baking his face. He hurt in places he didn't know he had. His head throbbed, but when he tried to rub some of the pain away, he realized his hands were tied.

"Can't move, eh, Punk?" asked Cisco.

Billy squinted in the direction of the voice. The sun was so bright it hurt. Cisco was little more than a menacing shadow sitting in a bit of shade.

"Can't let you get away again," Cisco explained. "Whooeee, it sure is hot in here. I don't know how you spent so many hours in here pulling nails. Don't you think it's hot?" he asked, almost conversationally.

Billy nodded. He tried to speak, but his mouth was so parched he couldn't move his tongue. Cisco had just confirmed what he had guessed. He was tied up in the old Rattlesnake Ranch building, on the rubble from when the roof had fallen in. That meant anyone looking for him wouldn't see him because he was inside the building, but he was still exposed to the direct, burning sun.

Cisco continued talking, and Billy could hear the oily gloating in his voice. "Can't talk, eh? That must be a first. I bet you're really thirsty."

Now, feeling more alert, Billy refused to give him the satisfaction of nodding.

"Yeah, it must be over a hundred in here, and it's still early. I'm sweating like a pig, and I ain't even wearing a hoodie like you are. You know what would taste great right now? A nice, big bottle of ice cold water." Cisco pulled out a bottle. Billy could hear him open it and drink greedily.

"Oops. I spilled some on my shirt, but I guess that don't matter. It cools me down." He continued to drink. "Just a bit left. I bet you really would like some, wouldn't you?"

Billy glared at Cisco. He knew where this was going and wasn't going to play.

"Well, if you don't want it, I guess I'll just pour it out." Cisco leaned forward and held the water up close, so Billy could see the bottle, could see the beads of condensation on the sides of the plastic. He was so thirsty! He watched in silence as Cisco turned the bottle upside down and slowly poured the water out onto the dirt floor, just beyond Billy's face.

Cisco laughed. "You messed with the wrong guy, Punk. You brought a lot of trouble down on a lot of people. Now it's your turn to feel some pain." Cisco looked down at Billy and shook his head. "Still, I'm not doing what I could do – what I should do. I *should* turn you over to the guys who fronted me the money. Then, no one would ever see you again. *Poof*, you'd be gone, just another runaway. But like I said, you remind me of me, and so I'm gonna do you a favor. I'm going to teach you a hard lesson. Maybe you'll learn," he said, tilting his head. "Maybe not."

Cisco got up and started walking around, kicking at the junk that littered the floor. Billy thought about snakes. All that kicking was sure to stir up any snakes that had slithered in to get out of the heat.

"You're going to juvie," said Cisco. "For a long time. What's better, you actually did me a favor. I had Matt fire up that old dozer and it fried, just like you planned. What you didn't know is that I'm insured against vandalism. You get juvie, and I get a new dozer. We both win." He stopped, thought, and smiled again. "Oh, I guess that's wrong. You lose, but I win twice." He laughed.

Billy closed his eyes, willing the pain to go away. Cisco walked over to him and kicked him in the stomach. "Pay attention when I'm talking to you." Billy opened his eyes and focused on the man.

Cisco smiled. "That's better. Now, you cost me a lot, but I'll make it up with the dump. So, now I get to watch the sheriff take you away and then wait for delivery of my new dozer. Only problem is, Matt got a little carried away last night. Your bruises are a bit too big. It might look like we didn't just subdue you." Cisco shook his head. "Sheesh, Kid. You cause me problems even when I'm beating the crap out of you."

Cisco smiled. "No worries, though. The only good thing about kids is they heal fast. We're gonna leave you here for a couple of days. Let those bruises look like you got 'em from some other trouble. Then, on Monday or Tuesday, we'll haul you out to the dozer and call the sheriff. Pretend we discovered you just then. I figure a kid like you will be able to last for a couple of days locked up here." He walked to the door, turned and looked around at the rubble covering the floor. "As long as the snakes don't get you."

Cisco smiled a final smile. "See you later, punk. Matt and me are going to spend a couple of days out of town. We've got to make nice with the money guys and explain how I'm fixing the trouble you caused. Plus, it's too hot around here. We need to be in a nice, air conditioned hotel with lots and lots of ice cold drinks. Think about us enjoying ourselves. We'll be thinking about you."

Cisco slammed the door. Billy heard the chain on the door rattle and the padlock click shut. He closed his eyes and tried not to think about snakes or how thirsty he was.

THIRTY-TWO 32

"This is really amazing," said Rory as he looked at Tima's richly textured painting. Through the abstract swirls of brilliant color, he could see their journey. The roaring fire blazed behind the glowing fog and the twisting serpent. The bird leapt across ribbons at the opening to another dimension. Beneath, nature's earth pulsed as the buffalo beat their song. Through everything danced the web of light. "Seriously. Amazing."

"I didn't mount it, so you can roll it and take it with you," explained Tima. "I'm hoping it protects you."

"It will keep everyone close. That's what I need. Thanks," he said, clearing his voice after it caught on the last word. He gave her a one-armed hug. "We aren't doing anything – we're all too down." He looked at Tima, the pleasure of the painting dispelling quickly against his sadness of leaving.

"Maybe the challenge tonight …"

"Will do what? I'm on a plane tomorrow morning. Even if we finish the challenge, nothing will change that."

"We're so close, but I don't know, either. I can't see how the challenge can fix everything that's wrong." She sighed. "Mom isn't budging on her plan to move. She called an agent this morning about the house. We had a huge fight." She wrapped her arms around herself. "She apologizes. She cries. But she won't change her mind."

"Where is she now?"

"Said she needed to calm down, so she's taking a bath." Tima sighed. "I'll try again tomorrow."

"Have you heard from Billy?"

Tima shook her head. "Not since he called Wednesday night to ask what happened with your dad. Then he said he had things to do and would meet us for the challenge. Have you heard about the Nomuras?"

Rory nodded.

Tima looked sad. "James told me his dad has almost stopped talking. James isn't much better. He won't even come over and talk about it, and he told me not to go there because he doesn't want to bother his dad."

Rory looked around and said in a near whisper, "I keep smelling Kroledutz. This has got to be their work."

"They're around here, too. My mom would never have come up with this idea to move on her own. She hates Cleveland. Any time we have problems, she says, 'At least we aren't in Cleveland.' But when I remind her of that, she starts crying again."

Rory's phone belted out a familiar tone. He looked at the screen and made a face. "Kathy. She's been calling all day."

Tima stood up. "You should talk to her. Get it over with. I need to check on my mom."

Rory sighed. "You're probably right. Don't take too long. You'll be my excuse for getting off the line."

Tima nodded and headed out. Rory answered the phone. "What?"

"That's not a very friendly way of answering your phone, Rory."

"Yeah, well, I'm not feeling very friendly. You know I don't want to go live with you."

Kathy sniffed. "I guess I shouldn't expect gratitude, not yet, but we used to be close and I want us to be close again. You're my son, and I love you. And, I think you will see that I really want what's best for you. Pastor says you will."

"Don't hold your breath."

"Please Rory, don't be so mean. What happened to that sweet little boy who made up stories in the woods with me?"

"Kathy, you know how I feel. You also know I have no choice. I'll come, but you can't make me like it."

She sounded hurt. "I only did it for you. Pastor says …"

Rory rolled his eyes. He knew he should keep his cool, but he hated what she had done. He'd thought he and Javier and Leon had finally found a home here. He didn't want to leave them or his new friends. Impatient and angry, he interrupted her. "Why did you call? These are my last days here. I'm trying not to think about you and where I'm going."

"Well, Rory, you may not be thinking about it, but we have been."

Rory stiffened, a flicker of hope stirring. "What do you mean? Have you changed your mind? Can I stay?"

"Oh no, Rory. I would never do that. It's a mother's duty to protect her child."

Rory lost it. "You ran away, and Dad stayed and raised me and loved me! Now you have the nerve to say you're protecting me? The only reason you're doing this is because someone else told you to. Think for yourself for once. You *know* Dad. You know me. You *know* this is wrong!"

"Rory! You will not use that tone with me. You will show us respect. It's time you learned how to act around decent people."

Rory could hardly see, he was so mad. "I'll show you respect when you deserve it. You need to think for yourself, not just follow the orders of other people." He straightened up, trying to gain control of his emotions. "Now, do you have anything else to say before I hang up?"

Kathy took a breath and spoke sweetly. "Yes. You have just shown me that I was correct. As of now, it is more than I can handle to teach you to behave."

"So you're giving up?"

"Oh no, Mister. I am not giving up. We've decided that once you arrive, you'll be attending a school that comes with military training. It's a wonderful school. The pastor's best friend runs it so we know it's a good place and we'll know right away if you misbehave. You'll be able to visit us on holidays and, if you improve, we'll let you live with us next year. Until then, you will live at the school."

"What?" Rory yelled. "You're taking me away from people who want me and love me and then sending me away? You're letting them tell you what to do with your life and my life? Can't you see how wrong ..." A deadly calm rose in him. He realized yelling was not going to accomplish anything. He took a deep breath, and spoke again, calmly but coldly. "Keep your distance from me, Kathy. Keep that pastor away from me, too. I'll do what the courts say because I don't want them to hurt Dad, but there's not going to be any mending between us. You get my body, but you don't get my mind or my heart." Then, before she could respond, he hung up.

"Rory!" Tima's scream echoed down the hall. "Rory! It's so ... Rory!"

Rory bolted down the hall. Tima was in the bathroom off Grace's bedroom, screaming. Rory slammed through the door.

Blood.

Blood was on the floor and on the walls of the bath. The water was red as it swirled around Grace, who was covered in blood. Tima had grabbed a towel and wrapped it around Grace's wrists. She was applying direct pressure, like they had learned in first aid. The towel was quickly turning red.

"Help me, Rory!" screamed Tima. "Help me save her!"

THIRTY-THREE 33

"Where's Billy?" asked James.

"Dunno," answered Rory, numb from finding Tima's mom and from preparing to move. "I've been home packing most of the day. I thought he'd come over to hang out, but …"

"That's not like him. Something must be wrong. Have you heard from him, Tima?"

Tima shook her head. "I was at the hospital all afternoon so I don't know if he came by, but he didn't call or text."

"How's your mom?" asked Rory.

Tima shrugged. "Still pretty out of it. My aunt's coming tomorrow to stay for a couple of weeks."

Rory, his anger rising, threw down the stack of clothes he was packing. "So this is it? I'm leaving. James' family may lose their farm. Your mom is in the hospital, and you're moving to Cleveland. Billy gets beat up and now is gone. We're all screwed."

James shook his head. "We still have a chance. Maybe if tonight …"

"If tonight, what?" broke in Rory. "Everything will be wonderful? Get a clue. It's over! My dad drove by Rattlesnake Ranch today. No one was around, but he said the kiva's got a big hole dug into it. Belecha's power is tied to that kiva. We're not going anywhere tonight."

James stood. "Look, I don't see any way out but forward. We came this far. We've got to try."

"Try what?" asked Rory. "We can't do anything without Billy. We need all four to travel, but that doesn't matter. Belecha isn't here. He's probably stuck in his own time, if the Kroledutz haven't eaten him yet."

Tima looked up suddenly. "Wait a minute! Rattlesnake Ranch! I bet that's where Billy is. He said he had something to take care of. I bet he went there to try to stop Cisco."

"So what?" said Rory. "He didn't stop him, did he?"

Tima stood up. "I don't know, but I have a feeling he's there. We should go look for him."

"I agree," said James. "Besides, that's Belecha's point of power. Maybe he can't leave, but if we go there ..."

Rory sighed. "I don't know."

Tima glared at him. "Rory Hurtado! You may have to leave tomorrow, but we still have tonight. Isn't it worth a try?"

Rory looked at James and Tima and shrugged. "Yeah. At least we can say we did everything we could."

The moon was huge over the empty yard. They skirted the fence, looking for signs of Cisco or Billy.

"Over here," called James. "I found his bike."

Tima hurried over to where James was standing. "I knew it! He's around here somewhere."

"How do we get in?" asked Rory.

"Look," answered James, pulling up the bottom of the fence.

They squeezed through and looked around.

"I don't see him," said James.

Rory had an idea. "The old Ranch building. If Cisco grabbed him, he could have locked him up there."

They hurried over to the decaying building. An old, low window frame splintered with a few kicks and Rory poked his head through.

"I think I see something," he said.

"Careful," said Tima. "There may be snakes."

Rory nodded and disappeared into the building. Walking carefully around piles of debris, he aimed toward the dark shape on the floor. He bent over. "Billy?"

"If you don't get me some water quick, I'm gonna barf," croaked Billy.

Rory grinned. "Nice to see you, too." He quickly untied his friend. Reaching into his pack, he pulled out a bottle of water and handed it to Billy.

Billy took a sip then looked at the bottle. "God, I want to down this whole thing, but then I'll just puke it up." He took another sip and massaged his wrists.

"What's going on?" called Tima from the window.

"He's here," replied Rory. "I think he's fine." Turning to Billy he asked, "*Are* you okay?"

Billy nodded. "I've been better, but I'll live. Cisco and Matt caught me trying to break the dozer last night. They kicked my butt and left me here." He smacked his dry lips. "Longest, hottest day of my life."

Rory shook his head and gave him a smile. "Have you ever wondered why so many people want to beat you up?"

Billy took another sip of water, considered the bottle again, then gulped half of it and poured some over his head. He stood and stretched, wincing at the pain, then managed a weak smile. "I figure they're jealous of my youth, stamina, and rugged good looks."

Rory rolled his eyes and called out, "He's delirious. Maybe we should put him out of his misery."

"What?" asked James. "Is he hurt?"

"No," said Rory. "He's as stupid as usual."

"Then get out here," called Tima. "If Cisco comes back, we're up the creek."

"Cisco won't be back for another day," replied Billy. "He and Matt went off to celebrate. But you're right. We should get moving. Is Belecha here?"

"Haven't seen him," said James.

Billy took a step, grimaced, and took another. "Give me a minute to work out these kinks." He walked around slowly. Then, leaning on Rory, he went to the back window. Stepping over the sill, he was immediately grabbed by Tima, who gave him a big hug.

"Billy Fuller, that was a stupid thing to do."

Billy grinned. "I do what I'm good at." He looked at the three. "Thanks. It is very nice to see you."

James shook his head and smiled. "Good for you we need four to go on a challenge."

"You know you need me around." Billy grinned at the four. "Hey, anyone got anything to eat? I'm starving."

Rory rummaged through his backpack and pulled out a granola bar. Handing it to him, he said, "Alright, we got Billy. Now, let's see if Belecha wants to come out and play."

"Agreed," said Tima.

They headed over to the pit that Matt had started.

Rory looked closely at the edges. "I'm pretty sure he didn't get down to the level of the kiva, so there's a chance. It looks like he was aiming for the center of it, even though he had no idea it was there."

"He didn't know," said Billy, "but you know who did."

"Radelam and the Kroledutz," said James.

Billy nodded. "Matt and Cisco aren't this smart, but they make good puppets when something like that is pulling the strings."

Tima sighed. "Let's get down there and see what happens."

They climbed into the shallow pit.

"Do you have the Stone, Rory?" asked Tima.

Rory nodded and pulled it out. Laying it on the ground, they sat around it at their respective glyphs. Rory looked at the others. "At least we know the Sodrol for this challenge. I just hope I know what to do when the time comes."

"I should have guessed you were the whale," joked Billy. "Fishy smell and always shooting air out your blowhole."

Rory punched him in the arm. "Shut up."

Billy grinned. "What do you think we should do?"

"Use what we learned last time," said James. "Focus on Belecha, and sing his song."

Tima nodded. "That makes sense."

They sat around the Stone and began to chant, drumming on the ground. Rory started to feel, then see the ribbons of light coming from the earth around them.

"Something's different," said Tima, looking around. "Can you see? The threads are blowing and ragged, like they've been torn."

"Keep your intention on Belecha," said James. "Reach out toward him and sing."

James resumed drumming on the ground. The others joined in. Rory saw more threads and a few ribbons rising. He thought about Belecha and began to chant. He aimed his intention to the kiva as he remembered it on his visits, with Belecha sitting on the rock in the center. He listened for the rattle. He felt the vibrations as James beat on the earth. One at a time, they began to chant, sitting under the moon, calling to the old man who had watched and guided them.

Rory felt a rumbling from underneath them. "He's coming. It's working."

The moon darkened like a storm cloud had covered its light. Then, an overpowering stench of rotten meat, burning plastic, and sweat filled the air. Rory's eyes watered at the smell, and he gagged. He heard Tima cry out. Opening his eyes, he groaned, hopelessness and fear washing over him.

Massed around the edges of the pit, grinning down at them with horrific intent, an army of Kroledutz pulsed, like thick, rank smoke from an oil fire. Rory looked for a way to escape, but there was no break in the wall of deathly creatures. He could sense row upon row of the foul things, pressing in toward the four friends as they sat exposed and defenseless. Destructive, vicious glee oozed from the horde, rolling toward them, freezing them where they sat.

Unable to move, they watched as the huge form of Radelam rose from the masses, his red eyes burning with triumph. Looming over them, his hideous voice shook and battered their bodies.

"The snacks have returned!" he roared to his followers. Then, he turned to the four. The dark hole of his mouth stretched under the cruel beak as if he were trying to smile.

"I see you were trying to call your friend Belecha," he said. "Unfortunately, the old man is busy now. We have been chasing him for days, and he is trapped back in his time, awaiting our return." The shapeless head seemed to shake. "We will wear him down there, and it will be a feast of a lifetime, but for now, a little nibble to crush his hopes would be lovely." His form seemed to gesture to the kiva.

"Especially since you were nice enough to deliver yourselves to the table." Then, laughing a twisted laugh, he grew larger, spreading out over the four.

Rory looked hopelessly at his friends. "At least we tried," he croaked.

"Goodbye," Tima murmured, her face twisted with sorrow and fear.

James and Billy nodded their farewells.

Rory steeled himself. *I hope it's fast*, he thought. *I hope it doesn't hurt.* He took a deep breath and closed his eyes.

A roar split the air. Through his closed eyes, Rory saw a brilliant, blazing light.

"Chem. Atem. Astalah!" The ground shook with the sound.

Rory opened his eyes and saw, towering above them, Belecha in full battle regalia. Huge and bright, he lashed shining ribbons of energy out at the gathered masses of Kroledutz. The dark creatures fell back with screams of agony. Belecha then hurled fiery balls of shimmering light at their retreating forms.

"Troledutz! Chamtelah! Petraldak!" he bellowed, the sound of his voice transforming into bolts of burning fire. Shrieking, the Kroledutz writhed and fled.

Gasping, the four teens scrambled to their feet.

"Quick!" said Belecha. "Get out and get to your kiva. I can hold them until you get there, but no longer. Do not leave your kiva, any of you, for any reason."

"What about you?" asked Rory.

"I'll pull back to my power time, but I can't come here again so you've got to get out now. It's up to you. This is it. We live or die on the full moon. Now go!"

With that, he gathered himself together, and again roared curses at the Kroledutz, hurling balls of energy.

"He is weak!" Radelam bellowed, calling his followers back. "He is old. Come back! Let us kill the old one. We will finish the others later."

The beasts began to turn.

"I see a way!" yelled Billy, pointing.

"Lead. We'll follow," called Tima. "Grab the Stone, Rory."

Tearing their eyes from Belecha, they sprinted after Billy, out of the pit and toward Rory's kiva, their only hope of surviving the night.

THIRTY-FOUR 34

Dropping into the kiva, the foursome fell back against the walls, gasping for breath.

"What do we do now?" panted James.

"We have to stay here," said Rory. "That's what Belecha told us to do."

"But what if he doesn't come?" asked James. "I don't see how he could get out, not with all those Kroledutz."

"That was way more than we saw in Albuquerque," said Billy.

"How are we going to fight those things?" asked James. "Even with what we've learned, what can we do against them?"

"Let's focus on what's in front of us now," said Tima. "We didn't know how bad it was, but Belecha and the others had to know. They wouldn't have made us go through all this if there wasn't a chance."

"I don't know," said Rory. "I don't see any way out. How about you, Billy?"

"No," admitted Billy, "but I also don't see any alternative. Either way, those things are coming for us."

"Great," said Rory. "So we wait. And, if we don't get torn apart by Kroledutz, then first thing in the morning, I go to Florida." He kicked at the dirt. "Life just keeps getting better."

"At least we get to spend our last hours together," said Billy, as he began to build a fire. "I've never really had friends before, you know, so I can't say this is worth it, but …"

Tima smiled and nodded. "It's something."

Rory thought a minute and shrugged. "Yeah. You're right. It's a nice place to end it."

"Billy, I don't know if you should build a fire," said James. "It might attract attention."

Billy shook his head. "They saw us with no light at all. Plus, they heard Belecha tell us to stay here. Hiding isn't an option. We might as well be comfortable. Speaking of …" He looked at the others. "Anyone have any food or water? That granola bar didn't go far, and in case you've forgotten, I spent the past 24 hours tied up in the baking sun."

Rory pointed across the kiva. "There's a pack with bottles of water, some fruit bars, and trail mix over there. There are a couple of blankets, too, in case it gets colder."

Billy struck a match and lit the fire. Then, he rummaged through the pack, pulling out four bottles of water and some trail mix. He threw some of the mix in his mouth and handed out the bottles, then settled back down by the flames.

"Now what?" asked James.

Rory looked at his bottle of water. "Now, we wait."

They leaned against the walls, drinking water and watching the fire, content to sit quietly, soaking up the calm silence of the New Mexico desert as the moon slowly worked its way across the sky.

"Rory! Are you down there?" Javier's voice came from the lip of the kiva.

Rory shook himself awake and looked around in confusion, wondering how he came to be in the kiva in the early dawn. Seeing the others sleeping where they sat, he remembered.

"Rory?" Javier called again, looking down at them. "Are you alright?"

Rory stood, stiff from sleeping against the kiva wall. "No. I'm not all right. I'm going to Florida. What time is it? Am I late for the flight?"

Javier smiled and shook his head. "It's early. Very early. When Leon said you weren't home, I knew you were here. I came to tell you the news."

"What news?"

Javier smiled again. Rory realized it had been a while since he had seen him smile. "About your flight. It's been canceled."

Rory straightened. "Canceled? I don't have to go?"

"You still have to go, but there was a meltdown with the computer systems at the airport. They had to shut down the terminal and the control tower and route the planes to other airports. All flights are canceled for at least today."

Rory hooted. "That's great! I hope they never fix it."

"They'll fix it, but it will take a while. Now, explain. What's wrong?" Javier started to climb down into the kiva.

"Dad! Stop! You can't come down here. It's not safe."

"What do you mean?"

"You're going to have to trust me on this. The Kroledutz are all around, and they're after us. Belecha said he'd come on the full moon and take us on the final challenge, but he didn't show last night. I think they got him. It's not safe for us anywhere but here, and I'm pretty sure it isn't safe for anyone else to be here with us."

"If you are in danger then I'm ..."

"Dr. Hurtado," said James, "I know you want to help us, but I agree. This is our battle and what we need, you can't provide." He looked down in embarrassment. He wasn't used to telling adults what to do. Then he looked back up at Javier. "We have to stand or fall on our own. Your world isn't going to save us."

Javier looked at the four in the kiva. "Do you all agree with that?"

They looked at each other, then back up at him and nodded.

"Well, if you are going to spend the day in the kiva, I'm going to get Leon to fix some food and bring you a case of water."

"Dad, I don't know if that's safe," said Rory.

"I don't care. I'm not going to let you sit here hungry all day."

"But ..."

"No arguments."

Rory looked at the others. Billy shrugged. Rory nodded to his father. "Okay. Thanks, Dad."

James spoke up. "Dr. Hurtado?" Again he hesitated. "Would you call my folks, for me? Just to let them know I'm okay, but don't tell them what I'm doing. Please?"

Javier nodded.

"And if things don't work out, would you tell them … tell them I was thinking about them?"

Javier nodded again and looked at Tima. "I'll do the same for your mom when she gets out."

Tima smiled her thanks. Billy looked down at the ground, knowing that, for good reason, the same would not be offered to him.

Javier turned to go. Then he stopped and turned back. "Rory? Did you just say that Belecha told you he'd take you on the challenge on the full moon?"

"Yeah, but he didn't show. That's why we don't know what to do. We waited all night."

Javier shook his head. "The calendar doesn't match the full moon cycle. Last night wasn't the full moon." He smiled down at them. "The full moon is tonight." Then, he turned and left four very surprised and suddenly hopeful teens with their mouths open in shock.

THIRTY-FIVE 35

By nightfall, they were restless and worried. As the full moon rose, they sat around the Stone and reached out with their intention, trying to call to Belecha. Nothing happened. After a long while, James sighed. "I don't think he survived. I don't know how he could. He's not coming."

"Hush! Focus on the Stone," said Tima.

"This is ridiculous!" said Rory. "We're just sitting here waiting for the Kroledutz to come and wipe us out. You saw that army. There's no way he could fight them off."

"I can feel them all around," said Billy. "I keep trying to feel for Belecha, but there's nothing."

"Even if they don't kill us now, we've lost," said Rory. "I'm going to Florida once the planes start flying again, Tima's going to Cleveland, and who knows about you two." He thought back to when he first came to this spot and decided to dig a hole. "I wish I had never stuck a shovel in the ground."

"Shut up!" yelled Tima. "Stop right now. Haven't you learned anything?" She stood up and faced the three boys, her eyes flashing. Rory saw the fiery snake in her face. She seemed to grow taller and stretch up to the sky.

"We've been through three challenges. On the first one, I learned the power of the snake is to see what's essential and what can be left behind." She glared at them. "We are essential. Our work is essential. We can leave behind this place, our bodies, our worries, but who we are … that's essential."

She looked at Billy. "Trust yourself. That's what we learned on your challenge. We didn't know how you'd get us back, but when it was essential, you saw the thread and you got us there."

She looked at James. "Stop thinking short term. Atomasa told us nature takes a long time. The Kroledutz have been here for over 5,000 years. That's long enough! This is bigger than any one of us. That's why they had to have all four of us work together."

Tima shook her head sadly. "I hate to see my mom the way she is. I hate what each of us is going through, but we have the power to do something about it. We're the only ones in the web at the right place and time who have that chance. They didn't set this all up to let us crash before we finish. Somehow we'll get to the fourth challenge, and we'll get through that, too. Sure, it's impossible, but we've gotten through impossible three times already. What makes you think we can't do four?"

"Well spoken, fire serpent!" said a voice from the fire.

Turning, they saw a ball of smoke had formed over the fire.

"Look!" cried James. "He's coming."

"Belecha!" Billy called out. "It's about time you got here, you old slacker. What happened? Did you forget how to drive?"

"Tinglen, if you ever call me an old man again, you will regret it."

"That's not Belecha," said James.

"Certainly not," said the ball, expanding and taking shape.

Billy's eyes widened. "Mealim!"

The old woman's form, as smiling and welcoming as she had been at the beginning of the first challenge, emerged and solidified. She smiled and nodded. "Second time right."

"What a relief!" said Tima. "But why are you here?"

"We cannot stop for explanations," ordered Mealim. "We must leave quickly. The Kroledutz are all around, and my entry will not go unnoticed."

"Where's Belecha?" asked Rory. "Is he ...?"

Mealim shook her head. "He is not gone, but he is trapped in his kiva in his time. We must act quickly, for he has little strength left."

"What do we need to do?" asked James.

"You must complete the fourth challenge, if you can, and activate the portal. Unless you can do that, you will be unable to bring the power that can defeat the Kroledutz to this time." She looked at Rory. "You know what is needed."

Rory nodded, thinking of the double pyramid, the Oloho, that Belecha had shown him.

"What can we do against that horde?" asked James. "We couldn't even take on one, much less an army."

Mealim looked at him. "You are not yet ready. A seed cannot give fruit until it has grown into a plant."

"You're asking us to grow pretty quickly," said Billy. "How long after the challenge are we going to be able to do anything?"

"Once the Stone is activated, you will be surprised how quickly you change from stupid," Mealim looked at Billy, daring him to protest, "to wise."

"I don't see how ..." began Rory.

Mealim broke in. "We have no time. You must face the fourth challenge. If you fail there, all matters not. If you succeed, all will be plain. Are you ready?"

"We are," said Tima, "but how will we travel? Can you be the pointer?"

Mealim nodded. "I can. However, we travel the dimensions and only a Watcher can provide an anchor and I am not a Watcher."

"Then what do we do?" asked Rory.

"I will stay here and anchor you," came a voice near the fire.

"Atomasa!" cried James.

The old man took form and quickly approached. "Leave right away. With a Watcher here, the Kroledutz will come quickly. I will try to keep them off."

Mealim turned to him. "You must hold the anchor, my friend. We will return as fast as we can."

Atomasa nodded. "I will do my best. Now hurry. The Kroledutz already approach."

Mealim looked for a moment more at the old man, reached out and touched his cheek. Then she turned to the four and nodded. She faded into a ball of light and floated above them.

Rory was surprised how easy it now was to shift focus. The threads became clear, circling around the kiva and shooting out from the Stone. He felt his body losing focus while Mealim reached out to a thread.

"Now," she called, and they were snatched up.

Soon, they were shooting along a ribbon, surrounded by the bright web of threads and spheres. Rory let out a breath and felt the delight of travel go through him. "It's like everything has been left behind. I wouldn't mind spending all my time doing this. It's much more fun."

Mealim spoke. "As pleasant as this is, we take on our forms for a task. To deny that duty is the seductive trap of this world. There is so much to experience, we are tempted … always tempted. But the result is dissolution. The result is setting aside creation in favor of stimulation. Action is not always pleasant, but deny your purpose at your peril and the peril of all."

Rory nodded and tried to prepare himself for the coming challenge.

"We are here," called Mealim.

They bumped down in a clearing, surrounded by thick forest. In the distance, they heard ocean waves crashing against rocks from every direction. Above them, a tall, cone-shaped mountain rose to the sky. Through the trees, they could see a plume of smoke billowing from the peak.

"Volcanic island," said James. He picked up some dirt. "Rich, but rocky. It's the combined ash and eroded rocks from eruptions in the past. The volcano started under the ocean and spewed out so much, it rose above the water. Lots of islands in the South Pacific were formed this way."

Billy looked at the plume. "That looks like it's going to blow again at any minute." He looked at Mealim. "I hope you can get us out of here quick if it does."

"As long as Atomasa holds the anchor, we can return in an instant. I will stay with you in case the mountain speaks." Seeing a sharp look from James she smiled. "Unlike the old raccoon, there is no one here I do not wish to meet. Quite the contrary. I believe you all know that the solution to the challenge must come from you, not from me, even if that means failure."

They looked at each other and nodded.

"Who do we meet here?" asked Tima.

Mealim nodded toward a figure approaching through the trees. "My mother."

"Your mother?" said Billy, staring at Mealim's ancient features. "How old is your ..."

Rory poked him in the ribs, not wanting to anger Mealim. "Remember, we aren't in our time or our dimension."

From out of the jungle came an exquisitely beautiful young woman. Her fine features suggested the royalty of ancient Incan societies. Her smooth face, framed by soft, black hair, was the color of terracotta clay. She smiled, and Rory felt a calm feeling of love sweep over him.

"Welcome, my children," said the woman. "Come, let me hold you again." She stepped forward and looked deep into Rory's eyes. He felt a huge bubble of joy lift through him. There was no doubt that this woman was his mother, his true mother, who had been absent for so long. He hugged her close and tight, a wonderful contentment filling him. He didn't want to let go, but felt her gently pull away and turn to Tima.

As Rory watched, the same act was repeated with Tima, then James, then Billy, and finally, Mealim. He could see in each face the same emotions of love and a separation now ended.

Finally, the woman straightened and turned to them all. "While it is joyous to again be with you in body, we have little time, my children. The mountain is nearly finished with its life and I with mine, and you have work that must be done. Sit."

They sat in a semi-circle in front of her. She smiled gently at them. "My name is Heyatoma. You are my children."

She gestured at the world around. "All that comes from the Spheres is alive and creates itself for the purpose of learning. On your three challenges, you have learned of the importance of things much bigger than you – Spheres, nature, creation." She smiled. "My story is shorter and smaller. It is about each one of you – about how important you are and the importance of each choice you make."

"I thought we could only follow the purpose the Sphere decided," said Rory. "That's what Arnalea said."

Heyatoma shook her head. "Purpose is much richer than that. You continually have the power to choose. If you did not, there would be little reason to take form. As you choose, as you act, you are creating your life. As you create, you learn."

"But what about what the Sphere wants?" asked Tima.

"The Sphere sets an intention. That is all," said Heyatoma. "Your choices and your intention allow the unexpected." She smiled. "If you knew it all, there would be nothing to learn."

"And it would be too dull to keep your attention," added Mealim.

Heyatoma pointed to a thick section of the forest. "See how dark it is there, even though it is bright day in the clearing?"

Rory nodded.

"Suppose a tree comes into form with the intention from the Sphere of experiencing slow growth in the darkness of the forest, the lack of sun for an extended period, until it finally gets tall enough to break through into the light."

"That doesn't sound like much fun," said Rory.

Heyatoma turned to him. "It might be difficult for years and years, but think of the excitement upon nearing the canopy of leaves and think of the wild joy of the first leaf that feels the sun directly on its surface after a hundred years of darkness. That joy can only happen out of the wait that came before."

"Sounds amazing," said Tima.

Heyatoma nodded. "It is a choice and an experience. However, once in form, with that original intention, what if the sun in this clearing beckoned so deliciously to the tree that it decided to grow sideways to reach out to the sun in the clearing? The tree is free to make that choice. Growing in that direction would block other plants, so they would have to choose a new path and take action with intention."

"So what would happen?" asked Rory. "Would the Sphere be angry?"

Heyatoma laughed. "The tree is of the Sphere. The Sphere can no more be angry with it than you could be angry with your foot. The tree is free to do as it pleases, based on its experience. When it returns, it will again become part of the Sphere and share its experiences. Then, all can decide if another tree adventure with the original purpose would be interesting."

"So, as long as it acts with intention, no harm, no foul?" asked Billy.

"Exactly. The choices the tree makes affect all, and all gain. So it is with you. Each one of your actions and choices enriches. Each of your choices offers new choices and paths to action for others."

"We're Sodrol," said Rory. "How does that fit in?"

Heyatoma smiled. "You are Sodrol because you formed around a seed. Because it is there, you tend to act and react in a certain way. When you are aware, its power helps you complete this task and, when this task is done, fulfill your purpose." She looked at them. "The seed has affected each of you since you came into form, even though you were not yet aware of it."

She looked at Tima. "All your life, you have guided change for yourself and others, showing the skins that must be left behind. You have channeled the fire to burn away all but the essential."

Tima nodded. "Truth."

Heyatoma looked at Billy. "You are often shunned for your perceptions, but you cannot stop that action any more than you can stop your breath. The shock others have felt at your insights has often cracked open their self-deceit, giving them the chance to become aware, though few have taken the gift you offered and even fewer have thanked you."

Billy grinned. "You can say that again."

She turned to James. He held up his hands. "I know. The earth and I go way back."

She smiled and nodded.

"What about me?" asked Rory.

She shook her head. "That is part of what you will discover soon, my son."

She looked at all of them. "Those are the seeds at your core. However, at each moment, you chose what to do and how to act, how to create. Each action affects the actions of others. You have complete freedom in those choices. It is your right. It is your glory."

She turned to Rory. "Belecha whispered to you to begin your kiva, but you took the action. You could have chosen to act or not act. Either action would have changed the world." She looked at James. "You decided to take part, even though you were inclined not to. You were not forced by outside pressure, by your seed, or by your own purpose. You had the freedom to choose."

She looked at them with love. "Each action is your choice. That is the wonder of being aware. That is why we must seek with intention instead of certainty. We cannot be certain, because we cannot know how each entity will choose." She spread her arms indicating the world. "That is the ongoing excitement of this experience of life."

"So we can do whatever we want?" asked Rory.

Heyatoma nodded. "You have that duty. However, to be aware, you must act with intention, and you must accept responsibility that you have made the decision and taken the action."

She smiled at them all. "Have you not wondered where the threads come from?"

Rory shook his head. "I thought they just were."

"No. When you create, you bring forth a thread. Each aware action brings a thread into being. Over your time, you will create countless millions of threads, which intertwine with the threads from others' creations. That is why we are called Adima – the Weavers of Light. We spin the threads into the tapestry of the web by creation and action."

They looked at each other, smiling at the thought that each one of them helped to create the web that they had traveled. Suddenly, the ground shook, a thunder from deep inside the earth. Looking at the volcano, they saw sparks fly through the thickening plume.

"The mountain announces its departure," said Heyatoma. "I must hurry." She picked up a stick and began to draw in the dirt before them.

"I have told you my story, and now I must give you the final piece of the puzzle. It is your role in the cleansing of the stain, and it tells you how you may succeed."

"Have you seen the Kroledutz?" asked James. "There are too many. They're too powerful."

Heyatoma reached out and stroked James' cheek. "My son, do you think I would send you to slaughter? You may not succeed, but you will not stand alone. The first piece of the puzzle is that you will not fight."

"Not fight?" said Billy. "Do you think we can just ask them to go away? Last time we saw them, they wanted to eat us."

Heyatoma shook her head. "No. They will not leave by asking. However, they cannot live where there is too much creation. Just as a small fire can warm you, a large fire can destroy a building or a forest." Another roar shook the island, more intensely than before.

"Or an island?" asked James.

"Or an island," agreed Heyatoma. "You can drive away the Kroledutz and cleanse the stain of the ancient mistake through the light of creation and through the power of your song."

"You don't mean we're supposed to stand up in front of that army and do a dance or something, do you?"

Mealim cackled. "Tinglen, you always did think too much of yourself. Even with your friends, you couldn't take on a single, sick Kroledutz without help."

"So what can we do?" asked Tima.

"You must channel the web," replied Heyatoma. "You must bring the creation of a million, million lifetimes of weaving into a single place. That alone has the power to turn them back and wipe clean the stain."

"Channel the web?" said Billy. "How can we do that?"

Heyatoma looked at Rory. "You know, Eliaya."

Rory said, "Eliaya? I thought I was called Techta."

Heyatoma shook her head and smiled. "Techta is what the old raccoon calls you. Your name is Eliaya. It means Beautiful Patterns. You are a most skilled weaver of light, my son. Now, tell the others of the power stone."

Rory nodded and turned to the others. "The night Belecha took me to his kiva, he showed me a stone hidden under the rock he sits on. It's a double pyramid. He called it the Oloho, an Energy Keeper. He said there were only three in existence. I'm supposed to bring it back when we activate the Stone."

"Why didn't you tell us?" asked Billy.

"He said I couldn't – that it wasn't time. Wouldn't even let me touch it. He said when we finished the challenges and came for it, I was the only one who should carry it."

"That is correct," said Heyatoma. "You must bring the Oloho to your time."

"But how do I use it?"

"Once your Stone is activated, it is more than a portal. It can do many things," replied Heyatoma. "When you have brought the Oloho to your time, go to Belecha's kiva. Place your Stone over the place where his rock lies. You will have to guess, as his rock will be deep beneath the sands. Sit around your Stone. Each of you, sit at the point of your glyph and sing the song of your seed."

"How will we know what the song is?" asked Billy.

Mealim tossed a rock at him. "You will have to think, Tinglen. Focus on your seed, and the song will come."

Heyatoma looked at Mealim. "Hush, little one," she said, as if scolding a child. The four were amazed that Mealim, like a child who had been scolded, bent her head and murmured an apology.

Turning to the four, Heyatoma continued. "Then Eliaya, release the Oloho over the Stone. Much will happen very fast, so you must keep your focus on your seed. You must provide a stable base so that the Oloho may do its work. Do you understand?"

Rory nodded. He felt a little worried. Story, puzzle, then challenge. That meant that something bad was about to happen and it was up to him to figure out a solution.

"Mother," he said, "I don't know about the chal-"

"IIIIIeeeee!" a scream tore from Mealim's throat, transforming her into a huge spirit and then dumping her into a sobbing pile. "Atomasa! He has been attacked. The Kroledutz! They massed and ripped him apart. Now they feed." She was sobbing and moaning. "They feed. They feed. Oh how, it hurts."

Wide-eyed, Tima shouted to Heyatoma, "What can we do? We have to help him!"

Heyatoma shook her head, her eyes wet. "There is nothing you can do. It is over." She went to Mealim and gathered her in her arms, rocking the sobbing woman.

James was stunned. Choking back tears, he said, "Atomasa was so strong. He was the teacher for my challenge. I didn't think spirits could die."

"I guess they can," said Billy, "and judging from Mealim, it was pretty awful."

Rory shook his head. "That's what we're supposed to face?"

"Maybe not," said Billy. "There's a problem. Remember why Atomasa was in the kiva?"

James looked at him with dread growing. "He was our anchor."

Billy nodded. "And without an anchor, we can't get back. We can only wander the threads."

Suddenly, a violent trembling shook the island. They heard trees crashing down. A huge explosion from the volcano pulled their attention upward. Fiery lumps of molten rock burst out of the top.

"It's gonna blow!" shouted James. "We have to get out of here before the lava starts flowing or we're done."

Heyatoma looked at James. "The lava will not cover the island."

"How can you say that? Look at that thing, it's erupting!"

Heyatoma nodded, her calm acceptance untouched. "That is true, but as I said, this place is nearing its end. The island will not be covered. It will explode and fall into the sea."

"Into the sea?"

Heyatoma smiled gently, seeing the event in her mind. "Yes, my son. This is the end of its time and the end of my time." She stood. "I must climb to the top quickly, so I may experience my last moments completely. It is my final action."

She wrapped her arms around each one of them and stepped away. "It has been a wonderful joy to be with you once more in the body. I will be with you again when you return to the Sphere." She smiled, turned and headed up the path toward the volcano.

"Wait!" screamed James. "You can't just ..."

"James, hush," said Tima. "This is it. It's the challenge." She turned to Rory. "I hope you know what to do, because we don't have much time and we don't have any options I can see."

As if to emphasize her statement, the island shook with another rolling tremor. A huge crash and roar told them a piece had broken away and plunged into the ocean.

Rory searched his mind for a way out, but nothing came. He was panicking. Billy stepped up to him and calmly gripped his arm. "No worries, dude. Take a breath. If it comes, it comes. If not," Billy grinned, "it's been fun." He gave Rory a quick hug.

Rory stared at his three friends, gathered around him, looking scared but also nodding their agreement. Mealim still rocked on the ground, moaning.

Rory looked around, feeling the place and experiencing a most curious sensation that he had been here, doing exactly this same thing, before.

And then, deep within himself he felt the seed glowing, whispering its secrets, filling him with its power. He knew. He saw. He was the whale, the Sodrol who crossed boundaries, who brought together the air and fire, the water and the earth. He felt the immensity of nature and of the Spheres. He felt the infinitesimal smallness of each body, acting on its own, creating and spinning the web of light until they could again become one with the Sphere and share the unique experience of their journey. He felt the time after time and life after life of the eternal creation and experience and learning of individual entities and the Spheres from which they came. He knew what it was to be a Watcher, and he knew that he had accepted that role.

"Mealim," he called. "Atomasa's pain was an experience. We will share our pain of his loss with him when we return, yes?"

Mealim looked up and took a moment to focus on his words. Recognizing the truth in them, she took a breath, then stood. "It was so sudden and sharp. I had never felt such a thing."

"It was well learned for both then."

Mealim studied Rory carefully, then nodded slowly.

"Can you summon Arnalea?" he asked. "I do not know yet how to reach out."

Mealim continued to study him. "You have decided," she said. "You are a Watcher."

Rory nodded. "I am a Watcher."

"Can you summon him?" he asked again. "We need him now."

Mealim nodded and faded out of body.

The volcano roared again and the island bucked. Another huge chunk tore free and fell into the sea.

Tima looked at Rory, hope mixing with rising panic. "Do you know what to do? We don't have much time."

Rory turned to his friends and nodded. He pulled the Stone out of his pocket and handed it to Tima. "I'm staying."

"What?" said Tima. "You can't do that. You'll be killed."

Rory smiled. "We don't die, Tima. You know that. I'll return to the Sphere and see you when you get there."

"But why?" asked James.

"You need an anchor. It can be there or it can be here. Only a Watcher can be an anchor. Belecha told me that I'd be faced with the choice. I've made it. I stay here with my mother and watch. I'll be your anchor."

"It's not worth it if you don't come back," said Tima. "We're in this together."

"I don't want to face your dad and try to explain," said Billy. "I don't want to …"

"Stop it. All of you. This is the last challenge and in every one it's worked out. I'm the Sodrol for this one, and I know this is what we need to do. It's not a choice, it's a duty."

Rory looked around at his three friends. He didn't want to stay without them, but there was no doubt this was the answer to the challenge. They looked back at him, then at each other, knowing he was right.

"You're the boss," said Billy, "but we can't travel with three. We need four."

"Mealim is getting Arnalea to be the fourth."

"But what about the Oloho?" asked James.

"Arnalea has the ability to hold the Oloho. He can take on the role of the whale, because he is aware."

"Are you sure?" asked Tima.

"I'm not usually a whale, but I can do it," said Arnalea, fading in next to Mealim.

Billy grinned at Arnalea. "Hey, there. I never got to thank you for the ride, and for scaring James so bad he almost peed himself."

Arnalea smiled and gave a little bow. "My pleasure."

The island gave another huge shudder. "I'd love to catch up," Arnalea said, "but I think we should do that later. This place is going to be under water pretty soon." He turned to Mealim. "Can I drive?" he asked.

Mealim drew herself up and glared at him. "Absolutely not! We have work to do, and you would have us swinging from here to the Sphere. Besides, you need practice as a whale."

Arnalea shrugged. "As you command, but when this is over ..."

"We'll see."

Rory looked at Arnalea. "Do you know where the Oloho is hidden?"

Arnalea nodded. "Under the old one's rock."

"And the other things? You know what is needed?"

"I'm guessing something small. Bracelet and necklace?"

Rory nodded. "Can you find them?"

"There's always storage behind the ladder."

"Then you can do it."

Arnalea shrugged. "Sure."

Tima came up to Rory and grabbed his arm. "But the Stone, Rory," she said. "Do you know how to activate it? Can you do it here?"

Rory looked at her, thinking back to the first day she showed up at the hole and started digging, not saying a word, just filling a bucket with dirt and hauling it over to the pile.

He looked at James and thought about the time he suggested James spend the night in the hole. "Sleep on rocks and let the 'skeeters eat me, when I have a nice bed just over the hill? No thanks."

He looked at Billy, remembering that first day at school.

He looked at his three friends, the first real friends he had ever had, and he nodded. "Give me the Stone."

Tima handed him the Stone and he looked again at his friends, knowing he would never see them again in this form.

"It's been fun," he said, and a tear rolled down his cheek. He held the Stone up to his face and the tear rolled onto it. "Salt water," he said, his voice breaking. Then, he held the Stone out for them to see. The tear glistened on the whale glyph and the entire Stone lit up, pulsing and glowing, like Rory remembered the Oloho had.

The volcano bellowed above and belched forth another volley of burning rocks.

Rory held the Stone out to Tima who took it and nodded.

"Time to go," Rory said. He took one last look at Tima, and James, and finally Billy. "See you around." Then Rory turned and hurried up the path that Heyatoma had taken.

THIRTY-SIX 36

"Eliaya. I am glad you decided to come."

Rory smiled. "You make it sound like I showed up at a movie, not the end of the world."

Heyatoma squeezed him. "Both are interesting experiences that can offer opportunities to learn."

"This seems like a bigger deal. I just said goodbye to my friends."

Heyatoma began to speak, but Rory held up his hand. "I know. I'll see them again, but not in this life. Not in this form."

"There are more things in the world than you now know, my son. You have much to learn."

"What do you mean?"

But Heyatoma quickened her pace. "Hurry. We must reach the top before the end. That is the best view."

"You sound like you've done this before."

Heyatoma nodded. "Many times, in many places, in many lives. It is my purpose. I am a kind of Watcher. I watch my family. And, at the end of a world, I send my children off to safety so that our knowledge can live again." She looked at Rory. "I have bid farewell to my friends and my children in life after life. It is what a Watcher does. And you, my son, have become a Watcher once more for a much wider family than mine."

"So I will have to say goodbye to friends again and again?"

Heyatoma nodded. "That is one of your duties. A Watcher takes on many tasks."

"But, saying goodbye. Seeing people die. I know they continue to live, but I can't help feeling sad. Not seeing my dad again, or Leon, or …"

Heyatoma smiled at him and gave him another quick squeeze. "Everyone and every physical thing dies. That hurts. It always hurts. Even when you see an evil thing die, seeing the life leave this world, this celebration of the physical, it is a sadness. You cry." She stopped, turned, and touched his cheek. "I cry every time." She turned and continued to walk.

"If I get out of this somehow, I don't think I want to have any more friends. If I have to stick around and watch people die, I would rather have some distance. It won't hurt so much."

Heyatoma shook her head. "You have it wrong. You can't escape by not caring; you will only make their experience have less worth. Entities die. Your only choice is how much of their creations you can share with others." She stopped and looked at Rory. "If you close yourself off, you will still feel the pain of their death. However, the more distance you put between yourself and others, the less you will experience their celebration of life. You have to experience the joy with the pain, Eliaya." She continued up the trail.

Rory considered her words. "Is it worth it?"

Heyatoma glanced at him with an eternity of love and smiled. "I have climbed this mountain or one like it countless times to bid farewell to my children and my world. I cherish each time and will do it again gladly. I am always amazed by the creation that is going on all around. Even in death, there is creation and action and learning. I am in awe again and again and again."

She touched his cheek gently. "And still I weep at each passing, even knowing that energy never dies ... knowing that the elements of each life have chosen to come here and that they choose when to leave. Even though I know they always return to their Sphere and are no more dead than you, I still weep."

Heyatoma smiled sadly. "I also know it is an honor to watch. I feel each death and weep as if I could not stop. Then, I sing of their life and their death so that the world can hear and know and learn." She looked again at Rory and nodded. "Yes, for me, it is worth it." She quickened her pace. "It is almost time. We must hurry."

Soon, they came to the end of the trail. Before them, the mouth of the volcano gaped. Inside, a boiling sea of molten rock bubbled and popped. Behind and far below them, the sea crashed on the rocks, tearing at the pieces of cliff that had just ripped free.

Heyatoma turned and gazed out at the ocean, breathing deeply of the cool wind that blew off the waves.

"In one life, I sent my children off in boats to the corners of the world. I stood here and watched until the sails disappeared over the horizon." She took Rory's hand, and he felt her calm joy flow through him. "It is a new experience to stand here with you." She turned and brushed a bit of hair off his forehead and cupped his chin in her soft hand.

"Eliaya, you bring me joy. The threads you will spin from this watching will be bright and full of color."

Rory looked at her, then pulled her into a hug. "I'm glad to have been here with you."

A deadly calm settled over the island. They turned and looked again into the volcano. Even the lava was still. It seemed the entire world was holding its breath.

Heyatoma nodded to herself. "It is time." She turned once more to Rory. "Try to hold form as long as you can, my son. The more you experience, the more you will have to share."

Rory nodded and opened his mouth to say goodbye.

A deafening roar reached from deep inside the earth, and the volcano burst apart.

Rory felt himself flying through the air. All around him were burning rocks and liquid blobs of lava. He saw thick ribbons of light shooting out of the volcano and the island as both shattered and fell into the sea. *I guess this is creation for a volcano*, he thought and laughed at the strangeness of it.

He plummeted as fast as he had soared. The sea closed above him with cold, refreshing violence. Down, down he plunged. *I must have left my body somewhere*, he thought, but wasn't sad.

As he sank deeper, the light grew dim, but then directly beneath him, he saw a burning red, glowing orb. He wondered how there could be a fire under water. Then he realized it was the volcano, still spewing lava. Pieces of rock, cooled by the crushing water, hurtled past. He saw a rock spinning by that was the same shape as their Stone, small and square. It even had a hole in the center. He reached for it.

THIRTY-SEVEN

"Rory!" Tima was shaking his shoulder. "Rory! Wake up! It's time to save the world."

Rory opened his eyes. Tima was smiling down at him. James and Billy were beside her, faces split with grins. He saw Arnalea and Mealim standing behind them. Rory shook his head, trying to understand what had happened.

"You just appeared, dude," said Billy. "We're in your kiva. We were aiming at Belecha's, but Mealim caught a whiff of lots of Kroledutz."

"She's a careful one," said Arnalea. "She checked before we dropped down. Good thing, too. I guess they went back to attack the raccoon."

Rory sat up and looked around. "How come I'm not dead? The volcano blew. Then I was under the sea." He remembered the stone he had seen. Looking down, he saw it was clutched in his hand.

Mealim spoke. "A Watcher can take many forms. You now have numerous duties. One of those is to witness a multitude of lives. You will return when you know it is time. This was not the time." She looked at Arnalea. "This one was sufficient to travel here, allowing you to make the decision. However, he is not of the body and will not be able to carry the items into this time."

Billy looked at Arnalea. "You mean on your return day, you didn't come back?"

Arnalea grinned and shook his head. "Psych!" he yelled. "Fooled you, didn't I?" He smacked his chest. "I left my body behind. I just had this one task." He looked at Rory. "It was a final act of service, to help you, my friend. You wouldn't, couldn't, take the step you had to take without knowing your friends were taken care of. They were okay, but not the way you thought." He grinned. "It's all about intention."

Arnalea began to fade. "Now I've completed my task. I've got places to be." He turned to Mealim. "I wish you'da let me drive." Then he was gone.

Rory called to him. "Wait! We still need a sixth. Atomasa said we had to use the double pyramid for the final …"

But Arnalea was gone. Rory looked at Mealim hopelessly.

"We're so close. We can get there, but we can't do anything without an anchor. We'll be squashed by the Kroledutz unless we can channel the dimensions. I can't be whale and anchor."

Mealim smiled. "The answer is close at hand."

"What?" said Billy, starting to get frustrated. "You're talking in riddles when Kroledutz are all around!"

Mealim shot him an angry look. "Hush, Tinglen. I am not talking in riddles." She nodded at Rory. "Maybe I should have said the answer is *in* hand."

Rory looked down at the stone in his hand. In the light of the full moon, he saw the stone was not only the same shape. It had the familiar glyphs in the corners. He looked up, confused. Turning to Tima he asked, "Don't you have the Stone?"

Tima nodded and held it out. The Stone in her hand glowed and pulsed as it did on the challenge. Rory looked at Mealim, holding up the stone he had brought back with him. "What is …"

She held up her hand. "Ask it, Watcher."

Rory looked at the stone in his hand. Then he looked at the glowing Stone that Tima held. He unfocused his attention and listened. After a time, he opened his eyes and smiled. Placing his stone in the middle of the kiva, he explained. "This is our anchor. It is an entity from another dimension. It will provide the sixth point. Now we have to go and go quickly."

Billy started to fade into a ball of light.

"Hold it, Billy," said Rory. "This time we have to take our bodies. That was the reason for activating the Stone. We have to be in physical form to bring back the things we need."

Mealim nodded. "You are correct, Eliaya. I have no body, but the pointer does not need one." She looked around. "Quickly now."

They stood around the stone on the ground. Tima held out the portal Stone, grabbing it by the corner with the snake. James and Billy each touched their glyph and Mealim, shifting into a ball of light, hovered above. Rory nodded and said, "Keep your focus on your body. We need to stay in form. Hold the Stone with all your intention. That will keep the base firm." They all nodded. Rory reached out and touched the whale.

Immediately, they ripped upward, then hurtled forward at a terrible speed. Rory was glad they didn't start traveling the ribbons with their bodies. This was harder. Almost painful.

"We approach!" called Mealim. "Kroledutz are gathered outside the raccoon's time, but have not been able to break through. We must gain speed to cut through the horde."

Rory felt his speed increase. Ribbons whipped by so quickly, they blurred. He had to keep his full intention on the Stone and the others as their passage threatened to tear them away.

"Now!" cried Mealim, and they slammed into the floor of Belecha's kiva.

Stunned for a moment by the impact, they stood and looked around.

Belecha sat hunched on his rock, fading in and out of form. When his form appeared, he looked desperately tired. His entire power focused on keeping a steady drum beat and chanting quietly. The threads and ribbons that wrapped the walls of the kiva were dim. The efforts of the Kroledutz were obviously taking their toll.

From above, a malevolent roar sounded. The threads shuddered and dimmed. Belecha jerked as if he had been struck and faded out of form. He resumed his chant and the threads began to glow a bit brighter.

"Old man," said Billy. "You look bad."

"Hush, Tinglen," ordered Mealim. "Do not take his attention. He must maintain this space a while more or all is lost."

"Oh. Sorry."

Mealim looked at Rory. "Do you know what to get?"

Rory nodded as another impact and roar shook the kiva. The ribbons dimmed to near darkness.

"Hurry, Rory," urged Tima.

Rory ran to the short wall behind the ladder. He stretched out his hand and felt for the pouch. Another crash and roar shook the kiva. The light was nearly gone.

He felt his fingers close around the pouch. Rory pulled it out, reached in and grabbed the necklace and a bracelet, and stuffed them into a pocket.

"Got 'em."

"Let's get out of here!" said James.

"No, wait," said Rory. "The Oloho."

"Better book it, dude," said Billy.

Rory raced to the center of the kiva. Belecha was gasping, and Rory could see the pain etched in his face, but still he kept the beat of the drum and croaked his song through cracked lips.

"Hang in there, Belecha," he whispered. "We're almost ready." He reached under the rock on which Belecha sat. Feeling the brick, Rory pulled it away and plunged his hand into the hiding place. Another roar shook the kiva, and lights from the threads went out. Rory looked up. Belecha faded into a dim sphere, its faint glow dying as Rory watched and the drum beat stopped. A terrifying bellow of triumph filled their ears.

Rory's hand closed around the Oloho, and he felt an enormous rush of power course up his arm. He pulled the Oloho out. It glowed and pulsed. Gripping it tightly, he plunged his hand into the center of Belecha. Instantly, the sphere lit up and the drum beat began again.

Rory stood, clutching the Oloho, and turned to the others. "Now!" he screamed.

Tima held out the Stone, and they all gathered around it. Rory looked at Mealim. "We need to end up in the same place, but on the surface and in our time."

Mealim nodded.

Rory looked at his friends. "We won't have a second chance. Those things are going to be massed and ready. They know we're coming."

"What's going to happen?" asked James.

Rory shook his head. "I don't know. All we can do is hold tight to the Stone with our intention. Remember what Heyatoma said. We are the base. We have to hold steady. Pay attention to the Stone. Sing our songs. Don't watch the fireworks."

"Let's do it," said Billy, the raptor ready to hurtle down, talons straining open, poised to strike.

"Yeah," said Tima, fire blazing in her eyes. "Win or lose, we'll do our part."

"Alright," said James, feeling the timeless power of nature course through his body. "I'm ready."

Rory looked at his friends. "I'm glad we're all here together, doing this."

"Rory, that's nice," said Billy, looking first at Rory, then Tima, then James. "But, shut up and dance."

All four of them grinned. Rory nodded to Mealim and touched the Stone.

THIRTY-EIGHT 38

"There they are!" Radelam screamed, looming above them. "Feed!"

The mass of Kroledutz rose up, blocking the sky.

Rory gagged as the stench of the creatures coated them in waves. The mob fell toward them, screeching and grabbing.

"Hold tight!" Rory gasped. "Sing. Concentrate on your power! Mealim, stay in position above the Stone."

Tima started the song, her clear voice chanting of the fire, the snake, the changes all must face, and the choices she had made. Billy's voice joined Tima's, chanting of the threads, the air, the bird soaring and seeking. James' voice began, low-toned, the slow, unstoppable movement of the earth. Rory heard the snorts and bellows of the buffalo, the timeless beat of nature.

The dark mass of howling creatures descended, and Rory fought a rising terror. He opened his mouth and began to sing of Heyatoma, of the volcano, of the sea, of the air, of the whale that brought all Sodrol together.

The Kroledutz swirled around them, roaring in triumph. Radelam rose above the Stone. "You puny specks think you can chase away your fears with a song? You think whistling in the dark does any more than tell the hunter where the prey is standing? Stupid creatures. You are wrong! And now you die!"

He opened his beak-like mouth, his burning red eyes gleaming in anticipation. A whirlwind of screams and rot from all he had consumed over the ages poured out of his mouth, wrapping the four in its filth.

Summoning all his power and intention, Rory thrust his hand, still gripping the Oloho, into the Sphere of Mealim, hovering above the Stone, and let go.

"Hold on!" he screamed to the others.

Everything froze in place. Then, with a force greater than the explosion of a hundred volcanoes, the Oloho cracked and burst wide. Searing bright lights of many billions of threads erupted as the full force of the web of light poured forth. The portal Stone exploded, hurling arcs of brilliant and devastating light at the Kroledutz.

Radelam fell back with a cry.

The teens continued to sing the song of their seeds. Rory felt the song of the whale coursing through him, vibrating the energy that poured out of the Oloho and spread all around him. He felt himself growing huge, expanding to the sky, his body taking the form of an enormous blue whale, pulsing with the power and songs of the sea, the air, the light, the dark. He called forth his song, and shock waves of sound and light split the Kroledutz with terrible power.

Rory looked at Tima and saw that she had become a python, uncoiling from the earth far below. Flames surrounded her, as she twisted and turned in the air. Thick ribbons and balls of burning light shot forth at the retreating army.

James was a towering buffalo. His powerful chest heaved as he bellowed at the dark forms. With each sound he made, vibrating bolts of energy flew at the Kroledutz, crushing the dark forms to the ground and grinding them beneath his hooves.

Billy had transformed into the mythical Thunderbird, his wings stretched across the sky. As he beat them, thunder and blasts of lightning tore through the darkness and rocketed across the world, lighting up the distant hills. He opened his beak and screamed his warrior cry. The ground shook.

And still the Oloho grew brighter and larger, a flood of energy and light blazing forth from its core.

The four sang their songs, their combined chants making the threads pouring forth from the Oloho swirl and pulse and glow even brighter. The sky lit like it was noon.

The smaller Kroledutz shrieked and vaporized. Soon, it was just the four and Radelam. Too large to vaporize, the evil leader hung before them, his shapeless body burning as he writhed, screaming empty threats.

"I will …!" He bellowed. "I will …!"

Rory looked at the creature as it burned and smoked before them. He had no hate for this thing that had brought so much darkness to the world. He only wished him gone.

"You shall die," Rory replied. "Your time has passed."

With a final shriek of pain and rage, Radelam vanished, raining a thick, black sludge onto the ground below.

Completely alone now, the teens kept singing, using their songs and power to bring cleansing light into the world. They chanted their songs as the Oloho channeled the energy of the web. Above them, the ribbons of light pulsed with their songs and formed and reformed into wondrous patterns of light and color.

They watched the weaving of light, adding to it with their songs and awareness, and all nature glowed with a beauty that had not been seen on this world for thousands of years.

"Did someone step on a cat?"

Turning, Rory and the others saw Belecha. Smiling at the teens, he reached out and pulled the Oloho from the glowing orb that was Mealim. It immediately closed upon itself, once again becoming a glowing double pyramid.

"That is the most horrendous screeching I have ever heard," said Belecha. "It's time you four got back down to your proper shape and size and put a sock in it."

Rory felt himself shrinking down. Soon, he was sitting on the ground, in a body he was much more familiar with. He stood and hurried over to Belecha, wrapping him in a tight hug, breathing in the animal scent of his weathered clothing.

"I didn't think you'd make it."

Belecha pushed him off with a grin. "Not so tight, youngster. I'm an old man. I break easy." He looked at the others and at Mealim, who had again taken form. "Thanks. I wish you could have done it sooner, but you did it."

Mealim stood and smiled. "You always have something to whine about, Raccoon, but I'm glad you survived." She looked at the teens. "You four did well, but now, I must go. This is a new time, and there is much to be done."

Rory looked at her and nodded. "Thank you, Sister."

She bowed her head. "Pay attention, Eliaya. You have a lot of work ahead." She began to fade out of form, but stopped and pointed at Belecha. "And don't trust everything that one says. He's a trickster." She faded to a ball. Rory saw her reach for a thread, and then, she was gone.

THIRTY-NINE 39

Before they could get too comfortable, they heard a shout coming from the gate.

"What are you pukes doing?"

A large car had screeched to a stop outside the gate, and Cisco was leaning out of it, screaming at them, while Matt hurried to unlock the gate.

"Get off of my land!" Cisco screamed, "Before I call the cops!"

"Uh oh," said James, turning to Belecha. "What do we do?"

Belecha smiled. "Sing." He looked at Rory. "Sort things out. Tonight, have everyone meet me at your kiva." Then he, too, faded to a ball and was gone.

"I thought Cisco would be different now that the Kroledutz are gone," said Tima.

Rory shook his head. "He doesn't have their power. He doesn't have their influence. But he still has his own mean."

"And he's drunk," added Billy.

As they watched, the gate swung open. Cisco jumped out of the car and ran toward them, waving his arms and yelling.

"That looks like it's plenty," said James.

Billy looked at the others. "Wait a minute. We just saved the whole friggin' world. I don't think this guy's a problem. Come on, Rory. Let's have a chat with him."

"What do we do?" asked James.

Billy looked at Matt, who was following Cisco, then at Tima and James. "What Belecha said. He wasn't joking. Sing."

Tima flashed a look of understanding. "I think our big friend needs to hear the song of the earth. I bet he'll want to give it a hug."

"You're right," said James, nodding. Then, he knelt down and started to drum on the ground, chanting slowly. Tima joined in, watching Matt. Like a buffalo hearing something he didn't understand, Matt slowed, then stopped and looked around, confused.

"It's working!" said Rory. "Keep it up. Billy and I will deal with Cisco."

James nodded, and kept going. They watched as Matt yawned. Shaking his head sleepily, he sank down to his hands and knees. Then he lay down on the ground and began to snore.

Rory dug into his pocket and pulled out the necklace and the bracelet. He handed them to Billy. "Belecha told me to give these to the Bird, that you'd know what to do with them."

Billy looked at them, thought a minute, and then a huge smile crossed his face. He nodded and shoved them in his pocket just as Cisco came barreling up.

"You!" he said, glaring at Billy. "Thick skull, huh? Here, I bet you'll understand this!" He cocked back his arm and got ready to swing.

Billy just smiled. Anger flared in Cisco's eyes, and he swung. At the last second, however, Billy turned, letting Cisco's punch pass him by, and then he gave the man a push. Cisco fell to the ground. Scrambling quickly to his feet, he cursed loudly and swung again.

Billy stepped aside again, this time kicking hard at Cisco's knee. Once more, Cisco was in the dirt.

"I'd advise you to stay down," said Billy.

"You little punk," groaned Cisco, struggling to rise. "I'm going to get you!"

When he finally got on his feet, Rory stepped forward. Summoning all the power he had gained over the past month, he raised his hand. "Stop!" he commanded.

Cisco fell back as if he had been struck.

Rory spoke with powerful intention. "It is now time for you to listen. We will go to your office, and you will sit."

Cisco stood frozen, eyes wide and uncomprehending.

"Now!" ordered Rory.

Without a word, Cisco nodded, pulled out his keys, and walked to the trailer. Billy and Rory followed. After he opened the door, Cisco went behind the desk and sat. Rory and Billy stood before him.

Billy looked at Rory, who motioned for Billy to talk, and then at Cisco. "Here's what's going to happen. You are going to give Rattlesnake Ranch to the county."

Cisco looked at Billy, the red rising in his face, but a glance at Rory stopped him from protesting.

"You're also going to sign that property you purchased over to Mr. Nomura, and you're going to pay me for the 24 hours I spent on your property. I didn't get much done, since I was all tied up, thanks to you, but ..." Billy grinned and dipped his chin. "I'm sure you understand."

Cisco jumped out of the chair, red rushing to his face. "You're out of your mind, you little crook! I ain't paying you nothing. And I ain't giving away my property, either! Nah, I'm calling the cops. Let them decide what to do with you."

He reached for the phone, but before he could lift it, Billy pulled the necklace out of his pocket and threw it across the desk. Cisco froze, looking at the ancient piece.

"Go ahead. Pick it up. Look at it." Cisco did.

"I'm not robbing you," said Billy. "Ripping people off is your talent. We're paying for what you're giving away." He nodded at the necklace. "With that."

Cisco bent over the necklace, carefully examining the delicate carvings, his face filling with greed. "Where?" he croaked.

Billy didn't answer his question. "I can see you're trying to figure out what it's worth," he said instead. "Pretty close to priceless, don't you think?"

Cisco was almost drooling as he continued to examine the necklace.

"Of course, an *honest* person would give it to a museum." Cisco shot him a panicked look, and Billy grinned and shook his head. "No, I won't make you do that. That is, I won't as long as you meet my terms. Right now."

Cisco's hand closed around the necklace. "Why don't I just keep it," he said, with a wry smile on his face, "and call the cops anyway? I'll say you were trying to steal it from me."

"That won't work," answered Rory.

Cisco raised an eyebrow. "Oh yeah, hot shot? Why not?"

"They'll never believe it's yours. My dad's an archaeologist, and I know about relics. There's never been a piece like that, inside a museum or out. You show that to the cops and you're going to jail for raiding antiquities. That's a federal crime."

Cisco considered. "So I'll just stash it, and then I'll call the cops. You and your friends have been mighty interested in that pit I've been digging. Now I see why. How about I have you hauled away and then go on a little expedition of my own?"

Rory smiled and shook his head. "I'll give you two reasons. One you'll believe and one you won't, but both are true."

"And what are your reasons?" sneered Cisco.

Rory looked at him, feeling his natural power rising inside. "The first reason is that my dad has already contacted the state historical commission. Once he sees proof ..."

Cisco began to speak and Rory lifted a hand, silencing him.

"We have proof," he said, understanding now why Belecha had wanted him to bring back the bracelet. "Once he sees it, this land will be locked down as an historical site for the rest of your lifetime. So, your choice is simple. You can keep the necklace, give up a fraction of its value, and make a fortune when you sell it, or you can try to be crooked and within 24 hours, you will have lost everything, including, very likely, your freedom."

Cisco weighed Rory's words and made a decision. He sat down, opened a drawer and pulled out his cash box and several documents. Then he looked up. "You told me there were two reasons. What's the other?"

Rory smiled. "If you do not, the power of the universe will crush you into dust."

FORTY 40

"Man!" said Billy, leaning back against the kiva wall. "Leon sure can cook."

Rory poked him in the stomach. "You keep shoving that much food into your face, and in six months, you won't fit through the door."

"That is a fate I am more than willing to accept. Leon is a magician!"

"He is, just don't get on his bad side. Mealim has nothing on him when he gets mad."

Billy nodded. "I promise. I'll be a good boy when I'm home."

"Home?" asked James.

"Yeah," said Rory. "My dad's lawyer and the sheriff had a talk with Georgette. She got a choice between giving up rights to her darling little boy or going to jail for child endangerment. Guess which one she picked? There are a few more hoops, but it looks like we're stuck with him."

Tima dropped over the side of the kiva. "Sorry I'm late. I was talking to my mom."

"What's the news?" asked Billy.

Tima smiled. "Once the Kroledutz left, she came around. She sounds like Mom again. I think she'll be home next week."

"And Cleveland?" asked James.

Tima smiled and shook her head. "I asked and she said she'd rather be staked out on an anthill in the sun covered with honey."

She turned to Rory. "Speaking of mothers …"

Rory clapped his hands and rubbed them together. "Seems Kathy's boyfriend had another girlfriend. Kathy called Dad in tears, saying he'd left her. The pastor decided to leave town, too. In the middle of the night, sounds like." He paused, thinking. "Talking to Kathy was different this time. It was like talking to Mom again, like my real mom."

"Awww," said Tima, wrapping her arm around his shoulders.

"That's not the best part. The boyfriend left his kids so she's up to her eyes in mom stuff." He tightened his forehead. "I think that part will work out okay. The kids are pretty young, and she was a good mom when I was little. But, right now, she said she's overwhelmed and not in a 'good place' to have me live with her. So, for now, the lawsuit is dropped."

Tima grinned. "So you're staying!"

Rory nodded, his eyes tearing, but unable to find more words.

They all turned to James. "And?" asked Tima. "Don't hold out, farmer boy."

James spread his hands and smiled. "Dad got a courier package from Cisco this afternoon. He nearly fell down when he opened it and saw the deed for the land next to us."

Billy smacked his still-full belly. "Lots more chilies for snacks!"

"Cackling and clucking like a bunch of old hens," interjected a voice from near the fire. "Wonder who'll lay the first egg."

"Belecha!" shouted Rory. "You're back."

Belecha formed and nodded. "I told you I'd be here, didn't I?"

James gave him a frown. "Thanks for the help this morning. We saved your buns and then, *poof* ... you were gone."

"I told you all you needed. Besides, it sounds like things worked out for everyone."

Tima nodded. "They did."

Rory looked at the old man. "Did it work? I mean, I know the Kroledutz are gone, but the stain? Did we do it?"

Belecha brushed his hands together. "Clean as a whistle and good as new." He looked at the four friends. "You came through. I wasn't sure you could, but I figured it was worth a try."

"I knew we'd do it," said Billy.

"You're smarter than that, Tinglen."

Billy shrugged. "I guess you're right."

Belecha grinned. "You know I'm right, but it might kill you to admit it."

"The only thing that bugs me is giving Cisco that necklace," said Tima. "I hate that he got one of the power objects from your kiva."

Belecha began to laugh and soon was doubled over and gasping for air. Wiping tears away, he said, "No worries there."

"What do you mean?" asked Tima.

"We used to spend lots of time in the kiva. Sometimes, we'd forget a birthday or anniversary or something like that. So we …"

Billy hooted. "You had a stash of presents you kept down there just in case you needed to get out of a tight spot!"

Belecha grinned and nodded. "Worked most of the time. Of course, I tried it once with Mealim …"

The teens laughed.

"I still had a body then," said Belecha. "I think I've still got the scars."

They all enjoyed the thought of Mealim throwing objects at a quickly retreating Belecha. After all they had been through, it was great to sit in the kiva and not have a world to save or a challenge to face.

Rory looked at his friends, thinking back over the past month. "Now what?" he asked Belecha. "We saved the world. What next?"

Belecha grinned. "Now, live. You came here to experience and learn. So do that. Enjoy yourselves. You've earned it." He wiggled his eyebrows. "Of course, with aware beings, there are always little jobs that pop up now and then."

Billy moaned. "Like this little job? Next time you better bring a big check, dude."

"Just a minute," said James. Looking at the others, he took a breath. "I'm exercising my option. I'm done."

"What do you mean?" asked Rory.

"You said at the beginning I could bow out whenever I wanted. Well, I want out. I did this, because you asked, but now … I want to be a farmer." He looked around, trying to judge their reaction. "And don't forget the other part of the deal. You said you wouldn't hold it against me."

Billy looked James up and down, a smile on his face. "You did what you said you would, even though you didn't want to. I respect that. I respect you." He reached out and shook his hand.

The others nodded their agreement. They knew their connection was solid. Now that the task was done, it was right that James would follow his purpose.

Rory turned to Belecha. "I guess we can't go traveling without James."

Belecha smiled and began to fade out. "Maybe, maybe not. When the need arises, someone always steps forward. For now, see what you can do with what you've learned. I'll be seeing you around, pelchas."

"Wait!" called Rory. "You've called us pelchas a few times. What's that mean?"

Belecha had nearly faded away, but they could still see his smile. "Oh, that's what we called the prairie dogs. You know – cute, dumb, skittish, and full of fleas." He faded away just before the pebble Billy halfheartedly tossed sailed by.

FORTY-ONE 41

It was the night of the new moon. Rory leaned against the wall of his kiva, gazing at the sliver of light peering around the edge of the dark orb.

The two weeks since their last challenge had flown by. Cisco had created a stir donating Rattlesnake Ranch to the county. For a few days, he'd been the most popular guy around. Then, he disappeared.

Rory breathed in the sweet smoke of the pinion sap and thought back to the first night he spent in the kiva. It seemed lifetimes ago. *Actually,* he thought, *it was.*

Since the challenges and opening the Oloho, Rory had been able to remember pieces of a thousand lives, and he knew this life, this path, and what they had done was a particularly special one. They had learned a lot. They had done some good.

He looked at the fire, at the flames wrapping around the wood, and at the smoke dancing up to the stars. As he watched, the smoke began to swirl more tightly above the fire. Rory grinned. He knew what was coming. He picked up some pebbles and tossed one into the center of the smoke.

"Ei cha!" he called. "I think an old raccoon got into the road kill and is trying to fart it out." He tossed another pebble into the smoke that was quickly becoming Belecha.

"Hey! Watch where you're throwing those stones." Now fully formed, Belecha picked up a small rock and pitched it back at Rory. "I'm an old man, and someone could get hurt – probably you."

Rory pulled back to toss another, then stopped.

"So, Eliaya, you ready to take a trip?"

"Trip? Where? I thought we were done."

Belecha smiled. "There's always more. There's more to learn. There's more to experience. There are challenges to be met. And you, Eliaya, are on permanent duty."

"Hey, you didn't call me Techta."

"Yup. The little toad is all grown up. I figure you earned your name."

Rory realized he already knew the purpose of this trip. He was getting used to the sensation of knowing a thing was truth without knowing why. "You're going to Return," he said. "Go back to the Sphere."

Belecha nodded. "It's been a long time. I told you I was a Watcher and a Singer. You made the decision to be a Watcher. Along with one job, comes the other. They can't be separated, and you owe me a song."

Rory felt solitude sweep through him. "I don't know if I can stand that, to do this without you ..."

Belecha reached out and wrapped his powerful, sinuous arms around Rory. Rory felt a glow inside. He felt and saw the web reaching to him and through him and off in every direction, vibrating and filling him with strength and the knowledge of myriad lives intertwined. Belecha stepped back and looked at him.

"It's that bad memory of yours. You forget you are always connected. You are always with the Sphere. You are always with every one of us from every time."

He rapped Rory's forehead with his knuckles. "You ain't this body. And you better be grateful about that! If this ugly hunk was it for you ...!"

Rory grinned. "Better looking than you ever were. It must have been awful looking like a monkey's butt for 5,000 years."

Rory thought of something and cocked his head. "You were here alone all that time. Is it going to be that long for me?"

"Nah. Activating the Stone was the turning point. Pushing back the Kroledutz and clearing the stain changed things. Now, more Adima will want to come through and make the place lighter and brighter. You won't be alone for long." He patted his shoulder. "Now, enough worry. We have to take a trip, and you have some learning to do."

"But, how am I going to travel now? The Stone exploded. James is out. Now you …"

"That's the first lesson." Belecha squatted and drew a square in the dirt. "To travel, you used the Stone. Each of you on one corner."

"Right."

"The Stone was your portal for that task. However, as a Watcher, you will have to work with many tasks. You have to be able to tune into lots of Stones. How can you do that?"

"I don't know," replied Rory. A thought came to him. He looked around at the round kiva walls. "Wait. Since a kiva is shaped like a circle, I can draw an energetic square inside of it, with its four corners touching the sides of the kiva."

Belecha grinned. "Gold star for you. Doesn't even have to be a square. You can connect to tasks from other dimensions with different numbers. The kiva is your base, and you take the position of pointer."

"Then what?"

"Aim your attention toward the web. Look for the threads and ribbons nearby. One will glow. Grab it from your belly with your intention. It will pull you up to it, and you'll speed along."

"How do I know when I'm there?"

"It's a feeling. If you think you're there, but aren't sure, ask."

"Ask who?"

Belecha rolled his eyes. "Ask whatever you want. Ask the ribbon. Ask the web. Ask your butt. The important thing is that you ask. An answer will come. Trust it." He smiled. "If you're wrong, that just means another trip."

"Makes sense."

"To land, first nod, that's physical. Say something, that's vibrational. Then, let loose with your mind and your belly, that's your intention. You'll pop right off."

"It seems like a lot is connected to the belly."

"Your belly is your connection to the web. It's the center of your being. Lots of people who are semi-conscious feel the tug of the universe in their belly and they think they are hungry. That's why they keep eating. It's not hunger, at least not for food. When you feel that tug, it's the web talking to you. It's a reminder of your connection to the web and the Spheres. Pay attention to your belly."

"But what about finding my way back? What about the anchor? I can point and I can anchor, but I can't do both at the same time. If you aren't coming back with me, how am I going to do it?"

"The kiva does it again, but in a different way." He looked at Rory. "What direction is the web?" he asked.

"Up."

"Nope. It feels like you're going up, because you are focused in a body." He sat down and motioned to Rory to sit. "Look around – use your heart and your belly."

Rory shifted his awareness. He saw and felt the pulsing vibration of the web of light, twisting all around Belecha, through him and shooting out in every direction. The kiva walls were alive with the dancing waves of the web, just like they had been in Belecha's kiva. He felt his body melt into the tapestry.

"Enough."

Rory opened his eyes. Belecha smiled gently at him.

"This kiva evokes the Sphere," said Belecha, gesturing toward the walls. "When you come to the kiva, what direction is the web? What direction is the Sphere?"

Rory looked at Belecha and smiled. He waved his hand at the walls, the ground, the sky. "All around me."

Belecha nodded and touched Rory's chest. "And it is right here, inside you. Your kiva is the anchor. Your intention is your pointer. Within the kiva, you are in any Stone, any task, and any adventure that is required. When you leave, your intention points the way, and the kiva, which you have filled with your energy, provides the anchor. You, with your kiva, are all of them. Four points on a Stone, a point that steers the direction above and a final point that provides the anchor. That makes you the double pyramid, an entity with 8 sides in one. Eight is the sign of the infinite. You are the infinite … in 1." Belecha wrote in the sand of the floor, "1=8=1."

"That's how you've been able to …"

Belecha nodded. "How I've done it all. And that is how you will continue to learn. You can travel to any place. Ask for a lesson and go. There are lots of things and folks who are waiting to show you more. But my time is done."

"Do I get to drive?"

"See if you can. First, connect to your kiva, be aware that you are putting down your anchor unless you want to go wandering the web for a very long time."

Rory looked around the kiva and felt his connection with the web pulsing from the walls. He looked at Belecha and nodded. "I'm ready. Let's go."

"You know where we are going?"

Rory nodded. "The cliff."

Belecha smiled his agreement.

Rory took a breath and set his thoughts aside. He grabbed Belecha by the arms and grinned at the old man. Belecha grinned back. Then Rory felt the familiar slipping of awareness. He felt, then saw the ribbons of light all around and reaching into the distance. More and more came into view, and he saw a sphere of glistening threads vibrating around, above, and below the kiva. Rory felt the threads around and then through him. He felt himself become part of the web and it was so vast, he nearly lost his footing. He was glad he was holding on to Belecha – an old oak rooted in the depths of the earth.

Belecha nodded. It was time to ride. Rory allowed his intention to reach out to the clifftop. He saw a thread gleam from the tapestry of ribbons all around. He reached for it with his intention and they whipped up the thread and shot along the path.

Hurtling through the blackness with threads and ribbons shining all around, he felt the web hum with the energies of millions of adventures from thousands of Spheres, each an experience, a life, a learning, a growth.

Just then, the image of the cliff top loomed in his mind. He knew they had arrived. He nodded, said, "Okay," and with his intention, let go of the ribbon.

They stood just down the trail from the clifftop, near the clear pool surrounded by soft, green moss. Belecha grinned at Rory's success. He went to the pool and walked in, washing himself as Arnalea had described, singing quietly to himself.

Rory stared off at the rich valley floor far below. He looked to the distant mountains, jutting up with their red, wind softened faces. As he watched, a red-tailed hawk rose from a rocky outcropping and circled down toward the valley floor. They were so high, the hawk was small beneath them, though it still flew high above the river bank that ran at the base of the cliff.

"Hey, Tomillo!" called Rory, realizing he had known the hawk before, not as a hawk, but as a friend in another time. Startled, he turned to Belecha to tell him what happened. Belecha had come out of the pool and was standing beside him.

"I know," he said, before Rory could speak. "Every time you ride, you learn. With every aware act, you learn. It opens doors. Then, you know more."

Rory nodded, and Belecha motioned with his head up toward the cliff top. Rory's eyes filled with tears, and he grabbed Belecha's arm. "I don't want you to go. I'll miss you."

Belecha smiled. "Yeah. It's something about the body. You know we will still be connected. You know you will see me again. You know I am, have been, and will be part of you. You know time is a trick. But there still are these moments. This moment changes both of our paths, and you feel it." He put his hand on Rory's heart. "You feel it here."

Rory nodded.

"That, Eliaya, is one of the main reasons we come here. To feel. To feel essential joy and pain, to laugh until our sides hurt, to cry until we can't breathe. These are the experiences we bring back to the Sphere, and that is why we keep returning. That is also why this planet is so sacred, because it allows us to feel."

Belecha looked at Rory fondly. "We've been through a lot of lives together. You're like a rock in my shoe -- a pain, but one I'm used to and one I miss when it's not there. This time, you took a lot on faith and pulled it together plenty fast. You've done well, but I'm ready. I deserve a dip in the big pool so I can share all I've learned."

"What do I do if the Kroledutz come back?"

"Not if," replied Belecha, "when. Darkness always finds ways to creep in from the corners. The web is too tasty for them."

"So, what do I do?"

"When there is darkness, you light a candle. If a candle is not enough, light a torch. Keep lighting candles. Get others to help. Don't stop. That was my mistake last time. The others didn't want to hear about the darkness at the edges, and I didn't push to get help. You see how long it took to clean up that mess. Take my advice: When you see the darkness start creeping in, use your natural gift – be annoying. Keep talking about it and get everyone to get busy – lighting, weaving, creating. But never stop lighting your own candles and torches. Even if no one else helps. Don't stop. Don't ever stop."

Rory looked at him, again knowing. "That's it, right? That's your last lesson?"

Belecha smiled, nodded, and lay his hand gently on Rory's head. Rory felt the strength of the forest of songs spanning thousands of years flow into him from the old Watcher. Belecha saw the Rorys of many lives stream by, and he felt each attempt, each learning experience that led them here. Again, he turned to gaze at the cliff and out across the valley to the shining web that filled the sky. His heart filled with contentment, and his arms raised toward the sphere. Then, in a very formal tone he said, "Now, Singer I call you to the Path. Aid my Return."

"What do I do?"

Belecha shook his head and said to himself, "He insists on staying stupid." Then he looked at Rory. "We walk to the top. I stand on the edge. You sit on the rock. Then ..."

"What?"

Belecha smiled. "What do you think a Singer does? You sing."

"But what do I sing?"

Belecha knocked him on the forehead with his knuckles. "Trust yourself. You are a Singer. You don't train. You are. It's like smelling bad. You don't have to study. You just do. Think about me with your head, your heart, and your belly. Think about the Sphere. Breathe in the purpose you have taken on. That's it. The words will come."

Rory nodded. "How long do I sing?"

"Well, in this case, you know I'm not coming back. For others, you sing until they come back to their body and tell you if they are staying or returning. For me, you need to sing me to the Sphere. You are providing the base. You'll know when you can stop."

Rory was unsure, but he knew Belecha wouldn't steer him wrong. He nodded.

Belecha straightened. "Remember, no talking on the way up." His eyes crinkled with the wisdom and love of thousands of years. "Hasta la bye bye, Eliaya."

Rory took a breath and looked again at his friend. "See you, Belecha. Thanks."

Belecha nodded, then turned and headed up the path. Rory followed. Soon, they were at the top of the cliff. Belecha stepped to the edge and looked out over the valley. Rory took his place on the wide rock. He looked at Belecha and past him to the hills beyond.

As he stared, he saw the red-tailed hawk fly up past Belecha and wheel around above him, screeching to the pulsing threads that filled the sky. From high above, a peregrine falcon swooped down and joined. From the direction of the village, a golden eagle flew and joined the dance above Belecha, splitting the air with its proud scream.

Rory saw and felt the lines of the web, glowing in a wonderful display. The pulsing vibrations of the web began to hum, and he began to chant in harmony. He picked up the drum from beside the rock and twined a rhythm through the chant. From deep inside, the words and sounds poured forth.

As he sang, Rory saw pictures of his time with Belecha – meeting him in the hole, the attack in Albuquerque, sitting in his kiva while he revealed the web of light.

A majestic, bald eagle joined the three birds wheeling, dancing, and calling above Belecha. They were flying over and under lines of the web, weaving a memory of his passing.

As Rory sang and the birds paid their respect, Belecha began to glow and shimmer like a thread of the web. He became a slow turning whirlpool of glistening smoke. A single ribbon reached out to lead him back to the Sphere, back home once more.

Rory's song rose to the sky and wove the web of light in glorious patterns. Pictures of other lives and other times with Belecha rose up and were gone. Still, he sang and watched.

The shining globe of Belecha glowed at the edge of the cliff, experiencing a final moment in this place. As Rory watched, it seemed the globe spun, and, once more, he could see the outline of his friend's weathered face, the wide mouth, the laughing eyes. As Rory sang and watched, the head faded away, leaving only two huge eyes, just as he had seen on the night Belecha had first appeared. Then, one of the eyes winked, and he was gone.

Glossary (Caution: many spoiler alerts!)

We recommend you read this glossary **after** reading "Adima Rising," to enhance your understanding of the book and the upcoming books in the series.

People (in order of appearance)

Rory Hurtado: 14, Javier and Kathy's son. He is the perpetual new kid in school, the first one to meet Belecha, and the digger of the kiva. Later, he becomes both a Watcher and a Singer.

Javier Hurtado: Rory's father, Leon's husband, and Kathy's ex-husband. He is an archeologist and teacher, who loves spending his summers excavating ruins. A loving father, his family is very important to him.

Leon Padilla: Rory's other father, and Javier's husband. He met Javier on an archaeological dig, while acting as the camp cook. Leon is as known for his mouthwatering Mexican dishes as for his ornate carvings. He provides a lot of heart to the family.

Billy Fuller: 15, Georgette's son, Suzie's brother, and Rory's first good friend. He is a math whiz and a smart mouth. He comes from a bad home, but he doesn't let it get him down.

Tima (Septima) Clark: 15, Grace's daughter, James' best friend, Rory's neighbor. Originally from Brooklyn, she moved to New Mexico with her mother about four years ago. An old soul, she often acts as her mother's caretaker. She is a talented painter, and an African American. She is named after Septima Clark, an early civil rights worker and educator.

James Nomura: 14, Franklin and Jocelyn's son, Lilly's brother, Tima's closest friend. A fourth-generation Japanese-American farmer, he lives and works on the family farm around the other side of the hill from Rory. His four favorite activities are farming, working on robotic and engineering projects, talking with Tima, and playing with his younger sister. He is very neat and organized, and always wants to know how things work. He is a reluctant participant in the adventure.

Cisco: Billy's short-term boss. An unpleasant, small-time operator, he borrowed money from some dangerous people to buy Rattlesnake Ranch.

Belecha: A Watcher and Adima. Known affectionately as "the old raccoon," he is the guide for the four teens as they go through the challenges. He was the Singer the day the stain was made.

Pelcha: Little prairie dogs and Belecha's mocking name for the four teens as a group … cute but skittish little critters full of fleas.

Tinglen: Billy's true name; what Belecha calls him.

Pecheme: James' true name; what Belecha calls him.

Heliotom: Tima's true name; what Belecha calls her.

Radelam: The leader of a nest of Kroledutz, and the main being hunting for the four teens. Thousands of years old, Radelam helped create the stain.

Kathy: Rory's mom and Javier's ex-wife. A restless soul, she gets bored easily and frequently travels from place to place. She has trouble with commitment and knowing who she is, but she genuinely loves her son.

Mealim: Teacher for the first challenge. An old woman who can transform into a fire snake. She has known Belecha for many lives. She explains the illusion of our bodies and where the Stone comes from.

Lilly: James' little sister. James is very protective of Lilly and tries to make special toys for her. She can get him to do nearly anything she wants just by smiling.

Grace Clark: Tima's mother. Grace is a well-published author. Her books include Having a Baby with Grace, Raising a Toddler with Grace, and Being a Mother with Grace. She's currently working on a book on recovering from mental illness called Having a Breakdown with Grace. The act of writing the book, however, has triggered another depression.

Jocelyn Nomura: James' and Lilly's mother, Franklin's wife. A short bundle of energy, she is kind to all and one of the best cooks in the county. Many people rely on her.

Franklin Nomura: James' and Lilly's dad, Jocelyn's husband. He is a third-generation farmer and serves as head of the county council. A quiet, principled man.

Arnalea: Teacher for the second challenge. He meets the four teens on his return day, and shows them how to ride the ribbons of light. He also explains how to travel with the Stone.

Georgette Fuller: Billy's and Suzie's mom. An unpleasant, violent woman, she has problems with alcohol and money. She doesn't mind conning people.

Suzie Fuller: Billy's older, mean sister, Georgette's daughter. More violent than her mother.

Atomasa: Teacher for the third challenge. A Watcher, he teaches the four about the long song of the earth and how to become part of the earth by singing its song. He also describes the secret of the Oloho and explains the importance of the pyramids and how they reach down energetically as far as they reach up.

Heyatoma: The mother and teacher for the fourth challenge. She is a kind of Watcher. She teaches the importance of each choice and the relationship between each entity and the Sphere. In one of the most important passages in the book, she talks about a plant that decides to act differently than the original plan. That is her greatest lesson.

Eliaya: Rory's real name from the spheres. Heyatoma first calls him by this name, as Belecha has been calling him Techta or "little toad." Eliaya means "beautiful weaver," and in the world of the Spheres comes from his ability to spin special and wonderful patterns in the web of light.

Things (in alphabetical order)

Adima: The Weavers of Light. Beings who create through intentional action. With each creative act, another ribbon of light is woven into the web of light. The Adima have rarely been on the planet since the stain; however, they are drawn here because of the ability to create and feel emotion.

Anchor: Traveling the web of light requires an anchor, a being who guides the way back. Although not revealed until the third challenge, Belecha has been acting as both pointer and anchor, a great strain. The anchor must be a Watcher (see Watcher).

Buffalo: An integral part of the Native American lifestyle, and the Sodrol at James' core, representing earth. Buffalo know the song of the earth and they know the power of singing the song, that it becomes a dance between two beings. The buffalo also understand that the earth takes time, great time, to change. Mountains rise and fall, seas fill and empty, and still the earth goes on, creating with intention.

Fire Snake: The Sodrol at Tima's core. The power of the fire snake is that it knows change requires leaving something behind, and it can make the hard choices of what needs to be left. Tima shows this in the first challenge when she demonstrates how to leave the concept of the body behind in order to go through the fire. The fire part of the snake is its swift, deadly bite, as fast as a flame and as completely deadly.

Glyph: A rough symbol or figure usually carved in stone. The four glyphs in the portal stone are the fire snake, the thunderbird, the buffalo, and the whale.

Kiva: A sacred place for Native Americans. A round hole in the ground, a kiva is usually 12 feet across, though they can be much larger. Traditional kivas had a wooden roof and a fire pit with a hole for smoke to exit. They were accessed by a wooden ladder.

Kroledutz: Energy suckers. Just as the Adima create light, the Kroledutz feed on it. They can wrap themselves around a human, feeding for many years, while the human gets weaker and darker in thought and actions. It is thought they also come from Spheres, but no Adima has seen such a Sphere. They exist to consume and spread darkness of spirit and action.

Oloho: A double pyramid and object of enormous power. Only two exist in all of existence. Belecha has one in his kiva. With it, the four are able to open a door to Adima from all dimensions and defeat the Kroledutz.

Pointer: Traveling the web requires a pointer, a being who rides above and directs where the travelers go. Without a pointer, the travelers would travel the ribbons of light forever without ever arriving anywhere.

Portal Stone: A stone formed by a Sphere that attracts Sodrol (see Sodrol). Each particular stone tells which Sodrol are necessary for a particular task. The number of sides tells the number of the world for which it is intended. Each corner features a glyph of the Sodrol that controls that part of the stone. The reason for the challenges is to make each Sodrol realize his inner power and how to activate the corresponding corner of the stone. The hole in the center represents the sphere that created the stone. By activating the portal stone, the four teens will be able to travel with their bodies through time and bring back the Oloho, which is required to defeat the Kroledutz.

Singer: A Singer helps entities return to the Sphere by traveling with the entity to the sacred cliff and then singing the song of the entity's life. The entity uses the singing to guide her back from the Sphere. If the entity finds that her work on this planet is done, she returns and thanks the Singer, then goes back to the Sphere permanently. If she has more to experience, she returns to the world and, with the Singer, comes back down the cliff. Watchers are Singers.

Sodrol: An Adima with a "seed" in his center, which gives special power and focus to the Adima. All four of the teens are Sodrol. Only Sodrol can bring a portal stone forward and activate it.

Sphere: The primal energies from the beginning of time. They come together for two purposes – to experience/learn and to share the experience/learning within themselves and others.

Stable Base: The number of travelers needed to travel the web of lights using a portal stone. The number needed to form the base depends on the number of the world. This planet's world is a four, thus the four teens: Rory, Billy, Tima, and James.

Stain, The: Human sacrifice to please a god, brought into the world with the influence of the Kroledutz. It separated humans from the knowledge that we are each responsible for creating the sacred through our intentional actions and convinced us that we needed someone else to act as the mouthpiece for God, someone who would tell us what is right, wrong, sacred, and mundane, someone who decides who lives and dies. It stole from humans our most precious right and responsibility.

This Planet: Our world. A particularly special place because of the emotions and creations it enables in the entities who have come here. A great source of ribbons of light.

Thunderbird: A mythical being of the Native Americans and the Sodrol at Billy's core. The thunderbird is a powerful hunter and destroyer of enemies. It has keen eyesight and can see the movement of its prey and aim for where it will be, not where it is. Billy's ability to see the games people play and call them on it is a result of the Sodrol at his core.

Watcher: An Adima who stays on the planet for hundreds to thousands of years, watching, bearing witness to the lives of others, like a recorder or history book. They are rarely able to suggest or interfere. Their purpose is to watch and return to the Sphere and share the experiences they have seen. At some point, they leave their physical body, but do not yet return to the Sphere. Instead, they manifest the body and travel the ribbons. Belecha and Atomasa are both Watchers. So is Rory.

Web of Light: Made up of individual ribbons of light, the web shows the creative intention of the universe. Every intentional, creative act creates a ribbon stretching from that act back to a Sphere. The threads weave together across the worlds and dimensions, ending up in a Sphere.

Whale: The Sodrol at Rory's core. The whale is the old being of the sea. It crosses boundaries. It is huge, but eats very small creatures. It is a mammal that lives in water. It sings. It breathes air, but lives in the depths. It sees the strengths in all things.

Places & Events (in chronological order)

Rattlesnake Ranch: An old tourist trap just outside of town that has been abandoned for years until Cisco buys it with the dream of reenergizing it, luring people off the highway and creating enough of a store that locals will buy there. Right now, it's a couple of falling down wooden buildings, a cracked parking lot, and a chain link fence that runs around the property.

First Challenge: Takes place at the Cave. Mealim, an old acquaintance of Belecha's, explains the significance of the Stone. She shows, rather than tells the teens of the difference between what we perceive as our bodies and the world and what truly is. She turns into a fire snake and the four must lose the illusion of their bodies to escape. Tima is the Sodrol.

The Cave: Scene of the first challenge. The cave is a place in the mountains where many travelers have found a safe place to pass the night. Its sand floor is comfortable for sitting and sleeping. Many glyphs from many travelers cover the walls. It is a sacred and safe spot for the Adima and Mealim's particular place of power.

Second Challenge: Up in the mountains in the Village of Aware Beings, the four meet Arnalea on his return day, the day he returns to the Sphere and decides if he has fulfilled his purpose or has more to do on the Earth. Arnalea shows the four the creation of the stain – a man seeking the power of the Aware Beings was influenced by Radelam and misperceived a girl's return as a sacrifice. Arnalea also explains how to use the Stone to travel and that different worlds have different numbers. Finally, he takes the teens ribbon riding through the cosmos, finally leaving them stranded. Billy, the Sodrol for this challenge, must see with the accuracy of the bird.

Aware Village: Scene of the second challenge. The village of people who live Aware Lives, who understand that they come from the Sphere to experience and learn and then return to share their learning. When they were on earth, the village was sought, as people thought it must be full of sorcerers and treasure. It was in the Aware Village that the trap that made the stain was laid – as a stranger watched a return and interpreted it as a sacrifice. The people of the village helped take the cliff to another dimension and live an Aware Existence. It is a world that would be if Adima held sway.

The Cliff: Also a scene in the second challenge. A sacred place used for Return Days, it used to be on the earth, but was moved to another dimension after the stain entered our world. This is where Aware people go on their Return Day. Protected by a steep, narrow mountain path and a protruding boulder, it contains a hidden pool surrounded by soft moss. A small path leads from the pool to a large stone where the Singer sits and drums and sings the song of the life of the person Returning. Beyond that, is the edge where the entity returning stands during the song.

Return Day: The day an entity, aided by a Singer, returns to the Sphere to share his experiences and learn his purpose. Then, he either returns to their existence in the world for further experiences or stays with the Sphere.

Third Challenge: This takes place in the distant past. Atomasa explains the duty of a Watcher and shows the four how singing the song of a thing (like grass) allows us to become that thing. He talks of the long cycle of nature and how nature is a balance. When he leaves the teens, a stampede of thousands of buffalo rushes toward them. James is the Sodrol.

Buffalo Wallow: Scene of the third challenge. A large, scooped out bowl in the earth, created by thousands of buffalo rolling there, scratching their backs.

Fourth Challenge: Unlike the first three challenges, which dealt with large matters, the fourth challenge focuses on the importance of each individual's act. Heyatoma, the teacher for the challenge, reveals that each person comes to existence with a distinct purpose in mind (from both the entity and the Sphere), but that as the existence progresses, the entity makes choices that can change things. Rory asks if that means they can do whatever they want, and Heyatoma says, in one of the most important sentences in the book, "You have that duty." She explains it is our duty to act with intention, that each intentional act of creation spins another thread in the web of light. It is during this challenge that Rory chooses to be a Watcher.

About Steve Schatz

Steve Schatz grew up in New Mexico, where he actually dug a kiva in his backyard. He has traveled all over the United States, discovering how other people see the world. He has been a tour guide, party clown, TV producer, business owner, and, for the last several years, a professor of learning theory. He has always been interested in things spiritual, and a life changing experience and spiritual guidance brought him to the idea for "Adima Rising." He is at work on the next book in *The Adima Chronicles* and spends most of his time writing in a little house in a little town next to Yokum Brook. Other poems and stories can be found on SteveWrites.com.

About Absolute Love Publishing

Absolute Love Publishing is an independent book publisher devoted to creating and publishing projects that promote goodness in the world.

We have published internationally renowned and Billboard-topping musicians, Olympic athletes, prominent media professionals and authors, inspirational and visionary figures, innovative change-makers, spiritual leaders, and more. Absolute Love Publishing is located in Austin, Texas, USA. It owns min-e-book.com and the trademark, min-e-book™. A min-e-book™ is a shorter-style e-book designed for a quick read.

Would you like to know about the latest Absolute Love Publishing releases? Join our newsletter by visiting www.AbsoluteLovePublishing.com.

Become a Fan: facebook.com/Absolute.Love.Publishing
Follow us on Pinterest: pinterest.com/absolutelovepub/
Follow us on Twitter: twitter.com/AbsoluteLovePub
Add us on Google Plus:
plus.google.com/102160404555181590431/
Join us on LinkedIn:
https://www.linkedin.com/company/absolute-love-publishing

Books by Absolute Love Publishing

Adima Rising: The Adima Chronicles by Steve Schatz
For millennia, the evil Kroledutz have fed on the essence of humans and clashed in secret with the Adima, the light weavers of the universe. Now, with the balance of power shifting toward darkness, time is running out. Guided by a timeless Native American spirit, four teenagers from a small New Mexico town discover they have one month to awaken their inner power and save the world. Rory, Tima, Billy, and James must solve four ancient challenges by the next full moon to awaken a mystical portal and become Adima. If they fail, the last threads of light will dissolve, and the universe will be lost forever. Can they put aside their fears and discover their true natures before it's too late?

The Chakra Secret: What Your Body Is Telling You by Michelle Hastie, a min-e-book™
Do you believe there may be more to the body than meets the eye? Have you wondered why you run into the same physical issues over and over again? Maybe you are dealing with dis-eases or ailments and are ready to treat more than just the symptoms. Or perhaps you've simply wondered why you gain weight in your midsection while your friend gains weight in her hips? Get ready to understand how powerful energy centers in your body communicate messages from beyond the physical. Discover the root, energetic problems that are causing imbalances, and harness a universal power to create drastic changes in your happiness, your well-being, and your body with "The Chakra Secret: What Your Body Is Telling You," a min-e-book™.

Dead End Date: The Adventures of a Lightworker Series by Caroline A. Shearer
"Dead End Date" is the first book in a metaphysical series about a woman's crusade to teach the world about love, one mystery and personal hang-up at a time. In a Bridget Jones

meets New Age-style, "Dead End Date" introduces readers to Faith, a young woman whose dating disasters and personal angst have separated her from the reason she's on Earth. When she receives the shocking news that she is a lightworker and has one year to fulfill her life purpose, Faith embarks on her mission with zeal, tackling problems big and small – including the death of her blind date. Working with angels and psychic abilities and even the murder victim himself, Faith dives headfirst into a personal journey that will transform all those around her and, eventually, all those around the world.

Finding Happiness with Migraines: a Do It Yourself Guide by Sarah Hackley, a min-e-book™

Do you have monthly, weekly, or even daily migraines? Do you feel lonely or isolated, or like you are constantly worrying about the next impending migraine? Is the weight of living with migraines dampening your enjoyment of the "now"? Experience the happiness you crave with "Finding Happiness with Migraines: a Do It Yourself Guide," a min-e-book™ by Sarah Hackley. Discover how you can take charge of your body, your mind, your emotions, and your health by practicing simple, achievable steps that create a daily life filled with more joy, appreciation, and confidence. Sarah's Five Steps to Finding Happiness with Migraines provide an actionable path to a new, happier way of living with migraines. A few of the tools you'll learn: which yoga poses can help with a migraine attack, why you should throw away your daily migraine journal, how do-it-yourself therapy can create positive change, and techniques to connect with your body and intuition.

Haunted Echo: The Soul Sight Series by Janet McLaughlin

Sun, fun, and her toes in the sand. That's what Zoey Christopher expects when she joins her best friend and fellow cheerleader Becca on an exotic Caribbean vacation. What she finds instead is a wannabe boyfriend, a voodoo doll, and Tempy - a tormented young ghost whose past is linked to the island grounds.

Zoey has always seen visions of the future, but when she arrives at St. Anthony's Island to vacation among the jet set, she has her first encounter with a bona fide ghost. Forced to uncover the secret behind the girl's untimely death, Zoey quickly realizes that trying to solve the case will place her in mortal danger. Shaken and confused by a menacing threat and by her budding feelings for the too-cute, too-nice Chris, will Zoey find a way to survive this vacation and put Tempy to rest?

Love Like God: Embracing Unconditional Love

In this groundbreaking compilation, well-known individuals from across the globe share stories of how they learned to release the conditions that block absolute love. Along with the insights of bestselling author Caroline A. Shearer, readers will be reminded of their natural state of love and will begin to envision a world without fear or judgement or pain. Along with Shearer's reflections and affirmations, experts, musicians, authors, professional athletes, and others shed light on the universal experiences of journeying the path of unconditional love.

Love Like God Companion Book

You've read the love-expanding essays from the luminaries of "Love Like God." Now, take your love steps further with the "Love Like God Companion Book." The Companion provides a positive, actionable pathway into a state of absolute love, enabling readers to further open their hearts at a pace that matches their experiences. This book features an expanded introduction, the Thoughts and Affirmations from "Love Like God," plus all new "Love in Action Steps."

Preparing to Fly: Financial Freedom from Domestic Abuse

Are financial worries keeping you stuck in an abusive or unhealthy relationship? Do you want to break free but don't know how to make it work financially? Take charge with "Preparing to Fly," a personal finance book for women who want to escape the relationships that are holding them back. Drawing on personal experiences and nearly a decade of financial expertise, Sarah Hackley walks readers step-by-step through empowering plans and tools: Learn how much money it will take to leave and how much you'll need to live on your own. Change the way you think about money to promote your independence. Bring control of your life back to where it belongs - with you. Break free and live in your own power, with "Preparing to Fly." Additional tips for women with children, married women, pregnant women, the chronically ill, and more!

Raise Your Financial Vibration: Tips and Tools to Embrace Your Infinite Spiritual Abundance, a min-e-book™
Are you ready to release the mind dramas that hold you back from your infinite spiritual abundance? Are you ready for a high-frequency financial life? Allow, embrace, and enjoy your infinite spiritual abundance and financial wealth today! Absolute Love Publishing Creator Caroline A. Shearer explores simple steps and shifts in mindset that will help you receive the abundance you desire in "Raise Your Financial Vibration: Tips and Tools to Embrace Your Infinite Spiritual Abundance," a min-e-book™. Learn how to release blocks to financial abundance, create thought patterns that will help you achieve a more desirable financial reality, and fully step into an abundant lifestyle by discovering the art of *being* abundant.

Raise Your Verbal Vibration: Create the Life You Want with Law of Attraction Language, a min-e-book™
Are the words you speak bringing you closer to the life you want? Or are your word choices inadvertently creating more difficulties? Discover words and phrases that are part of the Language of Light in Absolute Love Publishing Creator Caroline A. Shearer's latest in the Raise Your Vibration min-e-book™ series: "Raise Your Verbal Vibration: Create the Life You Want with Law of Attraction Language." Learn what common phrases and words may be holding you back, and utilize a list of high-vibration words that you can begin to incorporate into your vocabulary. Increase your verbal

vibration today with this compelling addition to the Raise Your Vibration series!

Raise Your Vibration: Tips and Tools for a High-Frequency Life, a min-e-book™

Presenting mind-opening concepts and tips, "Raise Your Vibration: Tips and Tools for a High-Frequency Life," a min-e-book™, opens the doorway to your highest and greatest good! This min-e-book™ demonstrates how every thought and every action affect our level of attraction, enabling us to attain what we truly want in life. Divided into categories of mind, body, and spirit/soul, readers will learn practical steps they can immediately put into practice to resonate at a higher vibration and further evolve their souls. A must-read primer for a higher existence! Are you ready for a high-frequency life?

The Weight Loss Shift: Be More, Weigh Less by Michelle Hastie

"The Weight Loss Shift: Be More, Weigh Less" by Michelle Hastie helps those searching for their ideal bodies shift into a higher way of being, inviting the lasting weight they want – along with the life of their dreams! Skip the diets and the gimmicks, "The Weight Loss Shift" is a permanent weight loss solution. Based on science, psychology, and spirituality, Hastie helps readers discover their ideal way of being through detailed instructions and exercises, and then helps readers transform to living a life free from worry about weight – forever! Would you like to love your body at any weight? Would you like to filter through others' body expectations to discover your own? Would you like to live at your ideal weight naturally, effortlessly, and happily? Then, make the shift with "The Weight Loss Shift: Be More, Weigh Less!"

Where Is the Gift? Discovering the Blessing in Every Situation, a min-e-book™

Inside every challenge is a beautiful blessing waiting for us to unwrap it. All it takes is our choice to learn the lesson of the challenge! Are you in a situation that is challenging you? Are you struggling with finding the perfect blessing the universe is holding for you? This min-e-book™ will help you unwrap your blessings with more ease and grace, trust in the perfect manifestation of your life's challenges, and move through life with the smooth path your higher self intended. Make the choice: unwrap your gift today!

Women Will Save the World

Leading women across the nation celebrate the feminine nature through stories of collaboration, creativity, intuition, nurturing, strength, trailblazing, and wisdom in "Women Will Save the World." Inspired by a quote from the Dalai Lama, bestselling author and Absolute Love Publishing Founder Caroline A. Shearer brings these inherent feminine qualities to the forefront, inviting a discussion of the impact women have on humanity and initiating the question: Will Women Save the World?

All books available at
www.AbsoluteLovePublishing.com.